The Waking Part

II:

Withstand in

The Evil Day

Cheryl McClamrock

This is a work of fiction. Names, characters, businesses, places, events, locales, and incidents are either the products of the author's imagination or used in a fictitious manner. Any resemblance to actual persons, living or dead, or actual events is purely coincidental.

Dedication

This book is dedicated to the survivors. You are strong, and loved, and seen. May you continue to let your voices be heard for those who can't speak!

Ephesians 6:13 "Wherefore take unto you the whole armour of God, that ye may be able to withstand in the evil day . . ."

Prologue

Geneva, Switzerland

Ha-Satan stood over the naked, bloody form on the floor.

"I'm disappointed, Adora." He shook his head and spoke gently as if he cared, "I thought you were smarter than Viktor."

He turned from her and smoothly slipped his arms back into the sleek, black Armani suit that fit like a second skin on his young and handsome chosen form. "I'll give you two more weeks to find your daughter and deliver her to me, or I will kill you and give the task to a more capable leader."

Nearby and showing no signs that they had heard or seen any of the violence that had just occurred, the three black-suited, almost featureless agents waited to escort their charge out of the building and into the awaiting armored limo.

When the door closed, Adora attempted to crawl to her dress crumpled in the corner of the room, but when she moved, pain shot through her arm, and she screamed in agony. Rolling to her back again, she cradled the mangled appendage to her scratched and bloody chest. "That bastard broke my arm." she croaked.

"Ninazu!" she called, "Ninazu, please help ..." The weak plea erupted into a fit of coughing, which produced a puddle of blood and phlegm on the floor.

Soon a dark form materialized in front of Adora, the square-bearded warrior's pupilless black eyes regarding her with an air of agitation. He wore thick black Sumerian armor and held an iron spear with a notched, iron sickle at the end. "Why have you summoned me, witch?"

Adora wasn't the type to beg and had ceased the use of tears decades before, so her cold blue eyes were merely glassy with pain and anger. "I'm of no use to you broken. Heal me and send the others away."

He glared at her, giving no answer.

"Please," she whispered.

The demi-god nodded. "Galdrar! Heiller! Take the others and go from us for an hour. Leave now!"

Adora began to convulse and cough again, writhing painfully for a few moments as the demonic legion left her body. Afterward, Ninazu waved a black armored hand over her; the bloody slashes immediately closed on her chest. The demon-warrior smirked when suddenly, Adora arched her back and shrieked as her broken arm popped loudly and painfully back into place and healed.

When she had recovered enough to stand, she glared at him as she dressed. "Take us to a place where we can speak freely."

"Do you wish for us both to be tortured for sedition? It will be worse for you, believe me." His voice, deep and emotionless, caused a cold shiver to race up her spine.

She nodded, noticing that her black dress was torn but still wearable as she slipped it on. "I understand the risks. You and I have been together for over twenty years. You understand that I'm about to lose my place in The Brotherhood, and if I fail, what does that mean for you?"

He considered her for a moment, then raising his sickle, he sliced downward, creating a slip, a barely perceptible line in the air in front of them. The demi-god grabbed her arm and pulled her with him through the portal. Adora yelped, then squinted and held her hand above her head, a feeble attempt to block the blinding glare of the blazing ball above. As her eyes adjusted, she realized they were in a desert on top of a dune with nothing and no one around for miles.

"I will speak quickly, as we have little time, witch." He towered over her five foot-seven slender form, his voice, like gravel and dark pitch, still made her stomach queasy even after twenty years of hearing it. "There is a faction of gods … dissatisfied with Ha-Satan's leadership. Recently, an elder god who has the power to overthrow the Nachash, was released from prison."

"Prison? Gods can be put in prison? By whom?"

He shook his head dismissively. "That's not important. What is important is that Azazel is now free, and he's gathering forces to overthrow the Nachash." Ninazu scoffed, "Ha-Satan is so arrogant, he thinks he's too powerful to now be overthrown."

"Nachash?"

"Lucifer, The Serpent. He overthrew your First-Father, Adam, in the beginning times and took his crown, so the Old Ones had to yield to his authority. Azazel and the others were just as powerful as he and had been creating armies of giant demi-gods (Us)," he roared, banging his chest loudly. "They expected us to rule humanity, but the Nachash had other plans. He took over himself and ruled all, The Nephilim and the humans, on this… prison planet," he scoffed.

"Prison planet? That can't be true. What about the times I was taken to Mars and Saturn?"

Ninazu smirked. "There is much that you do not know, witch. Ha-Satan is a master of deception. Even the low demons don't know the true extent of our limitations in this realm. In the beginning times, right before the Great Deluge, we had successfully corrupted almost all of the human bloodlines. The Enemy then judged us and the Old Ones. He cursed all Nephilim to be bound to the earth as spirits until the End Times. Azazel and a few other Old Ones were bound in prison under the earth for a hundred generations."

Adora now had sweat pouring down her face and back. She absently rolled her white-gold hair into a makeshift bun, her mind racing with questions. "Can I meet with this Azazel?"

Ninazu chuckled. "The ancient god is still hungry and eats almost all flesh who approaches him."

She grimaced at the sound of Ninazu's laugh as well as the thought of being consumed.

"Thousands of years in darkness will do that to a being." He said.

"So, what do we do?"

"Can you find your daughter?"

Adora nodded. "I still have trackers hidden in her. Also, she will do anything to save her sisters. I will get a message to her that they will be sacrificed if she doesn't turn up and she will come to me."

"Perfect, I will go to Azazel and offer Ha-Satan's bride to him in exchange for your safety and our joining his side."

"That sounds like a plan. When will you know? I only have two weeks."

He sliced the air again and pulled them both back into the room in Geneva. He looked down at Adora. "Your other demons will report that I sent them away. I'll tell the leadership that I was making sure you were telling Lucifer the truth about your daughter. We have to make this look believable."

Understanding his meaning, she looked up at him in horror.

He smiled. "Don't worry, I won't break anything."

The demon flung her across the room as she screamed.

Chapter One

Richmond, Texas

(6 Months after The Breach)
Gianna

A little over six months ago, I awoke in another realm with a group of strangers. The Almighty God had sent us there to overcome sin and lies in our lives and to form a team of specially gifted individuals. Diego, Darrel, Lincoln, Billie Jean, Lucy, and I were linked up with Bible heroes King David and Noah, as well as a handful of Arch-angels to prevent Satan from amassing and unleashing an army of Nephilim giants and nightmare monsters on humanity. The enemy had managed to open 13 portals across the world with help from international satanic groups using the power of blood sacrifice, star alignments and ley lines. Our teams managed to keep back and defeat many of the enemy giants and monsters and permanently shut down those portals. But not before some of the nightmare creatures had made it through. This was "The Breach."

***

Amora woke with a yelp. Her heart raced, almost beating out of her chest as she gulped, trying to catch her breath. Her eyes darted around the unfamiliar room, expecting to still be locked in the small, cold cell that she shared with her sisters in Geneva. Her breathing slowed as she

1

remembered she was instead in Texas with Gianna's family.

She heard a patter of small paws and a quiet meow before Tigger, Gianna's cat, sprang lightly up on Amora's bed and padded over, rubbing his downy head under her chin. She smiled and stroked the orange tabby who'd managed to always be right there to comfort her when she awoke from a nightmare.

Her mind swirled with images from the disturbing dream, fully aware that what she saw of her mother's torture was most likely truly taking place. She recalled fleeting terrible images of a dark figure throwing her against a wall as she screamed. Amora had never been shown an ounce of love or affection from the cruel woman who birthed her but knowing that her mother was being mangled by a Dark One still caused Amora to be sad and frightened for her mother.

More than that, she was afraid for her sisters. If her mother was being punished, she tended to take it out on her daughters because this somehow made her feel better. Amora recalled three straight days of rigorous combat training, topped off with ritual sexual torture by the coven on the third day followed by no food, sleep, or medical care. Adora was a vindictive taskmaster and at times, made her late husband and Amora's father Viktor look tenderhearted in comparison.

As Tigger settled into a purring ball between her crossed legs, Amora prayed for her sisters and, in the end, added a reluctant prayer for her mother as well.

Daughter, I'm with you, she heard the quiet voice respond.

A distinct peace settled on her, and she relaxed.
Prepare to leave.

She opened her eyes, worry suddenly dropping into her gut.

Do not worry, my daughter. Your new family will be with you.

Amora relaxed again.

Tell Gianna that Lucy is coming and to prepare.

"Yes, Papa," Amora said aloud.

***

Gianna stood on the precipice of a dark mountain top. Sweat dripped down her neck and back as strands of her long brown hair, freed from her braid, stuck to her face. She wiped at them absently with the back of her hand, which still tightly clenched a sword. Her black leather pants were slashed on one leg, and dried blood peeked through. Her arms were covered with dirt and scratches from a battle she couldn't seem to recall. From the side of the crumbling peak, she stared down into a black swirling abyss below.

The dark spiraling maw was wider than she could see, and occasionally, bolts of lightning streaked through it, briefly giving her a glimpse further into the mouth. The pitch-darkness seemed to stretch and grow, pulsate and move like a living organism. A shiver of fear moved up her spine from her gut, which burned with a dire foreboding.

Suddenly, the flashes began to reveal a shape forming in the inky blackness of the abyss.

Molten fire, blood, and shadow formed into a humanoid shape as thousands upon thousands of screams of agony echoed through the atmosphere. Gianna felt the torment of tortured souls ricocheting across her bones.

Her eyes grew wide as the molten figure stretched and expanded from the pit until it finally hovered like a

3

fiery mass just at her eye level. She couldn't tear her eyes from the sight as a humanoid face formed with eyes as black as the abyss it emerged from. Thick ram's horns burst from the creature's temples. Its body then materialized out of the fiery mass as thick and wide as a mountain, and coal-black wings of ash and fire exploded from its back to spread out seemingly across the entire sky. The being stretched its flaming arms wide, looked up at the sky, opened its mouth and roared. The mountain Gianna stood on shook with the fury of the flaming being until it broke apart, and she fell into the abyss.

Gianna kicked and woke up startled with a scream caught in her throat.

***

The next morning, when Gianna came downstairs, she was greeted with music blaring from the kitchen. Johnny Cash's deep ramble of "Ring of Fire" made her groan and roll her eyes. *Geez. Do they ever get tired of this one?* She wondered as she fought another yawn.

She turned the corner into the kitchen and caught David flipping pancakes at the stove and Amora stirring a bowl next to him, both on the tail end of a loud duet.

Dylan, she and David's eight-year-old son, was happily head-bobbing and eating pancakes at the table nearby. When David finally noticed her in the kitchen, his eyes lit up, and he grinned widely. "Hey Gigi! Did we wake you?" He put the spatula down, ambled over, and gave her a bear hug before kissing her on the cheek.

She stiffened and lightly shook her head as she stepped back. "Uh, no… No, it's fine. I was up--"

"David. The pancake!" Amora yelled.

"Oh shoot!" He jumped back over to the stove as a bit of smoke rose from the pan and quickly flipped it, "Crap. That one's burned."

"I'll eat it." Dylan chirped from the table. Johnny Cash still rumbled noisily from the speaker on the countertop.

Gianna took advantage of the distraction and shuffled over to the coffee pot.

Starting another pancake, David sheepishly looked over at her, "Did you want one, Gigi?"

She retrieved her favorite blue mug from the cabinet that boasted "Caution, I Have No Filter" and kept her eyes focused on pouring the steaming black energy into it. In response, she shook her head lightly. "No, thanks."

She heard him grunt, obviously disappointed at his spurned efforts. Acting as if she didn't notice, Gianna mixed cream and Stevia into her cup, stirring it as she walked over to hug Amora and then kissed Dylan on the head as she sat next to him at the table. The song then changed to Amora's favorite, "God's Gonna' Cut You Down." The drums and clapping started, and Amora whooped. David grinned as they started singing together.

Gianna was not a big Cash fan, but she liked this song. It had a catchy sound, and the lyrics were inspiring for many reasons. David had moved back in about a month ago, and Amora had taken to him right away. He was funny and good-looking, and most kids flocked to him. Gianna felt it was because he acted like a kid so much of the time that they just felt like he was one of them. Once he started playing his favorite music, Amora became as obsessed with the late "man in black" as he was.

Right now, after more than six months of separation, Gianna was still getting used to him being back. He was sleeping on the couch, and they hadn't been intimate or even kissed since his return. Gianna, more from the Lord's prompting, reluctantly agreed to give it a try, allowing him to move back in to help with Dylan and Amora. Lately, she spent much of her time out working with their "Giant Slayer" teams around the world, fighting pockets of monsters, training new members, and overall trying to keep the Apocalypse from overtaking the world. She could no longer leave the kids without adult supervision. In case a social worker ever stopped by, it had to look like this was a stable family unit.

David jumped at the chance to get close to her again and had hopes of reconciling. He was often disappointed that this seemed more an arrangement of convenience for her rather than a try at getting back together. She, frankly, wasn't intentionally "not trying" with him, but she did welcome the busyness of her schedule as an excuse not to have time to work on anything.

He wanted to go to marriage counseling and talk things out and had made some real efforts to show his desire to work on the marriage. He wasn't giving up easily and took each rejection in stride, rather than getting defensive and snapping at her or giving up totally and moving on. She had to admit, as she observed him over the last couple of weeks, he did seem to have a different demeanor and overall better attitude than he used to.

Amora interrupted Gianna's thoughts by placing a plate of pancakes on the table. "I know how to make pancakes now." She grinned wide at the accomplishment. Gianna patted her arm. "That's awesome, sweetie!"

Amora grabbed Gianna's hand with a sudden urgency in her eyes. "Lucy's coming here, and then we have to leave."

Chapter Two

Miami, Florida

Lucy leaned against her locker and glanced quickly at the news feed on her cell phone. She flinched at the first picture; a group of homeless people torn apart just blocks away from her apartment. The picture was a bloody mess, and she wished that she wasn't getting used to seeing scenes like this. The vampire population in her area was growing daily, and though she had taken care of quite a few of the roving bands, they were multiplying rapidly and getting bolder in their killing.

She was having no luck recruiting warriors from churches or Christian clubs. It was like they were blind to what was happening. She recently called Gianna and Billie Jean to talk about what was happening and to see if they had any thoughts about what to do. Just a month ago, Gianna had come to comfort her and helped her with a raid on a group nearby, but she had too much going on in her own area to keep coming to help Lucy. Lucy had been praying for a breakthrough here, but each day seemed to get darker, and she feared that soon, the whole area would be overrun with vampires and other monstrous creatures.

Just then, a group of goths walked by, eyeing her and she quickly pocketed her phone. A few of her former friends were in this crowd and seemed to sense her change from last year. Julia and (amazingly still alive,

Kevin) were amongst them. They had tried, unsuccessfully, multiple times to get her to hang with them again. Lucy didn't trust them, especially after catching an unwelcome glimpse of the entities controlling them.

Every once in a while, the Holy Spirit opened her spiritual eyes to see what was on or inside an individual and at first, it freaked her out and she ran from them. When she realized what was occurring and that they were afraid of her more than she was of them, she was then able to keep it together and act as if she wasn't seeing anything out of the ordinary.

The last time Kevin spoke to her in the hall before English class, she saw a spider-like thing the size of a cat sitting on him, behind his upper back and shoulders, its arms inserted into his neck and head. It seemed to be puppeting his mouth and briefly, his eyes changed to yellow reptilian slits during the conversation. She managed to finish the dialogue without retching and afterward ran into the bathroom, locked herself in a stall and prayed.

A couple of kids in the group nodded at her as they passed, and she discerned the hisses of their demons from behind the spiritual veil as well. She had come to understand that the demons could see her light and her angel guard, which caused much of the negative reaction to her from these kids, even if they didn't understand why they were reacting this way to her.

After they passed, Lucy quickly escaped to her next class, praying under her breath for more of a cover for her and her mother. Another worry was that her "extra-curricular" activities at night would draw revenge attacks. But so far, the monsters hadn't seemed to connect her to their thwarted efforts in the area.

She entered the History class and filed to the back corner of the room, as usual. Her teacher, busy at the white board, didn't acknowledge her or look up. There were still a couple of minutes before the class began, so she opened her textbook and took her phone out again.

She began to study the picture closer and planned an extra patrol at the homeless hangouts in town tonight. She didn't notice Julia slide in and sit down at the desk next to her until she spoke, "So, Lucy, we've been super bummed that you won't come to any of our get-togethers."

Lucy, startled, put her phone face down on the book, "I've been...busy."

Julia's tight smile didn't extend past her lips as her cold eyes drilled into Lucy's.

"We've noticed." She responded flatly. "Kevin really wants you to come tonight. We're having a bonfire at our usual beach cove hangout. You should be there," The snake-like entity wrapped around Julia's throat said. "And if we don't see you tonight, we'll come looking for you."

Lucy, unruffled, didn't respond. Julia, having finished her threat, grinned with her lips and dead eyes again, stood up and casually walked out of the room. The teacher finally looked away from her board after Julia left and announced, "Ok, everyone, have a seat and all eyes up here!"

***

Lucy, as usual, got home from school before her mother's shift ended at work and started dinner. She pulled the on-sale ground round out of the fridge and sniffed it suspiciously. It smelled ok, so she started browning it and pulled the box of instant beef stroganoff out of the cabinet, barely looking at the box as she prepared to mix the ingredients together. Her phone chimed, and she saw an alert pop up. She sighed and tapped a message from Kevin. "See you tonight." She shook her head thoughtfully, "Not a chance."

Just then, her mother, Laura, came through the door, throwing her purse and bags on the couch. She looked exhausted but managed a smile as she came into the kitchen, "Hija! Thank you for getting dinner started." She came over and kissed Lucy on the cheek and raised her eyebrows at Lucy's hair, "Blue streaks? I like it."

"Ma! You were here when I put them in yesterday." Lucy rolled her eyes.

Here mom laughed. "Of course, I was. But it looks different the next day. Today, I like it." Laura winked playfully at her daughter.

Lucy giggled and snorted as she continued to stir the beef stroganoff, "Did you want to finish that Bible study after dinner tonight?"

"Yes! Let's do that! I'm learning so much! And you'll be proud of me, hija. I prayed with that depressed lady at work whose daughter left home." Laura announced as she set the table.

"Mommy!" Lucy beamed as she brought the food over, "That's amazing. Did she cry?"

"Yes, poor thing," Laura began to spoon food onto both of their plates, "I hugged her and prayed for her daughter to come home. I really felt peace and assurance that she would see her daughter again, too. And I told her that."

Lucy was ecstatic at the remarkable change in her mother over the last few months. Just like Jesus had told her after her adventures with Him and the others, he said that her mother would come to know Him through Lucy.

They had prayed and cried together numerous times over the last few weeks as Laura learned about having a relationship with God, and He started revealing Himself to her. She soon began to heal from past hurts and stopped using drugs and alcohol to cope, and soon, she and Lucy repaired their relationship and started to feel like a real family. Lucy had never been happier at home and was so thankful that she came back here instead of going to live with Gianna like she had wanted to.

After dinner, they finished a Bible study on the book of John. Laura stood up and hugged Lucy, "Thank you, hija, for showing me the truth and helping me to heal." Tears formed in her eyes, "I'm sorry for all the years with you that I wasted."

"Mommy, you already told me you're sorry!" She squeezed her mom's hand. "I forgave you, and I'm enjoying the time we have now. Ok?"

Her mother grinned as she wiped a stray tear away. "I know, I know sweetie. I just want you to understand how much I'm loving coming home and sharing with you and how much peace I have now that I can't describe."

Lucy hugged her mom tight, "I'm so happy to hear that, mommy. I love you."

Her mom sighed, "I love you too, hija."

***

A little while later, when it got dark outside, Lucy grabbed her backpack and headed towards the door. "Ma! I'm going to my study group at the library!"

Laura looked up from her book. "Ok, don't be home too late. And you'll be with a group? There's crazies out there!"

"Yes, Ma. Don't worry, I'll be safe." She kissed her mother's cheek and walked out.

She sprinted down the hallway and into the public restroom to change into her "Lord of the Rings" gear, as she liked to call her outfit from the other realm. After pinning her cloak and stuffing her street clothes into her backpack, Lucy took the employee elevator to the roof of the apartment complex. She stowed her backpack in a corner and took off into the night from the top of the building.

She still thrilled at every moment of flight that she could get. Flying at night was a lot safer, but she found that she could even get away with flying during the day at times. Lucy was amazed at how cell phones had so many people clueless and never aware of what was going on around them.

She could zip by right above the heads of crowds and no one looked up. She still didn't like to take too many chances often, though. And lately, she did have to stay a bit more hidden as the vampire crowd wasn't distracted by electronics and had spotted her a few times. She had managed to keep her identity hidden and hoped to continue to do so for her and her mother's safety. But she worried because it seemed, lately, that she was the only one keeping the city from being completely overrun by the undead. She prayed about leaving this area soon for a safer city.

Lucy prayed as she flew slowly over parks nearby, landing on tall buildings and houses to watch for activity. In the last couple of weeks, most of the parks were empty before the sun set as many people had become more alert and appeared to be staying away from these areas at night. She left a few empty parks with relief that there were no straggling groups or homeless settling in. Her thoughts flitted to the kids from school who had "invited" her to the beach hangout tonight, and she wondered how seriously she should take Julia's threat. Maybe she would pass by and see what they actually wanted. She could always translate away if things got bad.

Her eye caught something strange in the sky. Though it was night, she suddenly saw a dark mist form over The Ancient Spanish Monastery a few blocks away. This had always been one of her favorite places, and she knew it well. Her mom's cousin, Gloria had gotten married there a few years ago, and Lucy fell in love with the historic structure from Spain. She headed to the monastery.

She landed in the courtyard, which was dark and beyond creepy at night. She hid behind a large tree and listened. It was a typical sweltering Florida night, yet she shivered, and the hairs on the back of her neck rose. She slowed her breathing, listening intently to the darkness.

She thought she heard muffled voices and low snickering. Lucy inched and crawled toward the sounds, and it seemed to be coming from the wedding chapel. The chapel was dimly lit with some candles burning as well as a couple torches up by the altar. She hid behind a back pew, and as her eyes adjusted to the dim light, she saw two young women tied up and gagged, one lying naked on the altar and the other standing nearby, arms bound behind her with two dark figures holding her arms. Both women were whimpering and shaking as the dark figures, who appeared to be a gang of street thugs, laughed as they began to cut small incisions on the first woman's arm. They took turns licking and slurping the dripping blood, and she knew immediately this street gang was vampires.

Her stomach twisted with fear, but anger and justice overrode it as she was determined to save the girls and destroy these vile creatures. There were six men of various sizes holding the girls. Vampires could see in the dark and were very strong, so she had to be careful but act quickly before the women were either killed or turned. Lucy released a strong force that blew out the flames and threw all the bodies at the altar back explosively. She hoped the girls wouldn't be too hurt by it, but better hurt than dead. She flew over there while the men cursed and scrambled, not knowing what hit them and what was coming.

"I need you, Jesus." She prayed. Suddenly, a bright light appeared, causing the vampires to scream, cover their eyes, and back away from it. Lucy took the opportunity and untied the women on the floor and helped them up. "Go now!" She shouted at them loudly over the screams of the gang. The girls nodded, got up and ran.

Lucy was about to turn back to take care of the vampires when a tall angelic being emerged from out of the bright light. Her eyes grew wide with recognition as Raphael the archangel appeared. He nodded at her and began to swing his sword. She ran out with the young girls as the screams from the vampires rose into the night.

15

***

After she helped get the women to safety, Lucy flew home, unsure of how long she had been gone, until she looked at her phone and saw missed calls and a text from her mom from an hour before. "Crap! She's going to be so mad!" She landed on the roof and scooped up her backpack, not bothering to stop to change. *I'll just tell her we were practicing for a play or something.* She thought.

When the elevator opened to her floor, her blood ran cold as a wave of darkness swept over her, "What the—" Her eyes scanned down the hall towards her apartment, where the door was cracked open.

Lucy's mouth dropped open and her heart drummed loudly in her ears, "No. no…no… no, no, no…" she whispered. She engaged a force field around her body and ran to her apartment, pausing just outside the cracked door. The hairs on her arms rose; she smelled blood and evil. Her head swam and Lucy willed herself not to faint.

"Mom?" she called as she edged the door open.

She crept in and began to lose her breath. There was blood everywhere, splattered on the floor and walls and written in blood on the living room wall, "YOU DIDN'T COME LUCY!"

Her knees began to buckle, and she leaned against the couch. "Oh God…"

She swallowed hard and bit her tongue in order to not faint and quickly scanned the room. Then she saw a form in the dark on the kitchen floor. Lucy raced over and turned the light on, "Mommy. . ." She whispered weakly as the tears streamed down her cheeks. "Mom!" she choked out. Her mother didn't move and was on her side. Lucy carefully turned her mother onto her back, "Mommy?"

Her mother's eyes were dead windows of fear, a frozen scream caught in her open, breathless mouth. Her blood had been completely drained, and two puncture wounds gaped open on her neck. Lucy laid on Laura's body and sobbed.

Chapter Three

Hickory, North Carolina

A phone buzzed loudly on the side table. Darrel groaned and reached over, fumbling for a moment before he found it, his eyes squinting from the brightness of the screen. Lincoln's name came up on the caller ID and he punched the green button, "What's wrong?"

Billie Jean stirred next to him, and he put his hand on her lightly.

"D, there's been some activity near Asheville. Sounds pretty bad. We need both of you tonight." Lincoln was being short and urgent.

"Are you sure BJ needs to come? She's hardly sleeping with the morning sickness."

"Tell her I'm sorry, but we're going to need all hands on deck for this one. We got a couple of giants running amuck, and it's a bloodbath!"

"Understood. We'll be outside in 5 minutes."

"Ten!" Billie Jean groaned sleepily.

Already up, Darrel pounded the red button and tossed it on the bed as he went around to Billie Jean's side. He kneeled and took her hand, planting a gentle kiss on her cheek, "Mrs. Coleman, you are needed for service."

She grinned at him, her voice still raspy from sleep, "I'm never going to get tired of being called that." She sat up and kissed him.

Their whirlwind romance, marriage, and subsequent pregnancy announcement in "normal" times would have taken some by surprise, but since The Breach and the loss of so much life, many were living in fast forward, grabbing happiness where they could find it. The team had been very excited, and all showed up for the nuptials presided over by Diego.

A positive result of the constant fighting of invading monsters had led to Billie Jean quickly losing the stubborn extra weight that she had struggled with for years. Soon after returning from her journey in the other realm, she ended up actually becoming the lean beauty that she had felt like was just another of her shapeshifting forms. Though it had been months since she struggled, now that her body was growing again, she sometimes still felt self-conscious.

Darrel put his hand gently on her belly, "How are you feeling? Are you up for this?"

She smiled and stroked his dark, stubbly cheek, "I don't feel queasy right now. And when I transform, I don't feel any pregnancy symptoms anyway," She snickered lightly as she climbed out of bed, "Don't be surprised if you wake up next to a lion until I get through this morning sickness faze. I can't stand this puking!"

He laughed and patted her rear as she walked by, "As long as you transform *after* we've made love, you do what you gotta' do, girl!"

She laughed again as she headed into the bathroom.

***

About ten minutes later, they met Lincoln, Alvin and eight other Black Ops soldiers, as well as a handful of trained militia members, at the front gate of the compound. After the fall of New York six months ago, where two giants and a mass of nightmare creatures killed thousands of people, many New Yorkers and surrounding states' survivors migrated south to escape the carnage.

During the incident, Lincoln, Darrel and his new Giant Slayer team had managed to kill a number of the monsters, although the giants were too tough to handle at the time, one being at least 18 feet and the other a good 12 feet tall. Their defense had allowed many citizens to escape, but New York had been officially declared a disaster zone after the governor ordered a drone bombing of the whole city. Unfortunately, many innocent civilians were killed who couldn't escape in time, and although quite a few monsters were terminated, both giants survived with just a few bruises.

Soon after, Lincoln, who had inherited a 20-acre family ranch in the mountains of North Carolina. He had invited Darrel, Billie Jean, Alvin and the others to move out and help him fortify and make it a safe compound for Slayers and their families. With all their pooled resources and skills, they had so far managed to erect a strong perimeter gate with controlled access, surveillance cameras with night vision and thermal sequencing, and booby traps that would maim any enemy that approached by land or air.

They had also built barracks for the vast amount of people who had been coming and would continue to come. More recently, they had managed to move in numerous RVs and mobile homes for families, which is what Darrel and Billie Jean now occupied. The leadership, Lincoln, Darrel, Billie Jean, and Alvin, soon expected large groups of refugees as well as recruits for the Giant Slayer teams from military, police, and militia groups.

In the last two months, there were a few families and police, fire, and EMTs from New York who had joined them. Some had come by on a tip, and others had come because of dreams or visions about the place. So far, there were around 46 people living in the new community and The Lord prompted them to expect a lot more. Lincoln, who lived in the main 4-bedroom farmhouse with his wife and four boys, was amazed every day as new groups showed up.

He, Darrel and Billie Jean were careful to only bring people on the monster slaying operations who were not only trained with weapons and defense but also had been brought to a saving knowledge of Yeshua. The spiritual equipment for fighting these terrors was of utmost importance, as the enemy creatures not only fought physically but were also capable of mental and emotional attacks. Many people had died rushing in, guns blazing, to take out monsters, only to be easily defeated by mind control, fear, and the like. It was only individuals who loved and walked with the Lord that stood a chance at defeating these nightmare creatures and surviving to fight another day.

Another benefit for a few new believers was the addition of special abilities. Alvin and his team were the first to experience these phenomena. After meeting with Darrel and Lincoln and agreeing to join up, it wasn't long before Alvin experienced the love of God firsthand with a dream visitation from Jesus himself.

Alvin's PTSD had begun to manifest in recurring nightmares of the battle with the giants in Guatemala that had killed most of his team. In them, he would experience

21

the slaughter almost nightly and would wake up screaming in a cold sweat. One night, soon after teaming up with Darrel and Lincoln, Alvin had laid in bed exhausted but fearfully fighting sleep. At the time, he hadn't slept well in weeks. Eventually, he succumbed to his body's need for rest and soon found himself trekking through the wild jungle with his troop, tracking the stench of the monsters. Just as he was about to again relive a giant eating his best friend, Jesus came to him, and the dream paused like a movie. He looked into Jesus' eyes and his fear left, and a heavy weight lifted from his chest. Then Jesus, shining and magnificent, spoke, but His mouth did not move, "Do not fear, my son! I Am the Living One. I died but look—I Am alive forever! And I have overcome death and the grave."

Immediately, Alvin was taken to a heavenly realm and saw Jesus sitting on a great throne; the universe, stars, planets, and everything in all creation beneath Him, and He shined brighter than the sun. Alvin wanted to fall before His glorious throne, but incomprehensibly, he had no physical body to prostrate. All he could do was to yield all of himself to the glory and greatness of The Being that was above all things and who had called him "My Son."

He woke up as a new person, completely healed and forever pledged to One, and His will forever. Later, Alvin discovered he had acquired the ability to absorb any solid matter he touched like iron, stone, or wood and temporarily take on that substance, making his body as hard or soft as what he touched.

As the team's intelligence sergeant, Alvin had brought three of his closest surviving ODA, Operational Detachment Alphas, A-team members to join the Slayers,

Li "Cat" Zhang, Jesse "James' ' O' Brian, and Jacques Marcell.

Li Zhang, "The Cat," was a 28-year-old female communications sergeant, and fluent in Mandarin, English, German, Arabic, and Korean. Li was also a formidable fighter with Brazilian Ju Jitzu, Muay Tai, and Krav Maga. After joining the slayers and coming into a saving relationship with Yeshua, she also received special powers of night vision and extraordinary jumping and climbing skills.

Jesse "James" O'Brian was a 34-year-old sharpshooter Sniper and weapons sergeant, the best sniper since the famous Iraq war hero Chris Kyle. Jesse could hit anything and anyone within 1000 yards with over 350 confirmed kills of enemy combatants in Iraq and Afghanistan, over 50% of those being non-human entities. Jesse James is a 5'11, ginger-haired, stubble-faced, wise-cracking redneck with military tattoo sleeves on both arms. Like Alvin, the mission to Guatemala had changed his worldview on supernatural entities and God. It didn't take much to convince him to join his surviving team members in believing the truth of Jesus. He requested that Alvin do the honors of baptizing him in the ocean. Somehow, in the minute of earth realm time that he was dunked under the waves, he experienced days of an encounter with The Son of Man and came up from the wave in tears and humbled like a child.

His new special ability of camouflage was similar to an octopus, which they liked to call "octo-flage." Not only could he blend in, but he also took on the texture and scent of whatever he was around so as not to be detected even by enemy search dogs.

Jacques Marcell, a 30-year-old male of French Creole descent, fluent in French and French Creole, 6'1, muscular, caramel-skinned, sharp-tongued Assistant Operations sergeant. He grew up in the swamps of Louisiana and was not afraid of anything. He was known to have tracked a 10 ft. sasquatch through the Smoky Mountain National Park while it phased in and out of our realm and correctly predicted where it phased back in for capture.

Jacques' mother was a voodoo princess, and he was raised seeing and experiencing dark spirit beings. He decided early on that he wanted nothing to do with his mother's "religion" and left home for the army as soon as he turned 18.

His "seeing" skills were soon identified by the army, and he was recruited into special forces. Unlike Alvin and the others, his disillusionment with his childhood religion drove him to seek a counteraction in knowing the only fear dark entities seemed to have was of the name of Jesus Christ. After reading through the Bible with the local chaplain, Jacques gave his life over to the "Highest Power," as he called it. Before the last mission, where they lost half of their Alpha team, he had a series of dreams where an angelic being warned him of what was about to happen on the next mission. He spoke to command to no avail, and they still sent the team.

The horror of that mission was the first he'd ever been on to send him home with trauma. Soon after, he took a couple weeks alone in a house in Wyoming and hiked through the Grand Teton area. There, he had an encounter with the Savior that drew him even closer to the Father heart of God, healed him deeply from the mission and many childhood and family line wounds, and he came back renewed and with a supernatural gift.

Jacques had the ability to influence a person's thoughts, where a person or even creature believed the thought to be their own. The Lord Yeshua showed him that this ability was normally only used by spirit beings, i.e. demons and angels. This was how many people could not distinguish what was their own thoughts or what a demonic entity was projecting into his or her own head or, conversely, how an angel could influence a person to not get on an airplane that was about to crash. The Lord also told him that many entities would not believe that a human could possess this power and would never suspect him of it.

These three were Alvin's inner circle and quickly became part of the "A-Team" of the Slayers' leadership, which also included Gianna, Lucy, and Diego, who came frequently to meet up for operations and training with the others, even though they were not currently residing at the compound. For a couple of their newly trained recruits, this would be their first time-fighting side by side with the "A-team", and there was palpable excitement coming from the well-trained ultra-warriors. Lincoln gathered the group around him and another ten militia members who would be support and eyes for the core team of eight.

He began to brief them, "I'm going to make this quick," He stroked his thick chest-length beard as he looked soberly at each individual, "This may be the ugliest mess we've all seen since New York. Prepare for not only blood and carnage but also blasts of fear and chaos. For those of you who've never faced a giant before, this is no fairy tale. These are terrifying, evil,

Cheryl McClamrock

vicious, killing machines that have superpowers! This is why no one that is not supernaturally enhanced and got a relationship with Jesus will be coming."

A few of them nodded. He looked at a large, bald, salt-and-pepper bearded man named Drake, who was a militia member, "Drake, I'm going to need you to make us a portal to Asheville large enough to drive our vehicles through." The barrel-chested burly man responded, "You got it, boss!"

Drake had been a local restaurant/ bar owner whose encounter with a werewolf that killed his wife initially sent him on a monster hunt that left him bloody and mangled near Lincoln's property. Lincoln's dogs had alerted him to the intrusion, and he got to the scene just as the werewolf was about to feast on Drake and sliced it in half with his sword. Thereby lifting the 250-pound wounded man and carrying him like a child back to his house. Drake, mystified by the display, vowed to stick with Lincoln until death from that point on. Lincoln soon thereafter led his new best friend to the Lord, baptizing him in the creek running across the land. After becoming a new believer, Drake received the ability to create portals to transport himself and others to different places on the earth. Over time, he grew in his gifting to be able to transport groups of people and even vehicles through the portals.

Lincoln turned to Darrel and Billie Jean and nodded. Darrel called to the group, "Okay, team, gather in." He bowed his head, and they all followed suit, "Gracious heavenly Father, we ask for your divine protection and guidance as we go do your work to defend earth against the abominations of the Enemy. May we be focused, aware, and empowered to be your swift hand of

26

judgment against darkness. May Your Kingdom come, and Your will be done on earth as it is in heaven. In the Name above all Names, Jesus the Messiah, we pray. Amen."

"Amen." Agreed the group.

With that, his eyes became orange, and instantly his whole body became a flame. Nearby, Billie Jean transformed into a snow-white lioness. Lincoln, already dressed in his warrior attire with sword and shield in tow, jumped on the first of three black armored vehicles. The other team and militia members climbed aboard as Drake, seated next to him in the front vehicle, made a circular motion with his hand and suddenly, a giant round portal appeared.

Darrel flew through first, with Billie Jean bounding after, and then the vehicles followed. The portal disappeared as the last vehicle passed through.

Chapter Four

Richmond, Texas

Gianna tossed and turned, her mind racing and unwilling to quiet down so she could rest. The rain, pounding against the window, should have soothed her, but instead it made her nervous and anxious, and she couldn't understand why. She decided to go downstairs and make a cup of chamomile tea and read for a bit until she got sleepy.

She tip-toed into the kitchen, trying hard not to wake David, who slept on the nearby couch. As she prepared the tea, a familiar soft head rubbed against her leg and meowed up at her, demanding food and attention.

"Shhhh, Tigger! Can't you leave me be?" She whispered as she scooped him up and rubbed his belly. He purred loudly in her arms, and she kissed the top of his head.

"I never wished so much to be a cat." Quipped David behind her.

She put Tigger down quickly and rolled her eyes, "Sorry, I tried to be quiet but was unsuccessful." Purposefully ignoring his comment as she stirred honey into her cup. "Did we wake you?"

He strode over to the fridge, "Oh, no, no, don't worry. I was having a tough time sleeping, too." He got the milk out and drank from the carton.

She grumbled, "Can you please get a cup? That's disgusting."

He shut it and put it back in the fridge, shrugging, "Why waste a cup when I just want a sip or two?"

Gianna shook her head, grabbed her mug and was about to leave the room with it.

He stopped her, "Wait, Gigi. I'm sorry. I'll get a cup next time. Can you stay a few minutes and talk?"

She sighed, not feeling in the mood to talk but knowing she couldn't avoid it for much longer. She reluctantly nodded and padded towards the couch in her fuzzy slippers.

Once there, she sat, covered her legs with her favorite soft blanket and sipped her tea. David, looking encouraged, sat next to her, but not too close. She noticed he was being considerate of her space. She decided to try her best to engage.

He took a tentative breath, "Have you had a chance to think about what I asked you last week?"

Gianna played dumb and gave him a questioning look as she took another sip.

"You know, about the counseling?"

"Oh, the counseling!" She shook her head as a knot formed in her chest, "David, no . . . I–"

He nodded reassuringly, "Gigi, come on . . . it couldn't hurt, right? Just give me—*it* a chance—"

She inched away from him, shaking her head, "David. No, I'm not ready."

"Gi, it's been six months, and now I'm living here—"

She stood up quickly, pointing down at him, "Don't. Just don't David! I was very clear that you moving back in here did not mean we were reconciling!"

He went to grab her hand and she yanked it away. He quickly held his hands up in surrender, "Look, I'm sorry, I know you did, I get it. Please sit back down."

Gianna put her empty cup on the side table, turning from him and wondering how she could get away and not have to deal with him and his feelings. He looked up at her with pleading big brown eyes, "Please . . . please, Gigi, don't go, sit with me a little longer."

She blew a loud breath out of her nose and reluctantly sat back down, but well out of his reach.

He smiled and stayed quiet for a moment, running his hands through his dark, wavy hair, his new thick beard showing shimmers of gray. She liked the new shaggy look, but she would never admit that to him. Right now, she still wanted to slap his face more than appreciate it.

"Gigi, I know I have no right to ask or expect anything from you,"

She nodded but stayed silent. "I just want some time to at least discuss *something*. You won't talk to me. You won't even tell me you hate my guts!"

"Fine, I hate your guts." Gianna quipped with no emotion.

David paused and pinched the bridge of his nose, "Gigi, I'm being serious here."

She cracked a smile, "How do you know I wasn't?"

"Because you're closed off like a bank vault! At least in counseling, you can let it all out! You can tell them and me what you are feeling and going through. At least I'll know something. It will be a start."

Suddenly, her phone buzzed violently on the side table, startling her. Relieved by the distraction, she quickly grabbed it, "I should get this. It's Lucy." David nodded and leaned back on the couch.

"Hello?"

"Oh, good you're up. . . I hope I didn't wake you." Lucy sniffled and her voice cracked.

"No, I'm fine, I was up. Are you okay? You don't sound good. What happened?" Gianna asked, her concern mounting.

"I'm on your porch."

Gianna's eyes widened and she ran to the front door. David, curious, followed close behind. She threw open the door, and Lucy stood there, tears flowing and mouth quivering.

"Oh, sweetie, what happened?" Lucy rushed into Gianna's arms and wept. Gianna held her close and guided the young girl inside. She eyed David to close the door. He nodded and closed it as Gianna steered her over to the couch. She took her backpack and put it down, grabbed the tissue box nearby and handed it to the girl. Lucy continued to cry for a bit as she took a tissue and began to wipe at her eyes and nose.

"Take your time, Lucy." She looked at David again. "Can you please get her some water?"

"Sure, yes ... right away." He skittered out of the room.

Gianna took Lucy's hand. "Did you translate here or fly?"

"I translated," she cracked a brief smile. "I totally would have got lost if I flew."

Gianna smiled. "Oh my gosh, me too!"

Lucy wiped her eyes again and took a deep breath. David came back with a glass of water and handed it to her as he sat down on the other side of her.

31

"Thank you." She drank the whole thing, not realizing how thirsty she was until just then.

"Lucy, this is my husband, David."

"Hello, Lucy, I've heard so much about you." He said sweetly.

Lucy looked at him shyly. "It's nice to meet you."

Gianna motioned to the stairs with her head as Lucy blew her nose. David nodded slightly, "I don't mind going upstairs if you ladies want to talk."

Lucy seemed to relax at that. Gianna smiled at him, thankful he was understanding of the circumstances. She did appreciate that about him lately. He didn't push too hard and seemed to give her space when she needed it.

He excused himself, "I'll just head upstairs then."

After he left the room, Lucy looked at Gianna with her big brown eyes, and Gianna was instantly taken back to when they first met, and Lucy had asked her if she knew how to get out of the weird realm they had woken up in.

Lucy's mouth quivered. "My mom's dead." Tears began to flow again, and she cried into a tissue.

Gianna put her arm around the girl. "Oh no! Oh no! What happened?"

After a bit, Lucy was able to give Gianna the whole story between nose blowings and more tears. Gianna cried with her young friend and quietly prayed while holding her. Finally, she could see that Lucy was exhausted, her eyes puffy from crying and droopy with fatigue, "Sleep here, sweetie. You look exhausted. I'll get you something to change into if you want." Lucy shook her head. "No, I'm fine. Thank you." She had already laid on David's pillow and had his blanket wrapped around her.

Gianna turned off the lamp, and as she headed to the stairs, she smiled slightly as she heard Lucy's breathing change and knew she was already sound asleep. Gianna prayed it would be a peaceful one.

Not until entering the bedroom did she realize that David was laying in her, rather, their bed already sound asleep. She bit her lip as she contemplated her options. The least fuss would definitely be crawling into bed next to him and letting it go. She wasn't sure that she was ready for that. It had been over seven months since he had shared her bed and she did miss him most at night. It was why she had trouble sleeping at times. But letting him get close to her again bothered her, and she didn't want to open a door that she couldn't shut again.

He seemed to be asleep, so she took her chances and slipped in on her side, taking special care not to get too close to him. She lay for a few minutes praying, as was her routine, and instantly noticed the warmth of having another person in the bed. She listened to the rhythm of his breathing and soon fell into a rhythm of her own as the scattered thoughts mixed with prayers soon sent her into a comfortable slumber.

A warm arm slipped around her as images careened through her mind: Lincoln running from a serpent beast, Jezebel squeezing David with black tentacles, emaciated children in dark cages, and Uriel's urgent silver eyes boring into hers, "Gianna! We must go now!" She ran towards him, two children in her arms, her heart pounding. She couldn't look away from his eyes. The angel's silvery brows furrowed, boring into her very soul, "Now Gianna! You must go now!"

She shot up to a sitting position in bed, heart pounding, with a scream caught in her throat. David woke up startled, "What's wrong?!" He had been holding her, and he turned her face to his. "Did you have a nightmare?"

She looked into David's brown eyes but simultaneously saw Uriel's as the angel's voice echoed loudly. "Go now!"

She jumped out of bed. "We have to go!" Her heart dropped into her stomach, and the hairs on her arms pricked up.

He sprang out of bed and didn't question her. They both began dressing on the run. She grabbed her phone. It was 5am. She took her emergency 'go' backpack from the closet, which was always ready with supplies and essentials. As she sprinted out the bedroom door, she yelled back to David, "Throw a few things into a bag. It's all we have time for and start the minivan while I wake everyone!"

Her gut burned with urgency as she woke Amora and Dylan, snatching their prepared 'go' bags and hanging them on the sleepy young shoulders.

"Come on, kids. Just like we've practiced!" She urged them.

Amora roused quickly and within moments was alert, her eyes filled with fear. She began to help Dylan with his shoes. Gianna, knowing that waking her up this way triggered her, knelt down and looked the girl in the eyes, "You're safe," Squeezing her shoulder reassuringly, "I have you. Okay?" Amora visibly relaxed and nodded.

"Okay, finish helping Dylan and meet us downstairs, sweetie." The little girl nodded again. Gianna walked towards the stairs and called down to Lucy to wake up as the children followed behind her. She herded the three young ones through the kitchen towards the garage door and shoved water bottles in their hands as she sent them into the waiting van inside.

Dylan looked back. "Wait mom! Tigger!" On cue, the orange tabby rubbed up against her leg and meowed up at her for food. "Tigger!" Her mind raced with the need to leave as she scooped the fur ball up and grabbed the container of cat food and a bowl as she shooed everyone into the van. Handing the cat to the now seated boy in the back, she jumped in the passenger side. With her face flushed, she put her hand on David's arm, "Drive."

He backed out into the morning darkness, tires squealing. She was thankful that he didn't ask questions. There was a rumbling, and she couldn't tell if it was from outside of the van or inside her trembling body. The spiritual noise she was feeling was like pin pricks up and down her skin, and her stomach quivered. She felt darkness encircling them.

Something's coming, Gi! I feel it!" Lucy remarked, putting words to Gianna's feelings.

"I know, I know," Gianna pulled her cell phone out and found Diego's number in her favorites. She pressed "call" and turned towards David, "Take 59 towards Dallas. We're heading to Missouri."

He raised his eyebrows, but again didn't ask anything and she thankfully sighed. It was now close to 6am and after two rings, Diego's deep and surprisingly alert voice came on the line.

"Hello, Gianna, what's happening?"

"Diego! I had a dream. It was Uriel and he told me to leave now. I don't know where to go except to you."

"I've been up for hours, too. Do you have Lucy and Amora?"

She nodded, "Yes! Can we come?"

"Of course, but you must do something before you come. It's imperative that you bind Amora's demons."

"What?"

Suddenly, a beastly growl came from the back seat. "YOU CAN'T STOP ME!"

Dylan screamed in fright and the cat jumped from his lap, spitting and hissing at Amora.

Gianna quickly turned her head to look back as Amora's face contorted, and the innocent little blue-eyed beauty was gone. Something horrible was now wearing her face. Her eyes were pitch black and her mouth opened at an impossible width as 'she' glared at Gianna and growled, a sound that couldn't possibly come from a little girl's throat.

"Oh my God!" Gianna whispered.

"What's back there?" screamed David.

"Gianna, what's happening?" asked Diego.

She turned to David. "Pull over, pull over!"

They were on the freeway, but luckily, it was early on a Sunday morning, and few cars were on the road. David jerked the van to the nearest exit as *the thing* that was Amora began to writhe and howl. The atmosphere felt impossibly heavy. Gianna struggled to take a breath and she wondered if she was experiencing a panic attack.

Dylan was crying now, and Lucy had begun to pray over Amora, which seemed to intensify the unholy writhing and howling. David quickly found an empty parking lot next to a long shutdown movie theater. He looked back at the small child with a monster's voice emanating from her foaming mouth and back at Gianna, "Whata' we do!?"

"Diego! What do we do? She's manifesting! Something horrible has got a hold of her!" She screamed into the phone.

"Keep me on the phone. Listen, Gianna, you have authority. It's been exposed, and it's afraid —"

"*It's* afraid?! You're kidding, right?" Her heart was pounding, and her mouth was dry.

"Gianna! Do not give in to fear! Fear empowers it! This is all it has to keep control of her—"

The hair-raising squealing grew louder as Diego talked. Lucy's prayers under her breath intensified, and she laid her hand on Amora's arm, causing the "girl" to yowl and pull back as if she had been touched by fire. The teenager responded with a sharp, "Shut up, right now!" Immediately, the squealing and growling ceased.

Gianna's mouth dropped open.

"What's happening, Gianna?" Asked Diego.

Lucy continued to pray inaudibly, her eyes boring into the now completely black eyes of Amora, "Now, I bind you! You cannot use Amora's voice. I forbid you from doing anything more to harm her. In the name of Jesus, I forbid you to report anything you've seen or heard. You are bound by the power of the Holy One!" Amora shook her head, mewling and whimpering like a hurt animal.

"Gianna!" came Diego's voice from the phone. Gianna had watched all this in amazement, "Hold on, Diego…" She responded breathlessly. She almost immediately felt her lungs relax and was able to take a full breath.

Tigger stopped spitting and was curled up on Dylan's lap, who also had calmed down considerably and was now also watching Lucy and Amora intently. Lucy finally broke eye contact with Amora, looked at Gianna and David and said "Pray."

Gianna nodded. "Pray, Diego." She immediately heard the Seer praying in the Spirit on the line. Gianna joined him, David also nodded, eyes wide but prayed under his breath.

Lucy, with the strength and fortitude of a woman beyond her years, turned back to Amora, who immediately looked worried again and began to shake her head.

Suddenly, the atmosphere was brighter, like the sun bursting through the dark clouds, and Yeshua stepped into the van through the side wall. Gianna's caught her breath. He looked at her, nodded and knelt next to Lucy and the little girl. The black eyes of the beast that had taken over grew wide in absolute terror when He entered. Gianna noticed the others didn't move, turn or seem to notice the King's entrance onto the scene. Lucy was still speaking, but Gianna now only heard what was taking place in the spirit realm.

Jesus reached inside of Amora and pulled out a thick, dark, writhing mass. It slowly took the shape of a hideous goat-footed, horned entity with thick arms. It was bound in golden chains and gagged with a golden rope. The ugly beast looked absolutely terrified as Jesus then delivered it into the hands of a glorious 15-foot, golden armored angelic being. The angel dipped his head to the Master, took his prisoner and disappeared.

Gianna couldn't tell where this was actually taking place but understood the spirit realm did not take the same "space" as the physical world. Jesus then turned back to Amora, who's body looked smaller than before for some reason. The little girl now appeared relaxed, and her eyes were blue again. As Lucy continued to pray, Jesus knelt over Amora again and her exhausted face lit up when she saw Him. He placed his nail-scarred hand on her forehead and said, "Peace, daughter." She smiled weakly and a single tear slid down the side of her face.

He turned back to Gianna, "They can no longer track her, but she has more healing to do yet." Gianna nodded. "Diego will continue to work with her when you get there. Go now. They will not see you."

"Yes, Lord."

Then He was gone, and with him, the sunlight dimmed a little.

Gianna suddenly remembered Diego on the phone, "Diego…"

"I saw it all." He interrupted; his voice was choked with emotion. "Get here as soon as you can, Gianna. Let's get her free."

She nodded. "We're coming."

Chapter Five

Asheville, NC

The city was in flames. The team had entered the area on the outskirts of Asheville. Darrel could just make out the dark rolling hills behind the city, made prominent by the flames rising from the buildings. The ground shook as the shape of a mile-high humanoid monster marched heavily through the blazing streets. The creature was easily double the size of the tallest building in Asheville, and as it walked it scooped up a bus, crushing it in its fist, then pitching it through a glass building blocks away.

"My God, I've never seen one so big!" Cat exclaimed next to him as she unholstered her M9. She was wearing a black suit with multiple compartments, each containing deadly items. Her hair and everything but her glowing cat-like eyes were hidden under a black head cover. "Hey, big guy, mind dropping me on a building close to the giant?" Darrel smiled and nodded, then turned to Billie, who had just transformed into the dazzling white gryphon, "Babe! You ready?"

Her giant eagle head nodded, and she clawed the ground. The team members who hadn't yet seen her in this form stared in awe. Billie Jean waited; her opalescent white wings still folded into her lion body. Darrel addressed the team, "BJ can take three of you in. The rest will have to walk; we can't risk the vehicles getting destroyed by getting any closer."

Jesse James raised his hand, "Drop me on a building nearby so I can get set up for my shots."

Alvin and Jacque climbed up behind Jesse and his large equipment bag on Billie's back.

Lincoln got their attention and laid out the plan, "I'll run in. Drake can transport two more. The rest of you come in from the other directions, so we're circling it," He looked at each seriously. "We'll take care of the main giant. The rest of you address the other trash who are usually nearby. Watch out for vamps, who can get you from above or from the shadows. I can't emphasize enough your need to rely on the Holy Spirit to be your extra eyes and to cover you."

They all nodded. With guns cocked and swords drawn, the team took off in six different directions heading into a hell of a war zone. Men, women, and children were everywhere, fleeing on foot with whatever they could carry. Bikes, motorcycles, and vehicles flew past them, heading out of town as the heroes headed towards the danger, they all were fleeing. A pair of teens had a group of hideous goblins pursuing them. Lincoln swiftly sliced through the predators, dropping heads before the monsters even noticed him. The teens hugged each other and cried in relief. They looked for their savior, but he was already hacking through a band of zombies. He shook his head, still unbelieving that this horror film had become a reality.

Each time the Slayers came upon a new nightmare scene, the new "reality" slammed them in the face. They began to notice patterns in the attacks as well. Of course, cities were more likely to be targeted because of the population density and the more death and destruction, the better for these fiends. Also, Lincoln had noticed that

41

it seemed the "big bads" spawned other monsters. They almost always were accompanied by masses of ghoulish creatures, werewolves, minotaurs, goblins, and other terrors there were no names for. The zombies were a new thing that he'd only been seeing recently, and they had questioned how the enemy was creating them. Were actual people getting turned, or were these just some other sort of abomination? They didn't really know and had no time to examine details on it but destroyed all of them they came across for safety's sake.

Minutes later, Lincoln had made it to the downtown area using his super speed. He immediately felt the ground rumble from the super giant's activities nearby. One of their usual strategies was to take out the biggest Nephilim; the other creatures would then flee or disappear. He stopped near the federal building, which was on fire, but beyond the smoke, Lincoln got a whiff of the putrid odor that he'd begun to identify with the Satanic Spawn. It was like Sulphur sprinkled over a trash dump.

Suddenly, a flaming car flew just inches above his head, crashing into the federal building behind him. The thing that threw it was a football field further down the road, looking like a gigantic dark shadow from where Lincoln now stood. Angry, Lincoln hardened his skin, which protected him from bites and blades, and ran towards the fiend.

Seconds later, he was standing within a few feet of an eight-foot monstrosity sporting four arms and a really bad attitude. The dumpster smell was overwhelming, which made Lincoln even angrier. The ugly beast grinned, showing a maw of gnarly blood-stained razors.

"Did you just throw a car at me?"

Instead of answering, it cackled wickedly and balled up its four jumbo-sized fists.

Lincoln pointed his sword at it, "You're going down, dumpster-fire!"

Behind him, Lincoln heard a crash and screams beyond. He needed to dispatch this pile of excrement quickly and get to the other victims. He ran at the fiend, who punched down at him too slowly for Lincoln's enhanced speed and missed every time. Lincoln easily dodged the slow punch and sliced through one of the offending arms. The beast howled in pain and rage. It immediately began to pound at Lincoln with the other three fists like a kid playing Whack-a-Mole.

Lincoln's hardened skin and speed powers made it nearly impossible for the giant to land a blow. The hero soon succeeded in quickly dispatching the other three arms, which were now littering the ground. Amazingly, the fiend's thick black blood smelled worse than the monster did before it was injured. The giant howled with rage, causing Lincoln to cower as the guttural noise seeped into his bones. He groaned as his head suddenly throbbed with intense pain.

Now defenseless, the monster was resorting to sensory attacks. Before it could catch its breath for another scream, Lincoln leapt in the air, decapitating it cleanly. The head dropped to the street with a sickening thud and rolled into a nearby alley.

***

Cat spotted a flat-topped building that wasn't on fire close to the center of downtown and pointed. Darrel flew near, and she jumped, landing easily and lightly on her feet, quickly disappearing into the shadows. Billie Jean had also just dropped her passengers close by. A military helicopter hovered at a seemingly safe distance yards away. Darrel saw the remnants of other choppers on the ground below and wondered if there were survivors. He waved Billie Jean forward towards the biggest giant they had seen yet.

The darkness, as well as the fire and smoke, obscured its features, but based on the carnage surrounding it, they knew it was more dangerous than any they had dealt with before. It was definitely the biggest. Darrel pushed down the fear that clawed at his insides like a beast wanting to escape. He prayed against fear and for angelic help. He hadn't seen angels since coming back from the Other realm and wondered, at times, if they were even really around.

The sky-scraper-sized beast had spotted them and left off its previous business of trashing every building in site. It was dark-skinned with a wild beard and tall horns sticking out of both sides of its head. Its glowing yellow eyes were all that Darrel could clearly see through the haze. Billie Jean swooped down, her white wings almost glowing in the darkness, as the giant slowly looked down on her, either curious or calculating. Darrel moved in closer and enveloped its head in a cast of flame.

***

Cat, Jacque, Alvin, and Jesse were connected with the others on coms and had coordinated a perimeter around the mountainous beast. Jesse James settled in a broken office building on the east side that no longer had a roof but still enough walls for coverage for him to set up his "beast sniping" arsenal, which consisted of a Barret M-82 semi-automatic wall blaster sniper rifle equipped with a Night force scope, and his Styr IWS 2000 anti-tank single shot bolt action rifle. He found both to be integral weapons in the giant slaying business. He had taken out quite a few towering beasts in the last few months with his deadly combination of weapons, sniping skills, and his new "octo-flage" abilities.

From his angle, he didn't see any way he could miss hitting the beast's massive head, especially since Darrel had set it on fire. Since it was occupied with trying to swat at Darrel and BJ like annoying house flies, he didn't think it would be able to see where the bullets were coming from before he took it down.

***

Lincoln ran towards the screams he'd heard earlier, hoping that it wouldn't be too late to help someone in peril. Most of the streetlights had been trashed, and the only light he had to work with was from sporadic fires coming from nearby buildings and cars. Halfway down the dark road, he stopped to listen for the person in distress. As if right on cue, a shrill scream came from up ahead, and he ran with super speed to the sound. As he turned the corner, a sudden wave of dark energy stopped him abruptly in his tracks and sent ice shooting down his spine. He crouched low, leaning on his sword to keep himself from falling over, and shook his head, trying to recover from the shock of it.

Once again, a woman cried out and he recovered enough to look up. To the right, where two cars had hit head-on, a significant fire creepily illuminated the once bustling area that recently boasted museums and great food. How long would it take the city to recover from this attack? Would they even be able to? His mind and emotions were in hyperdrive. As he scanned, he soon found the source of the screams. A young woman was

45

bound to a tree while what looked like a handful of vampires feasted loudly on a couple of bodies nearby. When she screamed, they looked up from their meals and laughed.

Lincoln growled, his anger as well as his stomach churned from the macabre scene. He was definitely going to put these monsters down. Somehow, they hadn't noticed him yet, and he was able to pinpoint at least three that he could see on the bodies. He was more worried about the ones he couldn't see that were possibly scouting from above. He hardened his body and ran at them. They only had a brief second to see him before he had relieved them of their heads. The three appeared to be young men, one with a beard and the other two would have looked like basic frat boys had it not been for the two-inch bloody fangs protruding from their mouths. He waited a few seconds before he moved, ready for an attack from above. The woman was still tied to the tree but slumped over, weeping silently. He wiped his bloody sword off on one of the vampire's shirts before sheathing it and cautiously walking towards her. Lincoln stopped a few feet from her and whispered, "Hey, hey, it's okay, ma'am. They're dead, but I need you to look up at me before I untie you."

She sniffled and raised her head. She had shoulder-length blonde hair with pink streaks in it, her skin was pale, and her eyes were giant pools of fear. Another college kid. He tried to see if she showed any signs that she had been bitten. She seemed to be calming down a bit. Lincoln hung his shield behind him and addressed the girl, "Are you okay? Have you been bit?"

She shook her head, "N-No..." she stammered. "They said they were saving me for dessert."

Lincoln growled in disgust. "I'm going to cut you loose, but if you try to bite me or any crazy stuff, I will not hesitate to kill you. Do you understand?"

She nodded.

He took a knife from his belt and began to cut her hands free while watching her and their surroundings carefully, "Were these the only creeps that attacked you or were there more?"

She rubbed her wrists, "Just them." She looked at the bodies and put her hand to her mouth. He caught her as she swayed and began to fall to the ground, "Woah! I gotcha,' ma'am!" He eased her to a sitting position on the ground.

She buried her head in her hands, "That was my boyfriend and his brother!" She began to hiccup and cry.

"Miss, I'm so sorry for this horrible loss you are processing right now, but we can't stay here." He helped her stand up.

She wiped her eyes and stammered, "Tha-thank you for saving me."

He nodded, "That's what I do, ma'am." He began to ease her away from the scene, walking her to the end of the block, "What's your name?"

"Emily." She whispered.

"Emily, I'm going to walk you to the edge of the town. There's a lot of people heading out of town, and I'm sure someone can walk with you to a safe place. I've got to head back in and help my friends put a stop to the carnage."

"P-please don't leave me, I'm so scared," she sounded choked and on the verge of tears again.

He groaned as his thoughts were torn between helping her and helping his team fight the big baddies.

Lincoln shook his head and stopped, pulling her into the shadow of a building, "Look, where I'm going is much more dangerous than what you just experienced, and my friends need my help. I promise, the further you get from this city, the safer you will be."

She sniffled and whimpered, and he ran his hands through his hair muttering to himself, "You freaking dummy…what are you doing?" He whispered under his breath.

"What?"

"Nothing, nothing…. Okay Emily, you can come with me," he tilted her chin up to look at his face, "Look at me, I need you to understand something."

She nodded, wiping a stray tear and still sniffling.

Even in the darkness, he could see her big blue eyes still glassy with tears, "This is life or death! I will probably have to put you in a hiding place in a nearby building while I go fight some horrible monsters that, if you get too close, will kill you or worse, melt your brain in your skull before they kill you." Her hand clapped over her mouth and her big eyes got bigger.

Lincoln nodded, "I just want you to understand the danger. Above all, I need you to do what I say, when I say it. Got it?" She nodded vigorously. He pulled her out of the shadows by her arm, "Let's go! And no talking unless absolutely necessary."

She nodded again, and they jogged off back toward the center of the city where most of the fires and smoke were coming from.

Chapter Six

Somewhere in Oklahoma

Gianna and the van crew's travels had been fairly uneventful for the last few hours. What used to be an eleven-hour drive from Texas to Missouri would end up being closer to twenty because of the current state of roadways, cities, and towns due to the Breach. Some states and towns hadn't yet been touched by dark invaders, but others had either been completely taken over by monsters and villains or destroyed. Finding safe places to stop for fuel and breaks was now precarious and expensive. Most of Texas except on the western border with New Mexico where there wasn't yet a militarized wall, had made it through relatively unscathed because of Gianna and her teams, the Texas National guard and volunteer militias.

Once they reached Oklahoma, though, it was a completely different story. As they drove carefully down sideroads to avoid the danger of main thoroughfares, heaps of smoking ash greeted them where thriving towns had once been. Many major cities were now overrun with gangs, ghouls and gargoyles and had to be avoided as not to attract unwanted attention. David struggled weaving in and around abandoned, looted and burned vehicles that littered the roadways.

After a couple of hours into Oklahoma, they finally found a seemingly abandoned gas station with a large convenience store to pull in at. There were still dozens of cars in the parking lot and they figured they wouldn't attract too much attention there. They hoped they'd be able to siphon off some fuel from the abandoned vehicles or get lucky and find some fuel in the pumps. David parked the van next to an old pickup and a couple of cars. He went to work checking each one with some home-made siphon equipment they'd picked up at a Home Depot in Texas. Gianna and the kids carefully made their way towards the store; Gianna and Lucy equipped and ready if need be. They didn't hold out much hope for leftover food, but possibly other items of need and maybe toilets with toilet paper were a hoped-for possibility.

The store was dark and completely glass enclosed with a few smashed holes where looters had gotten in and probably gotten most of the valuable materials. The group saw no movement inside, so they carefully stepped through a broken doorway, "Stay together." Gianna whispered.

She didn't trust anything she saw, knowing that criminals and ghouls could be hiding quietly in the dark aisles. She motioned towards the bathrooms in the back of the store, and they all headed towards them, with eyes and ears alert to movement. As they approached the restroom doors, Lucy held her hand up, "Let me go in first, I can shield myself and take the initial hit if anything is hiding in the dark in there."

Gianna nodded and held Dylan and Amora behind her with her swords out and ready. Lucy quickly came back out, nose wrinkled, "It's safe, but it smells horrible."

Gianna had thought about this possible issue since the last few places they stopped were also disgusting. She pulled her neck gaiter up over her mouth and nose, "It's ok, we'll just hold our noses as long as there's toilet paper, we'll make it work. Everyone turn your phone flashlights on, there's no power."

As soon as they entered Dylan blurted. "Eww! I'm not going in there!" And attempted to turn around and walk out.

"Dylan, hold your nose and go, this may be the only safe place available for a while. Just try to make it quick."

"I can't be quick when I have to poop!" He whined. Amora giggled and pulled her t-shirt neck over her nose.

Dark and smelly were inadequate descriptions for what the multi-stalled sewage pit smelled like. Gianna dry-heaved a little. "Ok, everyone, be as fast as possible!"

After layering the seat with paper, Gianna sat, hoping to get her business done quickly and get out. She rolled her eyes as the girls talked through the stall doors about how lovely it was to have toilet paper and Dylan playfully mimicked their dialogue.

"Are y'all in here? Everyone ok?" David's voice made Gianna jump a bit. "Yes, we're fine." She answered.

"It smells terrible in here, I'm going to go outside, can you bring me some TP?" He quipped.

"Aww, why couldn't I go outside?" Dylan moaned.

"You're fine! Finish up in here!" scolded Gianna. The girls giggled.

Gianna finished and walked out with a roll of tissue, handing it to David. As she turned towards the sinks, he remarked, "There's no running water, but I found some hand sanitizer and a few other supplies, I already loaded as much in the van as I could find."

She turned back and followed him out, "Did you find any food?"

Gianna slammed right into his back as he stopped abruptly.

"David! What the- ?"

Her eyes widened and the hairs on her arms stood at attention.

A few guns cocked loudly, "Well, well, well what do we have here? Come out *pretty lady*." Gianna stepped out from behind David to the scene of at least half a dozen greasy haired, dangerous looking, men all with guns pointed at them, and with wide gap-toothed evil grins.

David, his hands in the air, attempted to negotiate with them, "Look, guys, we don't have any money, but you can have our van and anything in it."

"David, no they can't!" Gianna was angry and her limbs were twitching with desire to pound these idiots into the ground.

"Gi! Let me handle this okay?"

"No, I won't let them take our stuff!" She felt a surge of power fill her limbs, and she was assessing how she could deal with them without getting David shot.

The wild-bearded leader cocked his shotgun, "Well, I'm going to have to tell you both to shut the hell up. We'll be takin' whatever we please along with you, little lady." He said with a wink of one of his black eyes.

A shiver of revulsion crawled up Gianna's spine, and she knew she'd see these filthy pigs dead before she'd let them near her or her family. She prayed the kids would hear what was going on and stay quiet in the bathroom. As if on cue, Dylan popped through the bathroom door, "Mom, I—"His eyes expanded and he snapped his mouth shut. David grabbed him and shoved the boy behind him.

"Ain't that sweet? We got a whole happy family! What else you got stashed in there?" He snapped his fingers at the others and pointed at the family. Three of the other grease balls roughly grabbed each of them and pulled them to the side, "No!" Gianna shouted, "Lucy! ON POINT!"

The Native American man holding Gianna punched her in the mouth, she instantly saw stars as excruciating pain overwhelmed her and she fell back. David yelled and tried to come at him, but the muscled brute holding him got him quickly in a choke hold and David couldn't move. Dylan began to cry, and the skinny young guy that had him just laughed and held his arm tightly. The leader and another man headed towards the bathroom door and as they touched it, a wave of power pitched the two thugs so far that they hit the back wall of the store and fell face first on the concrete floor with a sickening crack. The others quickly laid on the ground as if a bomb went off.

Lucy flew out of the bathroom and hovered above the small crowd for a moment assessing the trouble. One of the men looked up, "What the hell!" She swooped over, grabbed him by the throat causing him to scream like a young girl. Gianna used the distraction to grab the man who had punched her and pin him up against the wall, he paled with terror, "What are you? Please don't kill us!"

As she looked him in the eyes, she got a flash image of him beating and raping multiple women and girls. Her face began to heat up with anger, "How many girls have you hurt and had no mercy on, huh, you filth?" She punched him in the face, he yelped, and blood began to pour from his broken nose. She was about to hit him again when a crash at the back of the store made them all turn. Out of the dark multiple sets of yellow eyes peered at them, and a collection of inhuman high-pitched giggles accompanied the creatures as they approached.

The man Gianna was holding began to shake and whispered, "Bhopoli..." She dropped the man and he scrambled away.

The smell of the small creatures came into focus before the dark shapes of them did, "David take the kids to the van, now!" She shouted. She grabbed her swords from her back as she transformed into her full gear.

"Let me stay here and help you."

"No, David. Let me and Lucy handle this, please!"

At least a dozen 2-foot-tall demon dwarves materialized out of the shadows. The hair on the back of Gianna's arms raised as the dark-skinned little people came into view. The little monsters were dressed in Native American garb, and on first glance might have appeared cute, except for the yellow-eyed demon faces and razor-sharp blood-stained fangs that would make any sane man's bowels loose.

Within minutes, the creatures made a horrifying quick appetizer of the two knocked out gang members, and soon looked at Gianna and everyone else like the main course. David picked up the now screaming Dylan and pulled Amora by the hand past the shrieking Native American man whom Gianna had punched earlier, out the front door.

Lucy had just come back in after tossing one of the gang members out the same door and into the parking lot. She quickly shielded herself and Gianna with a forcefield, and Gianna promptly began to slice the little monsters to pieces before they could get past them to the others.

Soon the girls were sweating, as more and more of the creatures continued to scamper forward, "Are they coming out of the freaking ground?" She kicked one into a cooler, shattering the glass, while slicing another one cleanly in half, "I thought there were only like ten of them!" She grumbled as at least twenty little bodies covered the floor around them.

Suddenly, the whole building shook, and she and Lucy looked at each other with open mouths. The little creatures abruptly stopped attacking, turned around and ran back the way they had come. "Holy crap! That's not a good sign." Lucy stated.

They both ran out the front doors. David and the kids, along with the two gangsters that were left stood looking up at the blackened sky. Dozens of tornadoes were coming towards them from every direction. "Holy…" Gianna whispered.

Amora ran over and pulled Gianna's arm, "It's a Dark One. We have to go now! It will take me back to him!"

Gianna didn't need an explanation. She sheathed her swords, "Everyone to the van!" The wind picked up, and thunder rumbled threateningly close by. The midday sun, blocked by the black, menacing storm clouds, had turned the atmosphere dark as night.

Amora pleaded, "Gianna, we don't have time! Can you just disappear us all like you did when you saved me and the others?"

Gianna shook her head as her stomach turned with fear and disappointment, "Sweetie, we haven't been able to disappear others since Switzerland. We've tried. We can only translate ourselves. We've *all* tried!"

"Please. Try again! It's coming!" Amora's blue eyes filled with tears threatening to spill over. Gianna turned away, her heart pounding fiercely and her mind filled with desperate prayers. The thirteen funnels on the horizon began to converge into one giant cyclone with fierce lightning cascading through it as it moved with ferocious intensity towards them.

"Lucy!" she called the teen who had been hovering next to David and Dylan, all three mesmerized by the enchanted storm.

Gianna and Lucy quickly decided it was worth a try, and they called the others over. The gang members had long since scrambled into an old red Camaro and sped away. The roaring wind accelerated, whipping their clothes and hair wildly. The howling gale forced them to shout to be heard. They grabbed each other's hands, "Ok, everyone, we're going to say a quick prayer and we need to concentrate on our friend, Diego." Gianna shouted.

Suddenly, Dylan broke away. "I have to get Tigger!"

"Dylan! Come back here!" Gianna's panic heightened as she saw her child run off to the van and yank it open. The cat darted out in fear and scrambled under a nearby vehicle. David ran after him, "Dylan!"

Amora, shaking, clung to Lucy and Gianna.

"Lucy, take her to Diego, now!" Gianna shouted.

"But—" Lucy's eyes were wide with fear.

"Now!"

Her eyes filled with terror, Lucy pursed her lips, nodded, and took Amora's hand. She closed her eyes and disappeared, but Amora stayed right where she was. The dark sky flashed white as a lightning bolt hit the middle of the parking lot, cracking the ground with an ear-splitting boom. The family covered their heads and hit the pavement.

Suddenly, an enormous humanoid being materialized from the darkness and lightning and began to solidify in front of them. Dylan and David ran over to the girls. Gianna grabbed her son and clutched him to herself. The skyscraper sized creature stood only a few feet in front of them in the parking lot: its humanoid body formed from the black storm clouds, and its head resembled a gigantic deer skull with flaming antlers.

Her heart beat wildly as Dylan buried his head into her chest, "Lord Jesus, we need you . . ." Gianna whispered.

***

Richmond, TX

Adora waited impatiently in the black SUV as the dark agents ransacked the house. The leader, dressed in black military garb, looked almost human except for the fact that he was wearing sunglasses in the middle of the night and never turned his head to look anywhere when he walked. He approached the vehicle to address her, his voice emotionless and robotic, "It appears they left in a hurry no more than a couple of hours ago. Beds are unmade and drawers out-turned."

She growled and slammed her hand down on the door, "They were tipped off! I'll tap into her tracker and see where they are going."

He nodded and made to turn back. She snapped her finger and he paused. "Torch the house." He nodded again and tapped his earcom. "Torch it." He then got into the driver's seat of her vehicle as Adora began to chant under her breath, her blue eyes rolled back, showing only the whites.

The lead SUV sped forward, and the other agents quickly piled into the other two black vehicles to follow as the flaming home disappeared behind them.

***

Oklahoma

The wind picked up dirt and trash and swirled around, smacking them as they huddled against a car. The ground vibrated, and Gianna could feel her body picking up the frequency so that her teeth rattled. Amora squeezed her arm and squealed, "It's calling me! I won't be able to resist for long!" Looking at David, Gianna screamed, "I'm going to fight it!"

He grabbed her, "No, Gigi. How are you going to fight that? It's clouds and wind, for goodness' sake! You do martial arts!"

"I've got to do something! I can't let them take her!" Her throat began to ache from screaming over the wind.

His eyes were desperate, and he clung to her hand. "Please." He shook his head, "Please don't!" Gianna turned from him and unsheathed her swords. Her clothes immediately changed to black leather armor; her skin vibrated with supernatural energy. As she stepped away from the car, a flash of light pulsed the air, and Diego and Lucy appeared beside her.

Oh, thank God. She nodded and gave a grateful smile to both of them. Diego robed, white glowing staff in hand, his gray hair and beard as thick and wild as when she last saw him. He winked at her, and all three of them stepped toward the Dark entity. The wind picked up force, forcing the warriors to squint and put their arms in front of their faces as debris whipped at them from every direction. The dark energy coming from the entity amped up and Gianna's head began to throb. Behind her, Amora screamed, holding her head in pain as David huddled over her. Diego held his glowing staff in front of him and stepped forward. The horned monstrosity angled its great head to regard the seer.

"I am a servant of The Most High and carry His authority! I forbid you from occupying this territory! You cannot stay!" Diego cracked the base of his staff against the ground and a flash of light whipped through the atmosphere. The giant entity moved back a step and the thick air rumbled in response. Diego's whole body glowed white as he strained against the force of the dark enemy. Lighting flashed every few seconds in the darkness around the fiend, and soon more funnel clouds began to form nearby.

Gianna felt a shift and the spiritual atmosphere immediately thickened, and she became short of breath. Amora screamed and tried to pull away. Gianna let go of Dylan and threw both arms around the girl to keep her from running. Surprisingly, Gianna struggled to keep her grip on Amora, whose strength seemed superhuman.

Suddenly, a loud buzzing filled her head as if a million angry bees were trying to break through a wall after a person struck the hive. Lucy crouched close and shielded them with a force-field. Her eyes became wide with panic, "I can't hold the shield!" She yelled. Gianna's heart began to beat wildly in panic, sweat poured off her, "Lord . . . Jesus . . .please!" She prayed as she clung to the 75-pound girl with all her strength.

In the distance, a trumpet sounded, and a stream of light penetrated the darkness. "The bees" sounded panicked, Gianna looked up and her mouth fell open.

"What the—" David's eyes widened as he witnessed another giant entity step through the light in the black sky. The being dwarfed the horned dark Elemental like a mountain to a hill. Its face was too bright to see, but its body appeared humanoid and made of light. It drew a great sword and as it stepped towards the fiend, Gianna felt the bee sound stop.

The flaming skull only looked up at the giant warrior angel for a moment before the great sword struck its head from its body. The flames immediately died, and the giant deer skull flew into the clouds and disappeared. In minutes, the tornadoes dissipated, and the black sky cleared. Amora relaxed and Gianna released her grip on the girl and plopped exhausted on the ground next to her.

The angelic being seemed to turn towards the group and nod its head. It then sheathed its great sword behind its back and disappeared from site.

Diego, who hadn't moved since he cracked his staff, turned towards them, "Is everyone okay?" He ran his hands through his wild gray hair as he walked towards them.

Gianna smiled at their old leader and friend, "It's so good to see you, Diego!" He reached down and helped her to her feet and into a warm embrace.

"Mom! Mom! Tigger's not dead!" As Gianna turned towards Dylan, he scooped up the meowing orange furball who had darted towards them when everything calmed down.

"Well, he's only got eight lives left now!" Quipped David as he ruffled Dylan's hair. Gianna rolled her eyes, "Diego, this is my husband, David." The men shook hands, "I feel out of place in my plaid and jeans." David chuckled, eyeballing Diego's robes.

Diego smiled, "Your upgrade is coming, my brother." David's eyes widened and he closed his mouth.

"I've never seen this dude speechless since I've met him," Gianna chuckled, "I'm impressed, Diego."

"You'll be more impressed when you see what enhancements he gets. Let's go!"

"Wait! When is he getting these and what is it?"

"You'll find out in time, sister. Come! We must get back to my place and I believe with all three of us here, we can successfully translate everyone."

"Even Tigger?" Asked Dylan.

Diego chuckled and stroked the cat purring in Dylan's arms. "Yes, my son. Even your beloved kitty. Let's gather together."

They all grabbed hands and immediately disappeared.

Chapter Seven

Asheville, North Carolina

Jesse James fired his M82 precisely at the giant's flaming head. It swatted at Billie Jean, causing it to move just enough for the bullet to miss the center and nick its pointed ear. As it roared in anger, the ground shook like an earthquake. The already demolished walls of the building around Jesse cracked. He rolled out of the way just as a piece of concrete fell, smashing to the floor next to him. His heart pounded like a drum in his ears. He quickly moved the M82 to another spot, carefully eyeballing the only still-standing but cracked wall to his left. He looked up just as the monster's glowing eyes scanned his direction.

Luckily, Darrel hit it with another blast of flames before it spotted the sniper. Jesse scoped the giant's massive head again and whispered a silent prayer, "Guide this round, and let the giant fall, Lord." He pulled the trigger again and watched as the round struck the beast directly between the eyes.

It froze, mouth hanging open from a halted roar; its large black tongue flopped out at an odd angle. A final windstorm of a sigh escaped the giant's gaping maw in a stink that can only be described as sewage a' la mode, and Jesse fell to his knees and gagged as he caught a whiff of it. Darrel and Billie Jean landed on the platform next to him, "Jess, get your crap together and let's go.

That thing is about to go down!" Darrel urged while he helped gather Jesse's gear. The sniper nodded, still coughing, he stood and made his way over to Billie Jean.

The gryphon crouched, waiting for him to climb atop her stunning form, a mix of lion's body and snow-white eagle's head, talons and wings never ceased to make him stop and wonder if he was awake or asleep. Her golden eagle's eyes watched him stumble over. She gently nudged him up as she unfolded her luxurious wings. He gripped her neck, and she took off into the smoke-filled sky.

The dead skyscraper-sized giant began to sway, and after a brief pause, the body fell forward, completely smashing the building that Jesse had just been on.

***

Lincoln and Emily had just made it to midtown when they saw the big giant fall. "Yes! They got 'em! Hallelujah!" Lincoln whooped.

Emily's eyes were wide with terror. "Oh my God, what was that thing?"

Lincoln's grin faded. He forgot that most people weren't used to seeing giants and monsters on the regular. He grabbed her hand. "That was a Nephilim, but It's okay, that's why we're here. We need to move so I can find the rest of my squad." To her horror, he pulled her towards the fallen monster.

She stopped abruptly. "I…I can't go any further." She leaned against an abandoned SUV nearby. Lincoln, feeling slightly annoyed at having to stop when he wanted to find his crew, sighed and faced her, "Hey, listen…Emily, I know this has been like the worst day ever for you, but it's really important for us to keep moving. I've gotta' find my team, and then we can get you out of this town to somewhere safe, okay?"

"Safe! Are you freaking kidding me right now, dude? Where is safe in a world where Giants and vampires are normal?"

Lincoln raised an eyebrow. She definitely had a point, but right now, he needed to get her to move. He grabbed her hand and attempted to pull her forward, and she jerked it back with surprising strength, "I'm not going anywhere near that dead monster! There's no telling if it's playing dead or for real dead!"

"Emily, I'm not going to argue with you. I'm here and I won't let you get hurt. I have got to go and if you don't want to, then I'll be forced to leave you here alone." Lincoln felt his face flushing with anger.

She folded her arms and turned her back to him.

"Look, I don't want to leave you, but you're not giving me a choice." With that, he turned from her and walked towards the downed behemoth.

After about a block, he heard footsteps running up behind him and he paused quickly, glancing back. Emily was jogging to catch up with a scowl on her face that he could see from a great distance.

"I know why God gave me boys." He said to himself as he shook his head.

"I'm glad you changed your mind." He said to Emily when she caught up.

She responded with a snort and a shrug and began walking at his pace.

Soon, they came to an area littered with concrete, glass, and building debris making it super hard to walk down the street. They began carefully jumping over twisted metal and moved around abandoned and demolished vehicles on a seemingly deserted, wide street. Lincoln noticed that after the giant fell, the other loud noises, screams, and explosions also stopped, and the city had become eerily quiet. They made it a few more blocks before hearing a whistle from a building above them.

Lincoln pressed his back against a brick wall, pulling Emily back with him as he looked up. Darrel was standing above, waving a flaming hand their way. He signaled that they were all circling back to the direction they'd come from. Lincoln nodded and he and Emily were about to change directions when a black Humvee pulled up next to them. Drake was in the driver's seat, "Get in, loser, we're finished here." Cat swung the door open to the back seat as Jesse James guffawed loudly from inside the vehicle.

Lincoln smiled as they climbed in, "Hey, I had my own action on the other side of town!"

They were still laughing. He shook his head and introduced Emily to the crew in the Humvee.

Drake drove on, maneuvering the Humvee carefully through the warzone that was Asheville. The team caught up on what had happened to each of them during the main battle while Emily sat quietly observing Lincoln's team.

Chapter Eight

Oklahoma

Adora's eyes glowed yellow as she crouched in the gas station parking lot, running her hand over the immense, smoking crack in the asphalt. She stood up slowly and her eyes soon returned to their usual cold, pale blue. The tall, thick, super-soldier guard turned back towards her, regarding her with a blank sunglass-covered stare.

"There was a great battle here, Ninazu."

The soldier holstered his weapon, raising his sunglasses to reveal the pitch-black eyes of the demon, "Your daughter was here, and those with her defeated a powerful Ancient Elemental."

"We only missed them by an hour, maybe two," Adora remarked as she smoothed her long, black skirt and returned her sunglasses to her eyes.

"The longer she is with them, the less likely we are to regain her, witch!" He glared at her as she casually strolled back towards the armored SUV.

"We'll have her soon enough." She responded dismissively as she opened the car door. Suddenly, he grabbed her arm and slammed her against the vehicle to face him again, his black eyes merely inches from her cold stare, "They are no longer in this state, witch." He spat, "They left through a portal to some place I cannot see."

She glared back at the possessed soldier. "I can find her without her tracker, Ninazu." She pulled her arm from his grip and opened the back door of the SUV and gestured towards it like a TV game show model. He grumbled menacingly as he looked inside. Laying in the backseat, drugged and asleep, were her other daughters, Anna and Alanna. "They almost look like little blonde angels, don't they?" She said with a sly smirk.

"How are they going to find your eldest daughter?" He snipped.

"Don't you know, Ninazu, that Amora is a clairvoyant and has been checking on her sisters to make sure they are okay? Alanna let it slip during an arduous ritual the other day. She's still recovering. The sleeping pills were a merciful convenience, really. As soon as we want her to come to us, we will merely bring my youngest daughter to the brink of death and cause her to call out to Amora to save her." Adora stated with as much passion as reciting a math equation.

She closed the door and faced the demon with crossed arms, "Now, where is this Azazel? I want a guarantee that he will protect me before I deliver my daughter Amora to him, or I will give her to Lucifer as originally agreed!" His eyes narrowed with anger. Suddenly, the soldier's body fell to the ground and began to foam at the mouth and convulse. Four other soldiers got out of the second SUV, and Adora yelled at them to get back in, which they immediately did.

Ninazu manifested physically in front of her, ten feet tall in complete black armor and roared in a demonic language, sending what felt like ice needles up and down her spine and a booming headache through her entire skull. She screamed in pain and fell to her knees. Her body quaked as she felt multiple entities leave it violently.

Ninazu then jerked her roughly to her feet and suddenly, they were in the desert. Before she had time to think, he grabbed her throat and lifted her in the air. She clawed feebly at his hand and kicked, "Witch, I should snap your worthless neck right now and be done with you and your entire genetically modified bloodline!" Her face began to turn blue, and her eyes rolled back. The demon opened his hand and let her drop like a sack of potatoes to the sand. She coughed and wheezed as she rubbed her throbbing neck.

The demi-god turned his back to her, his anger abated at the sound of her wheezing in pain. When he spoke again, he was much calmer, his voice a deep, oily rumble, "You must never say the name Azazel anywhere at any time except here where there are no ears. Let this be your last warning, witch. Next time, I won't hold back my impulse to kill you." Adora nodded as she attempted to stand.

"I've arranged a meeting with another elder god who serves Azazel. If that goes well, I will present your…proposal."

"When is your meeting," she croaked, "We have little time left."

The back of his armor-covered hand smashed into the side of her face, knocking her back onto the sand. Her vision blackened for a second and she groaned, which pleased him, and he grinned, "I know the time we have, witch. You do what *you* need to do, and I will take care of my part." He lifted her to her feet, his face within inches from hers, "*I* will tell you when we will speak of this next."

Adora nodded weakly. He grinned again and yanked her back through the portal to the parking lot in Oklahoma.

The super-soldier stood up, smoothed his jacket and winked at Adora with Ninazu's black eyes before returning the dark glasses to his face. He then got in the driver's seat and signaled to the other SUV that they were moving. The other vehicle's engine revved to life as Adora hobbled slowly to the passenger door and got in. "Where are we going?" She rasped.

He grinned wickedly. "Sedona."

Chapter Nine

Springfield, Missouri

Diego's quaint cottage farmhouse could have been on a magazine cover for "Modern Farmhouse Style." The red metal roof capped a pristine white cottage with red shutters, an oak door, and a wraparound porch with a cozy porch swing. Gianna couldn't help admiring the green landscape. Gorgeous, thick old trees spread their limbs in perfect spots around the property that was enclosed by a postcard-worthy white wooden fence.

Diego climbed the porch steps, waving the group in as his wife opened the front door with a warm grin, welcoming the odd bunch as if she expected and hosted large groups of strangers regularly.

"Hello! Come in. I'm Nita," she said as she hugged and kissed each one on the cheek when they passed through the door. She was small in stature with beautiful olive skin and features. Her salt and pepper short hair, perfectly styled, seemed to only add to her natural beauty as her kind eyes with just a hint of corner lines made Gianna only hope she would age as gracefully one day.

Dylan stopped at the door. "Can I please bring my cat Tigger into your house, ma'am?"

"You're such a polite young man," She grinned at Gianna, "Of course you can bring your kitty! Come in and get settled."

The boy let the cat jump out of his arms and the orange tabby, who never met a stranger, immediately began weaving in and out of Nita and Diego's legs. Delighted, she cooed, "What a friendly kitty." And began stroking him.

"Oh, he'll never leave now." Gianna rolled her eyes.

Diego soon began serving them plates of warmed up food and poured juice and water into the children's cups. In no time, they were all seated around a large dining table, eating and chatting as if at a family gathering. Nita and Diego's warmth and hospitality made their house feel like home immediately to the group. David chatted away with Diego as if he'd known him his whole life, which didn't surprise Gianna; David was always outgoing and the life of the party.

She smiled as she scanned the table. Amora looked content as she spooned potatoes into her mouth. Lucy still looked troubled but seemed to settle and eat, which was more than she had done in the past few days just picking at food. Dylan, like his father, loved being around people and grinned widely in between shoveling gobs of food from his second plate into his mouth.

Gianna could almost forget that they were on the run from an unknown dark pursuer. Almost. The worry began to seep in halfway through the meal, a gnawing feeling that settling anywhere long was not an option. Soon, she stopped eating and chatting altogether, and her stomach felt like a mix of ice and dread. She looked at Nita and Diego. They seemed happy, loving, and comfortable the way retired grandparents look when they are enjoying the part of their lives where they don't have much going on except visits from grandchildren and

71

travels to Florida in wintertime. She didn't want to bring anything here that would destroy that for them,

"We can't stay!" she suddenly burst out.

The chatter stopped abruptly, and they all looked at her.

Gianna shook her head. "It was a mistake coming here. I'm so sorry."

Diego calmly got up from the end of the table and walked over to her, gently placing his hand on her shoulder, "Gi, we understand the danger at hand and if you think by leaving you will protect us from it, you're wrong."

Tears began to fall from Gianna's eyes. "I don't want you to lose this, Diego," she wiped a stray tear. "Not because you helped us. You have Nita and your kids and grandkids." He hugged her, and she began to weep.

"Oh, daughter, you have been carrying the world on your shoulders." She gripped him and cried heavily. He held her as she did and continued, "You can't protect everyone, Gianna. This is too big. We were meant to do this together, our team, and others that have and will join us." He looked into her eyes as she wiped her nose with a napkin. "There are no more safe places, Gi. We're actually safer now that you and Lucy are here." Gianna shook her head in disagreement.

He nodded, "Yes, we are. We are stronger together. And we will stay together until the Lord takes us!"

***

Nita showed David and Gianna to a spare room and took Lucy and the children to the basement, where they had a pull-out bed and extra cot. She also brought in some clothes from her kids and grandkids' stash and apologized if anything didn't fit. "There's a bathroom down the hall stocked with towels and other toiletries. Please use whatever you need."

"Oh, thank you, Nita." She hugged the motherly figure tight, "You've done more than enough. I'm sure these clothes will be fine for us. I'm just glad I can put something clean on." David also gave her a squeeze on her way out the door.

He looked at Gianna, "Are you okay, Gigi?" He moved to hug her, and she let him for a few seconds, then wiggled out of his grip, "Do you mind if I use the shower first?"

He sighed, then looked down and stuck his hands in his pockets, "Go ahead." He said flatly. She quickly grabbed the clean clothes and scrambled out to the bathroom.

Two and a half days in the same clothes can make a girl grumpy. As she peeled off the filthy layers, she realized that these dirty garments were all she had left of her own things. They had only thought about getting away from that place in Oklahoma and didn't give a second thought to the fact that they were leaving the van behind with everything they had left in the world, which wasn't much, but now they had nothing. She paused, looking at the pile of dirty clothes on the floor, and blinked back tears, "No, stop it. You've cried enough today, girl." She said out loud to herself. She then got into the hot shower and re-focused on enjoying the warm spray and the silence.

***

Back in the guest bedroom, David sat on the bed, wrestling with the empty feeling in his chest. He tried to push back the sadness as he contemplated the mess he'd made of his life and family. He wondered if Gianna would ever look at him again without disdain and distrust, not that he blamed her. He was well aware of how he destroyed that with the affair. It was foul and ugly, and he hated to think of it. "Can You fix it, Lord? Can you fix me?" He whispered to the empty room.

Movement in his peripheral grabbed his attention, and he looked up. A human hand appeared in the air by the closet door. David rubbed his eyes with his fingers. "That's not weird at all."

He looked up again and the hand was still there. As he watched it moved over to the closet door, it proceeded to knock twice. It paused for a moment, then knocked again. Then the hand disappeared.

"No, not weird at all." He stated out loud to the empty room as he stood and walked over to the closet door. David took a deep breath and opened the door to a standing wall of red, lighted water. He put his hands on his hips and looked down, shaking his head, "I'm asleep in that bed right now. I'm sure of it." He looked over at the empty bed and shook his head again. Sighing, he faced the wall of water and stared into it, but all he could see was his own reflection staring quizzically back at him.

"I need a trim," he remarked, rubbing his unruly beard, "Okay, let's engage."

He put his hand into the water as his reflection did the same, then pulled it back out quickly, "Bone dry."

David took one more look around the empty room, took a deep breath and walked into the water.

***

Downstairs, Nita was serving up bowls of ice cream to Dylan and Amora who were eating with delight as Lucy sat nearby on the couch talking with Diego. She had just finished telling him about finding her mother's body and fleeing Florida. He listened patiently; his eyes filled with concern for the young girl who wiped a stray tear from her cheek.

"Hija, you've had no time to grieve this incredible loss. I'm glad we're beginning to talk it through, but let's plan to talk tomorrow about how you can properly say goodbye to your mother and begin to mourn her passing.

Lucy nodded, her lips quivering as she held back an outburst of pain. She took a breath, "Diego, I am thankful for the time we had the last few months," she paused, wiped her nose with a tissue and looked at him, "we really reconnected, ya know, and she got clean." Lucy smiled through her teary eyes, "My mom stopped using the last couple of months for sure."

"Really?"

She nodded, "Yeah, we were even doing a bible study and praying together! It was really nice…" she trailed off and the tears began to fall again. Diego hugged her, and she began to weep on his shoulder. He held her until she finished and blew her nose.

Nita came over. "You poor dear. Can I hug you?"

Lucy smiled and stood up. The grandmother hugged the girl to her bosom and stroked her hair. Lucy relaxed into the woman's embrace for a bit.

"You must be exhausted, Lucy dear." Said Nita.

Lucy nodded and wiped her eyes.

"Come downstairs, honey. You can shower and lay down. I can get you a change of clothes from my daughter's old things. She led Lucy to the furnished basement that looked like a small apartment. Lucy's eyes suddenly became very heavy, and her body ached to lay down.

After Nita left her with towels and clothes, she took a quick shower, and as she laid in the full-sized bed covered in a fluffy pink quilt, she noticed Nita had pulled a couch bed out for Dylan and Amora. Her breathing began to slow as she faded into thoughts of how kind Diego and his wife were and how she couldn't remember when clean sheets and pillows felt and smelled so good, and before she could think another thought, she melted into sleepy bliss.

***

David whistled admiringly as brilliant colors danced across the cave walls and massive stalactites and stalagmites that filled the cavernous room. The flowing reds, blues, and yellows mixed and waved on the floor and ceiling, each coming from the different water-filled doorways throughout the room. He vaguely remembered Gianna mentioning a cave that led to other realms in one of their few talks about her otherworldly adventures, leading to her current superhero status and persona. But now, seeing it with his own eyes confirmed the crazy tales and had him wishing he had probed more details from her.

"It is a sight that strikes awe into a soul, is it not?" stated a man who was suddenly right next to him. David jumped back in a fighting crouch with fists balled to strike.

"I apologize if I startled you." The man responded calmly as if he had bumped David in a crowd of strangers. He was dark-skinned, with dark, curly hair, dressed in middle eastern type garb similar to what David remembered seeing in movies set in Egypt or the Middle

East. The man was clean-shaven, with a chiseled jawline complimented by sparkling clear sea-green eyes and broad shoulders.

David hadn't relaxed his posture as he assessed the stranger, who seemed to be waiting patiently for a response. David, never one for long silences, decided to finally ask. "Who are you?"

The stranger nodded, and a friendly grin revealed a striking smile. "I am your guide to truth."

David raised his eyebrows and somewhat reluctantly dropped his hands as he no longer felt threatened by the evasive stranger. Again, the man regarded David with calm, thoughtful ease.

David's mind whirled with questions, nervousness, and some fear. "Okay, *sir*…Can you start by telling me what this place is and what am I doing here?"

The man gestured to the colorful cave. "This is the Cave of Worlds. Each doorway is a portal to another realm, time, place, or sphere. You, David, are here to understand your destiny and your *true identity*."

David stroked his beard thoughtfully. "My true identity, huh? Am I some chosen one," Here David used finger quotes. "This is where I say, 'it's not me. You got the wrong guy because I'm just a regular dude.'" The stranger looked at him more intently but didn't respond directly to what he had said.

David shrugged as he realized that his propensity to throw humor into difficult situations wasn't always the appropriate response. "Tough crowd. Do you know my wife, Gianna? Has she been here?"

The stranger grinned and nodded. "I do, and she is very familiar with this place."

"So, are you an angel? Did God send you to instruct me...to help me fix my mess?"

The man began to walk and signaled for David to follow. "Come and see."

They crossed the vast cavern of liquid doorways, passing by a multi-colored pool with a cascading waterfall flowing into it. Soon, arriving in front of a crimson-colored liquid passageway. David stared at the odd reflections of a disheveled, sad American man and shook his head. "Why do you shake your head, David?" The man's kind voice almost brought David to tears, and he rubbed his nose and looked away.

The stranger again waited patiently for a response. David took a couple of breaths and croaked out, "I'm a big mess..." He shrugged and shook his head, "I...I just don't know what I'm doing here."

The man looked at David with those deep, kind eyes and squeezed his shoulders assuringly, "Young man, you will soon see that you were made for so much more," He nodded, and David felt hope rise in his chest at the man's words. They again faced the ruby-colored waters. The man placed his hand on David's back, nodding at the reflection, and they both stepped through.

Chapter Ten

Hickory, North Carolina

Darrel and Billie Jean stepped out of the bathroom and steam from their long, hot shower followed them into the room. Wrapped in fluffy towels, they collapsed onto their bed. He covered her face and neck in light kisses as she wrapped her long legs around him. The light from the bathroom gently danced across their bed, allowing him to appreciate the contrast of their skin in their entwined limbs.

He looked into her eyes. "How are you feeling, Mama?"

Billie Jean smiled as she lightly touched his wooly beard. "I'm still not used to this furry thing covering your handsome face."

"It's gone if you don't like it."

She giggled. "I didn't say that I didn't like it, silly. I actually do. I'm just still adjusting to your new look."

"Okay," he began lightly, tracing his fingers over her face and neck, "You didn't answer the question."

"I'm fine. Not feeling bad at all, just exhausted from the battle earlier." She covered her mouth as a stray yawn escaped, "I could probably sleep a couple of days if anyone would let me."

"I'll do my best to keep you out of anything that's not absolutely necessary, Babe. I promise tomorrow is your rest day."

Billie Jean rolled her eyes. "Why do I feel like that kind of talk will guarantee a sasquatch or creature from the black lagoon will stroll through the camp tomorrow?"

Darrel chuckled. "If they do, you won't know it, I'll take them both down myself."

"See that you do, sir!" She laughed, then stifled another yawn.

He kissed her lightly on the lips, forehead, both cheeks and chin. "Go to sleep, Beautiful. Saving the world can wait while you rest and continue making a baby." She smiled and turned over. Within minutes, her breathing changed, and she was asleep.

Darrel wished he could fall asleep as fast as his wife, but his rampantly running thoughts kept him awake even though every muscle in his body ached and his eyes burned with weariness. Ever since Billie Jean told him that she was pregnant, he found too often his worry overtook his excitement. Would he be a good father? Could he protect his new family in this deadly new world? What kind of childhood would his son or daughter have with the apocalypse on the way and mom and dad flying off to possibly die every day? He sighed and ran his hand over his face.

You are not alone, My Son, the quiet voice quickened to his heart.

Darrel's eyes filled, and a single tear escaped, hitting the pillow by his ear.

"Is that you, Lord?" Darrel answered in his heart.

I'm here, my son and I hear each of your sighs, your clenched hands, your quiet brooding.

Darrel contemplated the Father's words for a moment. *"You see all of that, Father?"*

I see all, my son. Each groan of your heart is a prayer that rises to Me.

Darrel never imagined that God heard his emotions as prayers. His mind turned over this new revelation, and he was in awe of it.

Darrel, Darrel?

"Yes, Lord?"

You and your bride are greatly beloved. Am I not with you?

"Ye-Yes, Lord. Of course, You are." Darrel felt his face flush.

The child is a gift. She has chosen you and Billie Jean as her parents. All of you will do great harm to the kingdom of Darkness.

Darrel put his hand over his mouth in surprise. His heart beat fast with excitement. *A girl? She chose us?* "Thank you, Father. I… I don't know what to say."

More difficult times are coming, my son. Dark times. Don't forget that I am with you.

Darrel began to wonder what dark and difficult could mean if what they had already experienced wasn't that. Before he could think much further, he was fast asleep.

***

Lincoln walked Emily to the female bunk house, quickly explaining how the camp worked, "You can sleep here tonight, and if you decide you want to stay on long-term, you will be assigned a job and be put on a combat/survival training daily schedule. I'll introduce you to Mae, who is our resident coordinator and also like the camp mom and she'll get you situated."

Emily kept nodding; her pale skin almost translucent in the darkness. She seemed tired and withdrawn, which didn't surprise him after what she had witnessed earlier. When they got to the bunkhouse door, Lincoln knocked lightly. The door cracked enough for a gun nozzle to slip through, along with a groggy, "Who is it?"

"Mae! It's me. I have a refugee from Asheville that needs a bunk."

"One second." The groggy voice answered.

The door shut and Lincoln stroked his long beard as sounds of movement came from within. Emily looked up at him wide-eyed, "I'm not sure about this. . ."

He smiled and squeezed her shoulder. "It'll be fine. They're just cautious. Some ladies in there have been through some stuff."

"Stuff?"

Before he could reply, the door opened and a large black woman in a pink robe, with her hair wrapped in a sleeping cap, filled the doorway. Hands on her hips, she grimaced at Lincoln, then turned slowly to eyeball Emily, who inched behind Lincoln in fear.

"Mae, I know it's late—" before he could finish, she bear-hugged him against her ample chest, cutting off his protest, "Lincoln, the girls and I haven't slept a wink since y'all went off to Asheville. We have been praying for victory, and the Lord assured us that you would have it!"

He laughed as she finally freed him, "Thanks, Mae, that means a lot that you all would stay up praying for us."

"That's the least I can do…and the *most* I can do," she said with a wink at Emily, "and part of my job is to teach these ladies how to pray, and I intend to teach 'em how to win wars that way."

Lincoln nodded. "Yes, ma'am, it is imperative to have prayer support for every action that we move forward with."

Mae turned to Emily with a grin. "And what's your name, young lady?"

Emily still looked uncertain but answered, "It …it's Emily, ma'am."

"Well, Miss Emily, follow me, and we'll get you cleaned up and settled in a bunk for the night." Mae turned back to Lincoln, "Don't you worry. I'll take care of her, and we'll see you in the morning."

Lincoln nodded as Mae showed Emily into the bunkhouse. He felt a weight lift as the door closed, and he turned back toward the main house, his family and his bed. As he walked down the road, exhaustion was about to crash down on him full force, and he couldn't wait to crawl into bed next to his wife and sleep.

Chapter Eleven

Springfield, Missouri

Diego switched off the kitchen light and was making his way toward his office when Gianna came down the stairs, her hair wrapped up in a bath towel, "Diego, is David down here? He wasn't in the bedroom, and I thought he'd want to know I was finished showering."

Diego shook his head, "No, I haven't seen him since you both went upstairs a bit ago. Maybe he went downstairs to say goodnight to the kids, Nita just tucked them in." Gianna nodded, "Okay, I'll go down and check, I'd like to tell them goodnight myself." She turned to go that way when he stopped her, "Gianna, before you go, please join me in my office for a couple of minutes so we can catch up."

"Sure, okay." Gianna pulled her hair down and started to squeeze the moisture from her long brown tresses into the towel as she followed him into the study. As she entered, she gave the filled bookshelves an admiring glance, "I'd love to dig through all of your shelves," she shook her head and sighed, "but I doubt I'll get the chance or have the time."

Diego stroked his wild, gray-streaked beard and smiled. His now familiar, kind eyes brought some comfort to the deep sadness that was overtaking her by the hour. She ran her fingers along the spines of some old leather-bound commentaries before plopping down on a comfortable old chair in front of his desk.

"You're welcome to read anything in here and take as many with you as you can tote along your journey, "He glanced at the books stacked on the corner of his desk, "I have more than enough to keep me occupied for however much time the Lord grants me . . . in this realm." He winked.

Gianna laughed and nodded, "Well, if there's a way to stuff a few into my bag, know that I will, my friend." She ran her fingers through her damp hair and appreciated the comfort of being with an individual with whom she felt a deep connection through shared experience. Knowing there were only five others in the whole world who shared their particular life journey had made their connection stronger than they thought possible in such a short span of time.

"I know the last few months have been a whirlwind of activity, fighting, training, protecting and travel. We haven't had much time to catch up on what is going on in life. I'm sorry I had to meet David under such circumstances, but I'm glad to finally meet him."

She crossed her arms and nodded. "Me too. Me too. Did you get a chance to talk to him? What do you think?"

Gianna was hoping for more insight than 'he seems like a nice guy' from Diego since he seemed to "see" more than what was on the surface of situations and individuals.

"I think he's very unsure about his role in your life and in this journey," He looked at Gianna more intently. She blinked slowly, striving to keep her face unreactive.

Diego continued, "Are you reconciling?"

She shook her head. "No. Nope. I really don't know, nor have I really thought about reconciling. I let him move back in to help with the kids and thought," She looked at the wall of books behind Diego, "I thought that I would see how it felt to be near him again."

"And how does it feel?"

"Awkward, mostly." She chewed the inside of her cheek thoughtfully.

Diego didn't respond and just waited for her to finish her thoughts.

She sighed. "I realized, lately, that the monster-killing activity has kept me busy enough not to have to deal with my feelings," She laughed nervously, "I've been more scared of coming home to talk with him than fighting the beasts from hell out in the world." She rolled her eyes, "How crazy is that?"

Diego leaned back in his chair and nodded.

"He keeps wanting to talk and go to counseling," she rubbed her eyes, "and the more he asks, the more I feel like I want to run in the opposite direction. Diego, I just don't want to try right now. Like, I've let him back in the house and the kids love having him around. And Amora has really taken to him. You should see how he is with her. It's so heartwarming, especially after all she's been through with the ritual abuse," She shuddered, "We really need to talk about her and what to do since we know her family or whoever is going to find us eventually."

"I'm glad Amora is connecting with him, and yes, we do need to discuss her situation, but let's backtrack a step. What are you nervous about facing in counseling with him? If you don't want to work on reconciling, why invite him back home?"

She shrugged, feeling a tightness in her stomach, "I don't know what I want, Diego. Part of me still loves him and has forgiven him. I see how he's trying, but it's complicated. I sometimes feel dead inside when I'm with him, like not even hurt or anger, or desire or anything…just…nothing."

Diego stroked his beard thoughtfully. "You've cut off your emotions."

"What? No, I haven't. I feel emotions, just not for him." She started winding her thick, wet hair into a bun and tucked it in on top of her head.

"There's nothing wrong with protecting your feelings from someone who has betrayed you, Gianna. I'm not saying you are an emotionless robot. Of course, you have feelings for your kids and others. This "deadness" with David is a natural defense mechanism. If you've been wounded, a piece of yourself splinters off with that wound and holds it, so you can function in life without breaking down. It's similar to how SRA survivors, Satanic Ritual Abuse, like Amora will produce another personality to help survive the extreme abuse. It's a remarkable ability the Lord created in human souls to help us endure in this broken world."

She stared at him with raised eyebrows, "Are you implying that I have multiple personalities?"

He ran his hand through his long, almost fully gray head of thick hair, "No. No, not at all, and if you did, there would be nothing shameful about that. But no. I'm simply pointing out how the soul responds to trauma. Think of a glass jar dropping off a table from a short distance. It may slightly crack and a splinter or two of glass comes off, and if dropped from a longer distance, will completely shatter into hundreds of pieces and shards." She nodded.

"All of us are capable of splintering or breaking depending on the level of trauma suffered. Every human being suffers emotional and physical trauma in life because life is hard, and since the Breach, it's been extremely more traumatic. Most people need healing, even those of us who know the Healer personally. We still need our souls made whole again."

"Well, that makes sense. I think all of us that went on that journey a few months ago needed healing in some way, and we healed so much," She crossed her arms again, "Well, I thought *I* had healed so much...so why do I feel so lost and unsure and numb?" A few tears leaked from her eyes, and she wiped them quickly away.

"Gigi, did you think you were completely healed and whole after you awoke from the other realm? Did Yeshua tell you that?"

"Well, no...not exactly. But He said He'd take care of it...but—"

He grabbed a tissue and came around his desk, handing it to her as he kneeled in front of her chair. She took it and wiped her nose. He continued, "He began a great work in you and us while we were there, Gigi. But it was a beginning. We're partners with Him in our own healing, and through our participation, we knowingly and unknowingly help to heal others."

A few more tears escaped as she pursed her lips together and took in his words. He patted her arm gently and stood up, "You have a lot on your plate: a mother, a foster mother of a very needy girl, a hero...and if you want to put healing your own heart and possibly your marriage on a shelf for later, well then you do that."

Gianna blew her nose and tried unsuccessfully to hold back the overflow of tears that pushed through. Diego handed her another tissue, which she took gratefully and nodded.

He leaned back on the desk and crossed his arms. "Look at me, dear."

She looked up at him.

"Your own personal healing and dealing with your feelings for your husband and marriage are two separate things. I advise you to not neglect yourself, and in that process, I believe the Lord will guide you about your marriage."

***

David rubbed his eyes. He was standing in his childhood bedroom. He took a deep breath as he scanned the familiar *Return of the Jedi* poster, the rumpled, unmade bed, and the much smaller version of himself sitting on the floor, absorbed in an imaginary battle between Optimus Prime and Luke Skywalker. His younger self didn't see the stranger in the room with him, and David wondered what was happening; was this real or a vision? The room was much smaller than he remembered, so there was no possible way the child wouldn't have already seen him if he was visible. So, David assumed he was seeing some sort of interactive vision, and his analytical brain proceeded to calculate how it was possible.

Watch. A voice spoke in his head or out loud. He was unsure.

Suddenly, a woman walked into the room. His mother. David's heart beat wildly, and he instantly remembered this day. He'd forgotten how striking she was, her long dark hair feathered as was the prominent style of the 80's. Her large brown eyes, so much like his own, he had never realized before now how much he favored her. His mother's eyes were troubled. He hadn't noticed that as a child, but now he moved closer and drank in her face, her body language, hoping to gain a clue as to why she did what she did. He must've been eight years old that day. The last day he saw her. She sat on the floor next to him and leaned back against his bed.

"Hey buddy, whatcha' up to?"

He stopped his play for a moment and looked up at her, showing her his toys. "Playing, Momma."

"David, baby, I need to talk to you for a minute."

He looked at her. "Okay."

She smiled nervously. "I'm leaving for a little while, baby and I –"

"Where are you going?" Little David put his toys down and focused on his mom.

Older David saw for the first time that the little boy looked worried.

"I can't tell you where right now, but I need some time to figure some things out. And then I'll be back to get you and your brother."

"How long will you be gone? What about Daddy? Is he going too?"

"Not long, baby," She shook her head and began to stroke his hair. "No. No, Dad is staying with you guys. I won't be gone a long time, I promise."

Little David's eyes grew big with sudden fear, and he reached for her. "Mom, when are you going?"

She hugged him quickly and turned away. "I'm going today, buddy."

He put his toys down and clung to her. "Take me with you!"

"No, Sweetie, I can't." She unwound the little boy's arms from her, "I promise, I won't be gone for a long time, and I'll come back for you and Jake."

Before he could protest again, she stood up and started for the door. Young David followed her out of the bedroom. Older David swallowed hard, his stomach sour with emotion and something that felt like fear. As he stared at the floor in the now empty room, his mind flooded with old memories of waiting for his mom to come back and later for visits that never occurred. Until he had finally accepted the fact that she had lied and was never coming back.

Years later, his father finally told him and his younger brother Jake that their mother had remarried and started a new family with the man she had run away with, Conner Hawkins, from her work. He didn't want step kids and she, apparently, loved him too much to fight about it.

Reliving this memory stirred something deep inside that he wanted to push away, but before he could though, the bedroom disappeared, and the scene changed. He, Jake and his dad sat at the small square dinner table a couple years later. He may have been 11 years old and his brother 9. His Dad, as usual, looked pale and tired from long hours at work plus overtime as a crimes against minors detective at the local police department. He remembered his dad suffered from insomnia, a PTSD symptom from what he was exposed to daily at work. Even though his dad worked long hours, he always made a point to have dinner with him and Jake almost every night growing up.

David remembered that this particular night, his father told them that he had hired a babysitter to stay with them during summer break.

"Boys, summer break is starting, and I'm not going to be home much. I don't want you sitting in front of the TV all day and doing nothing, so I hired Heather Stephens to stay with you. She's going to take you to the pool, feed you and make sure you do your chores while I'm working."

David pushed his food around the plate with his fork and mumbled, "I guess mom lied again when she said we'd spend some of the summer with her."

Dad's mouth became a thin line under his dark, bushy mustache. "David, we've discussed this before. Your mother makes a lot of promises that she doesn't keep. She's yet to talk with me about getting you, and since summer break is in a couple of days, I must arrange for your care."

"Jason's mom said I can hang out at his house. They've got season passes to Water World and said I can go with them." Piped in Jake.

Dad nodded. "Mrs. Slater already talked with me about that, and I told her you can go with them."

David put his fork down and crossed his arms. "I'm not going to stay by myself every day with some strange girl."

"You can come with us, David! I'm sure Jason's mom will say it's okay."

David scowled. "No way am I hanging out with you babies every day either!"

"Hey, we're not babies, you jerk!"

"Sounds like something a baby would say!"

"Shut up!" Jake screamed.

The Waking Part II: Withstand in The Evil Day

Dad yelled, "That's enough. Both of you, quiet!" The boys quickly looked down at their plates.

Young David's stomach soured. He knew if his mom was around, he wouldn't have to have a babysitter. He couldn't wait to be older and do what he wanted to do. A few days later, Heather started to come over. She was eighteen and had just graduated from the local high school. It turned out that she was fun and pretty, and soon enough, David didn't mind hanging out with her. Sometimes Jake was there, and sometimes he wasn't. Soon, David had also developed a little crush on her. He didn't even tell his dad that she would smoke in the backyard and talk to boys on the phone for hours while he played Nintendo.

Sometime after he became very comfortable with her, she began to bring some magazines over and invited David to look at them with her. At first, he was embarrassed and uncomfortable, but soon, he couldn't get enough of seeing the images of naked women and men. Heather eventually asked him if he wanted to see a naked girl in real life.

***

Gianna paused outside of the bedroom door. She just wanted to lay down and get some much-needed sleep. She breathed a quick prayer that David was already asleep so she wouldn't have to talk to him, and immediately she felt guilty for praying it. "Okay, I'll talk to him. But can it just be short and surfacy?" she whispered.

Shrugging, she turned the knob and walked into the room just as David walked out of the closet. Gianna, eyebrows raised in surprise, paused in the doorway.

93

David looked a bit startled to see her. "Oh hey, Gigi!"

"David, did you just walk out of the closet?"

He smiled weirdly and ran his hand through his hair with a sigh. "I, uh, just had the strangest experience." He crossed his arms and sat on the bed, shaking his head.

Intrigued, Gianna sat on the wicker chair across from the bed. "Do tell." She noticed that he was still wearing the same clothes as when they had arrived at Diego's, and yet he looked and smelled clean. His face even appeared refreshed, like he had had a full night's sleep. David looked at her intently, his brown eyes glassy with tears he was struggling to hold in. He chewed the side of his cheek, and she could tell his mind was going a thousand miles an hour.

"When I was eleven years old, I was groomed, molested and raped repeatedly by my eighteen-year-old babysitter." He breathed out a long breath of air at that confession.

"Oh, David, why didn't you ever tell me? Oh my God, I'm so sorry—"

He held his hand up. "Before you say anything, Gigi, please. I have so much to share, and I'm weighing what to tell you and what you will even hear from me." He crossed his arms again and looked up at the ceiling. "I've never told anyone, *ever,* about what happened to me. I didn't even know I was affected by it... hell, I didn't even realize I had been raped until I was an adult and a father." He ran his hands through his hair and shook his head. "And I don't want you to think I'm using it as an excuse for any of my actions, either. I just know that I've not been honest with myself, or you, or God. And all of that's changed now. He changed me and healed me, and I want to tell you everything." A single tear escaped, and he quickly wiped it away.

Gianna was shocked and didn't know how to respond.

"You don't have to say anything except answer this question for me." He paused and looked at her without moving from the bed or uncrossing his arms.

She nodded.

"Can I tell you everything?"

Gianna nodded again, and he began to tell her his story.

Chapter Twelve

Sedona, Arizona

The caravan of SUVs pulled into the parking lot of a small unimpressive building right before sunset. Adora wasn't one to worry except when she didn't know what to prepare for in a situation. Her demons, who were usually non-stop chattering away at her or to each other, were unusually silent and had been the last few hours of the drive to Arizona. This put Adora on edge even more. The agent, who was also Ninazu, had said nothing since they left Oklahoma. She had decided to keep most of her thoughts and questions to herself since Ninazu's outburst had left her throat bruised. She would have taken her anger out on the girls had they been awake to cower at her abuse. This left her ruminating in her own dour thoughts. The so-called "god" she served and this unknown ancient god, Azazel, both, it seemed, would lead to her eventual and tragic demise. How could she cow to both and still survive to hold leadership and power in some way? Ninazu's revelation that there was a god powerful enough to imprison other seemingly powerful and ancient ones had her increasingly intrigued. What could she do to contact this other powerful entity?

Anna and Alanna had begun to stir only an hour ago but were still so groggy from the drugs that they stared with glassy eyes straight ahead, saying nothing. As they parked, Adora addressed the agent, "I need to get the girls to a bathroom and get them some water. Can we do that here?"

He simply nodded and then exited the vehicle. Adora frowned and grumbled to herself as she barked at the girls to get out of the car. Anna immediately perked up, found the door handle and ushered little Alanna out. They all followed Ninazu into the featureless building without saying a word.

***

After tending to the girls and herself in the dark lobby restroom, Adora, Alanna and Anna were led to a small reception area with only agent Ninazu accompanying them. Adora crossed her arms and grimaced at the site of the waiting room's abysmal décor, which sported one sad brown couch, poor lighting, and threadbare gray rugs. The room was small with no hallways, and they waited outside one large brown door. Everything about this place, from the exterior to the interior, seemed too purposefully unimpressive. Adora felt that trying this hard to be inconspicuous just made it more suspect. She scoffed internally.

"Where are we, Ninazu?" She grumbled.

"You'll know soon enough, witch. Let me do the talking unless you are addressed directly." He lowered his sunglasses and stared directly into her eyes. Adora nodded quickly and shivered as she turned away from the horrific inhumanness of his ink, black orbs. He returned his sunglasses, and they continued to wait for whoever Ninazu had arranged for them to meet.

After what seemed like an hour, the brown door opened, and a towering figure emerged. She was unnaturally tall, her head nearly brushing the top of the nine-foot door frame. The striking woman's long serpentine limbs and neck poked out from a smart black suit whose short skirt served only to further enhance the already unfathomably long legs ending in the highest red heels Adora had ever seen. She couldn't fathom how the woman balanced her enormous body in them. The woman's large, dark eyes darted menacingly from one of them to the other. Her long black hair and paper-white skin accentuated blood-red bubbly lips poised to either scold them or eat them.

Adora's skin pricked up at the sight of her, and immediately, her demons went berserk and began to scream profanities in her head. With great effort, she blocked their voices so she could concentrate. Ninazu didn't seem to react at all, and the girls, still holding each other's hands, stepped back a few paces at the sight of the giantess. Finally, looking down her nose at Ninazu, the woman spoke, "The Master is not yet ready to present himself in public and only takes special appointments."

Ninazu nodded slightly, "I have sent messages to the Master. He is expecting me. Ninazu of Sumer and Mesopotamia. He knew me well at one time."

She crossed her arms, "I've heard directly from him that he does not wish to be disturbed. I will bring him your message."

Ninazu removed the sunglasses and used his true dark, oily voice, "That will not do. He will hear what we have to say directly from us."

Even though Adora shivered at the sound of his voice, the woman seemed unimpressed. She raised an eyebrow, "I'll see what I can do. Wait here." She waltzed back through the doors, shutting them loudly behind her.

"Ninazu, who does she think she is talking down to you as if you are some peasant!" Adora snarled.

Ninazu turned towards her and whispered, "Quiet, witch. There are eyes everywhere. She is no one to be trifled with…I am surprised that she is his doorkeeper."

Lowering her voice, Adora prodded. "What do you mean? You know her?"

He rubbed his chin, "She's older than me. An infamous legend that I've only heard of for millennia, but no, I don't *know* her. She is Lilith."

Adora sucked in her breath, "The mother of demons? The first wife of Adam? She isn't a myth?"

Ninazu chuckled, "Haven't you seen enough in your life to understand that in all myths, there is a kernel of truth? Mother of demons? Yes, and to some of the worst of my kin, the incubi and the succubi. Lilith is a powerful and dangerous creature to cross. Azazel was wise to secure her. Let us hope all our travels and plans were not in vain." He replaced his glasses again.

Adora ground her teeth as she contemplated what to do if this meeting failed or never even happened. Before long, the door opened yet again, and Lilith stalked into the room, followed by what appeared to be two yellow-robed Buddhist monks. "The Master will see you. The monks will take you to him." She crossed her arms and again spoke down her nose at Ninazu, "I must warn you, if you displease him, he will torture you for one hundred years and eat the hag and her spawn." She smiled, turned like a ballerina on her sharp red heels and stalked back into the office.

Adora's mouth dropped open in shock. The door slammed before she realized she was also infuriated by the gall of the wench to call her a hag and smile with delight at informing them of being the god's next meal. Ninazu grabbed her arm and turned her towards him,

"Forget her. Now listen. That was no empty threat, do you still want to do this?"

Adora closed her mouth and nodded, "We must take the chance. Lord Lucifer will kill me anyway, I know it. At least with this god, I may have an opportunity to survive. . . or better yet, have a place in his kingdom."

Ninazu nodded. They turned towards the monks, who gestured at the elevator. Adora grabbed Anna and Alanna's hands, and they all followed the monks into the opened lift doors.

Chapter Thirteen

Hickory, North Carolina

After receiving a change of clothes and a warm shower, Emily settled into a vacant bottom bunk and contemplated her next move. There were about eight other women and girls besides her and Mae in the bunkhouse that easily could've housed up to twenty-five. So, there were many empty bunks surrounding her. She waited until all the small whispers and giggles ceased and heavy breathing and light snoring commenced.

Emily then slipped out of bed and walked through the side wall until she appeared outside the bunkhouse in the shadow of the trees. Her hair and eyes became red fire, her limbs stretched and filled out, and her borrowed cotton pajamas disappeared, revealing a tight black bodice that barely covered her full breasts and a strip of fabric that just concealed her bottom, followed by thigh-high black boots. Her teeth and nails were of a dangerous yet provocative length, and she was hungry.

***

Jesse James had just finished his shower. After a battle like tonight in Asheville, it took a bit of time for him to settle his mind enough to sleep. Lately, he would sit at his desk in his small room in the three-bedroom trailer he shared with Alvin and Jacque, reading Psalms until his eyes got heavy. Tonight, for some reason, he began to read and his eyes blurred. He struggled to concentrate on the words. He said a quick prayer and decided to lay down. His thoughts raced from bringing down the giant tonight to flashes of the jungles of Guatamala, the caves of Afghanistan, and then strangely to an old girlfriend, Tiana, that he missed when he felt pangs of loneliness. His mind drifted into memories of making love to her, her kisses, touch, and her beautiful body. His body responded with powerful longing.

Suddenly, the memories felt more real than he'd ever experienced before, and he became fully engaged in them. He could feel her, smell her, he grabbed her long beautiful hair and drank in her kiss. He began to pull away from her lips, but she became more aggressive and bit down, causing pain mingled with pleasure. He soon became short of breath and again attempted to disengage. She grabbed his head and continued to kiss him deeply while wrapping her legs tighter around him. Something in his gut told him to get up and run. He began to panic and opened his eyes, hoping to end the fantasy only to find he was fully awake and in his small trailer bedroom with a woman he didn't recognize kissing him and wrapped around him. His heartbeat quickened in fear and she finally stopped kissing him. Her wicked smile revealed a mouthful of razors. He tried to scream, but he had no breath, no voice. She had finished with him sexually while simultaneously absorbing his fear energy, she then bit into his neck and began to feed.

***

Jacque shot up in bed, a scream caught in his throat, his heart thudding hard enough that he heard it in his ears. He wiped cold sweat from his face as he fumbled to find his phone. 3:11. He'd only been asleep about an hour. His heart wouldn't stop and the hairs on the back of his neck were on full alert. Something was wrong. He reached under his side table where his gun was hidden, but easily accessible. Grabbing the gun, he slowly stepped to his bedroom door and pressed an ear to it. He willed his heart to slow down so he could hear. It seemed quiet, but all his senses said different.

Jacque slowly opened the door, staying hidden behind the wall, he waited a few seconds for any indication of an intruder. The darkness was still and quiet and full of evil. Leading with his gun, he walked crouched forward in a defensive position. In the shadowy hallway, he listened. A gasp from Jesse's room. Jacque turned quickly and proceeded the few steps to his friend's door. He listened again. Some movement and a groan. He decided to take the chance and kicked in the door with his gun before him.

Something on top of Jesse turned. Wicked red eyes on a deathly pale face filled with dripping razor like teeth. It hissed at Jacque, and he emptied his gun into it. The creature screamed but showed no sign that the bullets affected it at all. It then began to come at him, and he yelled, "I rebuke you in the name of Jesus!" A louder hellish scream came from its throat, and it disappeared through the wall.

***

Lincoln's phone buzzed near his head, and he groaned. Charlotte stirred next to him but didn't wake. He fought the sleep that kept his eyes from opening knowing that a late-night call was usually an emergency. He found his phone and squinted at the name on the screen, Alvin. He pressed the phone to his ear and whispered, "Hello?"

"Boss, the camp is breached. There's been a casualty. Can you get over here ASAP?"

103

Lincoln was now wide awake, "Yeah! Yeah, I'll be right there."

***

When Lincoln joined Alvin and Jacque outside their trailer, he noticed the military vets' normal business cool demeanor was replaced with what he could only call "ghost shocked."

"What happened? Where's Jesse?" He asked, hoping to break the thick sense of dread that was building by the minute.

Jacque answered, his eyes glassy with unshed tears. "Dead. I didn't get there in time. It's my fault."

Alvin squeezed his friend's shoulder and shook his head. "You can't go there, man. You'll never get out of that hole once you go in that place of blame."

"Oh my God. What happened? Show me."

They led Lincoln into the trailer and when he entered Jesse's bedroom, he stepped back gripping the doorframe to keep him from collapsing. "What the hell happened here? What did this to him? Did you see it?" Jesse's bloody corpse had multiple bite and scratch wounds with chunks of flesh missing. The most prominent wound was at his throat, where they could only surmise the creature had drained him of most of his blood. What was left of his blood was splattered on the body, bed, and walls.

Jacque shook his head, the shock of what he witnessed still apparent in his face. "It was a female demon creature. I've never seen anything like it before. It was on top of him," He closed his eyes and ran his hands through his short, wiry curls.

". . .eating him. I shot it, but that did nothing. When I rebuked it, it screamed and shot out through the wall."

Lincoln's stomach twisted with disgust and anger. They had to find the monster before it killed again. "Wake some of the others and have them scour the compound until we find it and kill it."

Chapter Fourteen

Springfield, Missouri

David, curled in a fetal position, clutched his stomach, and wept uncontrollably on the cave floor. As the tears poured out, the lights from the colored doorways moved across his form. He didn't realize he was back in the Cave of worlds until he saw the colors. The memories of his mother and the sexual abuse overwhelmed him to the point of collapse. The knots in his stomach, so severe that they began to well up until they burst out in screams and then a travail of moans the like he had only heard when Gianna was birthing their son Dylan. But this time it was coming from his own mouth, and he couldn't stop it.

Once the tears came, he yielded fully to the emotions. He let himself cry for the first time since his mother left. He cried for the boy who hurt so deeply that he stuffed the pain down in his belly for years only letting it come out in fits of rage at his brother and father. Then he wept for the young kid who was so naïve and vulnerable, that he didn't understand the abuse from a woman in charge of him wasn't love and affection like he had once thought. He wept for the loss of innocence and a childhood that was stolen. Then finally he wept for his sin. The hurt he had inflicted on his father, brother, and then his wife and child who he'd sworn to love, honor, and protect.

In the midst of a sob, a hand squeezed David's shoulder and he looked up. It was the stranger. "I'm here, my son."

David wiped his nose on his sleeve and began to sit up. "I'm sorry. What did you call me?"

The man looked into David's eyes, "Do you not know me, my child?" He wiped a stray tear from David's cheek, "I am and have always been with you."

David gasped as warmth filled his belly and suddenly, he knew, and became aware that he had always known that this man was Jesus. A sob overtook him, and he pressed his face against the Lord's chest and wept again. David's heart cried out, *Forgive me. Forgive me. I'm unworthy.*

Yeshua held him close and whispered, "It is forgiven, my child. You are mine. I make you worthy."

***

Gianna sniffed and wiped tears from her own eye, "Oh David, how did you feel after hearing that?"

David, who had been looking at the ceiling while sharing, turned back to his wife, shook his head slowly, "Indescribable. I've never felt so loved and accepted until that moment, Gigi." He put his hand on his chest. "I mean, I . . . I felt that I knew God before that, ya know? Like, I've been to church and sang the songs, prayed the prayers, and felt the good feelings. But this. This was flesh and blood real. He was really holding me. And there's nothing in this world like seeing Him face to face."

Gianna nodded, knowing all too well that feeling of being wrapped in Jesus' arms and seeing Him face to face. She began to tear up again. David took a deep breath and said, "There's more." She nodded and waited for him to continue.

"Jesus told me that I could only really get healed if I forgave. That the enemy had access to the places of wounding in my life and set up strongholds in those places that keeps the love and freedom He purchased for me out." He looked at her, his lips a flat line of frustration. "I guess before then, I thought if I forgot about the past, that in a way that was like forgiving. I didn't understand that it was affecting me. That my hurt was also causing me to hurt others and it blocked me from fully receiving God's love and forgiveness myself." He shook his head and ran his hand through his hair.

"He helped me get to a place of true forgiveness, which I finally understood wasn't about absolving those who hurt me of what they did, but instead freed me to be forgiven myself." David's eyes watered and he stared down at his empty hands and then back up to Gianna. "Gi, after I forgave my mother and my abuser, I was able to see that the person I most needed to forgive was myself." His mouth trembled and a few tears escaped. She was about to go to him, and he stopped her, shaking his head. "No. I don't want you to comfort me. Please let me finish." Gianna nodded and sat back down.

David stepped over and got on his knees in front of her. Gently taking her hand as he looked up into her eyes. Her heart pounded and she tried to look away. "Gigi, please look at me." She forced herself to look into the eyes that she fell in love with years ago, now filled with pain and tears, and she was afraid. She was so afraid of being vulnerable to him again, of beginning to trust and allow the possibility that he could destroy her again.

But she couldn't turn away from him now, amid what God was possibly doing in him. "Ten years ago, I vowed to love, honor, and cherish you and only you until death do us part. I broke that vow, Gianna. I betrayed you in the worst way possible. You have biblical grounds to leave me and move on. I'm not even asking you to take me back right now. I'm asking one thing only, and I know I don't deserve it any more than I deserve the forgiveness of God. But I'm asking if you will forgive me for what I have done and how I've hurt and betrayed you."

Gianna put her hand to her mouth to cover an escaping sob. She felt the dam of her hardened heart beginning to break and was unable to hold it back. She hated being vulnerable in front of him and allowing him to see how much he'd hurt her. But as she began to cry, images of Jesus flooded her mind, from when she first yielded to him months before as she watched him sacrifice himself for her on the cross. She cried and allowed David to hold her as she let almost a year of unshed tears go.

***

After about two full hours of tossing and turning, Diego quietly got out of bed careful not to disturb Nita. Apparently, there would be no rest for him tonight, he felt an urgency from the Spirit. He left the room and began to pray as he walked the dark, quiet halls of his home. Twenty minutes of quiet waiting as he paced in front of his office brought to his mind's eye a strong word. *Amora.* Diego stroked his beard thoughtfully and nodded. *So, it is to be tonight, Lord?*

He felt a strong confirmation.

Diego made his way downstairs to the basement. Lucy was sound asleep in the bed and two little forms were breathing slow and steady on the couch bed. He went to Amora's side and was unsurprised to find her eyes open, almost as if she were waiting for him. She whispered, "Papa said you were coming to help me." She reached her too small for her age hand out and he took it, helping her up from the bed.

Upstairs, he sat Amora down on the living room couch and sat down in a chair in front of her.

"Tell me, little one, what Papa wants me to help you with."

Even in the dimness, Diego could see Amora's large blue eyes were troubled. He couldn't imagine the pain and horror she had experienced in her short eleven years, and yet she had survived and now seemingly so open and sensitive to the voice of the Spirit. He perceived how powerful and great her calling and giftings were. The Spirit also gave him a small sense of Father's great love and passion for this one and that slight sharing felt enough to burst his heart. Diego placed his hand on his chest and steadied his breathing while Amora spoke. "Satan has sent my mother and others to find me and bring me back to him."

"Why does he want you so much?"

"My father's and my mother's family are both related to some great king in the past that had a blood covenant with Lucifer. My father and mother were put together to make the purest bloodline child and I was born to be a high priestess and Queen in the secret dark kingdom and to eventually bear a child that will be the most wicked world ruler ever created."

Fear laced with dread dropped into the pit of Diego's stomach and sat heavy like a cold stone. He had no idea the child they rescued was such an important chess piece in Satan's cosmic match. He began to pray in the Spirit with deep urgency as he spoke to the girl, hoping for divine wisdom and understanding to come to himself and their group quickly.

Amora continued, "I don't want to be found, but I'm afraid of what will happen to my sisters if I stay hidden."

"Will he not be able to use your sisters for this plan of his if he can't have you?"

She nodded, "Yes, they are the same as me for the bloodline, but they are very young. Only 9 and 7. I will soon be able to bear a child, whereas my sisters won't for a few years yet. Satan wants to implement his plan immediately." Amora looked thoughtful and worried. "I... I've seen my sisters. Like in a waking dream. They are being brought to a place of great darkness."

Diego nodded, "You see visions. Do you also dream about things before they happen?"

"Yes. I have always done that. But the visions began about a year or so ago. My father would force me to tell him what I saw and dreamed," Amora looked down. "I hated him so much that I would lie about what I saw or keep some information to myself."

Diego tipped her chin up, "He hurt you more than anyone else, didn't he?"

Amora nodded, then turned away, "I saw him die. Satan killed him. It was horrible, but I was happy he was dead."

"I'm not going to tell you that it's okay to hate, little one, but I understand why you feel the way you do.

111

How a father could hurt his own child is beyond me." He shook his head sadly, "But I think you have begun to understand that you belong to a Father in heaven who is perfect and loves you with love deeper than the oceans and wider than the entire universe."

Amora nodded, "I'm so happy Jesus sent you all to rescue me and I've been so happy these last few months living with Gianna and David but…" Her lips began to quiver, and she quickly wiped a tear away. "I want my sisters to feel loved and safe too. My…happiness has only brought them more misery and pain. I've got to save them!"

Diego was silent as he thought for a bit. "Amora, we've been charged with protecting you and helping you heal from your past, so Satan can't use you for his nefarious plans. I think first we should work on this now, then you and I will pray about what to do for your sisters. Are you agreeable to that?" She sighed and nodded slowly.

Diego patted her hand gently. "Now, I'm just going to invite the Holy Spirit to protect and guide us in the first steps of healing for you. Just relax and know that you're safe, and we'll only do as much as Father shows us tonight. Okay?" Amora nodded again, and Diego began to pray, "Holy Spirit come. We invite you to shield us. We ask that you blind and deafen the enemy. We ask that any spiritual trackers, reporters, snitches, sneaks, and spies that are human or demon will not be able to hear or see us. I pray in Jesus' name."

"Oh! I felt something lift off me just now." Amora said.

Diego nodded. "I figured someone of your import would have more than we could anticipate on you. Even though we got the biggest demons out of you before you came here, there's still residue and attachments that need to be addressed." Diego looked into her eyes for a moment, waiting for any shifting or a prompting from the Spirit. Amora held her breath, a nervous habit when she didn't know what to say. When Diego finally nodded, she blew it out with relief.

"Listen. Satan and his demons will continue to have rights to you based on access you and your family have given them by word and action. So, first things first are breaking off the bloodline covenants and oaths that were on you from the womb through your parents and forbears. I'm going to lead you in some prayers to renounce the oaths and covenants. Are you ready?" Amora nodded.

Chapter Fifteen

Sedona, Arizona

After a very long and silent ride down, the elevator doors finally opened. The hairs on Adora's arms immediately stood at attention, and she smelled blood and darkness. She, the girls and Ninazu followed the monks out into a hallway carved through a mountain. There were rows of overhead yellow lights along a lengthy passage that was wide enough to be a road two cars could travel down. She instantly recognized this was an underground military base. Many of which she had been to throughout the world since childhood. They were all the same in many ways. All located deep underground, in or near a major city, with vast subterranean levels in which it was above top secret to even find out how far down the levels went, not to mention what was done on those lower levels.

Adora, as a member of an old blood family in the Satanic brotherhood, had been involved in rituals done around the world to program children for MK Ultra mind control and other government super soldier programs. Most of these bases were used for Lucifer's experiments and schemes and she wasn't surprised by any of it having been a product of the experiments herself. What did surprise her, was the deeper evil that she felt here as well as her own demons' chattering nervously to herself and each other. She suddenly had doubts that she would come out of this meeting alive.

The agent who was Ninazu said nothing as they waited silently beside the monks. Adora looked over at Anna and Alanna. They were almost exact replicas of each other, one slightly shorter, but both too small for their age probably because of lack of proper nutrition and sunlight, their long white-blonde hair was disheveled from the lengthy sleep in the vehicle. They clung to each other; eyes wide with fear. The girls rarely spoke to her, and for her part, she only yelled commands at them when necessary. Funny how only now she had some small regret of the lack of human connection with her daughters. After all, she had been forced to reproduce, as with everything else in her life. Adora was told what to do, who to service, who to kill, who to marry, and eventually to have children for Lord Lucifer. Her only free thought was to survive. Now, with the possibility of death at hand and looking at her two youngest daughters, she wondered if there was a different path she could have walked that would have led to a more normal life for herself and her children.

A black Humvee pulled up, and Adora shrugged, letting the strange thoughts slide past and disappear into the abyss of fear and dread. She raised her chin and squared her shoulders, willing her face to exude strength and power. A soldier exited the driver's side door and, without saying a word, opened the back doors for them to climb aboard. Ninazu sat in the passenger's seat. She, the girls and the two monks got in the back.

After about fifteen minutes, the vehicle came to a stop in front of a guarded electronic steel door. The driver showed his ID, one of the guards then proceeded to look into all the windows at the passengers. He nodded, the other guard opened the electronic doors and they drove through. This happened three more times and took at least another thirty minutes before the hallway opened up and soon they couldn't see walls or ceilings. It seemed like they had driven into a great cavern. Adora couldn't even see where the dim lighting was coming from. Soon they stopped completely, but she had no indication if they had actually arrived anywhere.

They got out of the vehicle and the Humvee drove off. Adora's demons again had grown eerily quiet, and she could sense their fear. She whispered, "Ninazu, I've never felt this kind of evil before, even around Lord Lucifer."

He shook his head, "This is millennia of ancient darkness restrained. Even the strongest of us shudder to approach the Old Ones. Remember, witch, only speak when spoken to."

Anna and Alanna began to whimper and held each other tightly. The atmosphere was thick in the spacious, empty cavern. The stone floors radiated a cold that sent shivers through Adora's bones. As her eyes adjusted more to the gloom, she could see that the small slivers of light came from slits and cracks, possibly a hundred feet up in what looked like the ceiling of the cavern. She imagined it was sunlight peeking through the top of a mountain.

Suddenly an icy, thick blackness slammed down on her, and she fell to her knees with the weight of it. Her eyes began to water, and her nose filled with the pungent odor of sulfur and wickedness. She noticed Ninazu and the monks were also on their knees beside her, and the girls had passed out and lay in each other's embrace nearby. For a second Adora was glad they would not be awake to witness what may be coming.

Then a voice rumbled through the cavern like thunder preceding a storm, "Ninazu."

Adora squeezed her eyes shut as the voice penetrated her mind.

"I have come, Lord Azazel." He answered.

"Is this the woman you spoke of, Ninazu?"

"Yes, my Lord, this is Adora von Braun and two of the children."

"I wish to speak to her."

"Yes, my Lord." Ninazu looked at Adora and nodded.

Adora attempted to look upward, and a brief viewing of the ancient god came across her mind's eye as if she were seeing him in full daylight. Azazel's full form reached to the ceiling of the cavern and filled the whole space. His visage was of fire and shadow in a humanoid shape and yet something like ram horns protruded from his head. Fire, terror, and rage were in his eyes. It was but a couple of seconds flash, but enough that it overwhelmed her, and she desperately tried to shake free of it. When the viewing finally passed, Adora attempted to raise her head again and nausea overtook her.

The rumbling voice fell on them again, "You are gifted with spiritual sight, Adora. You can see me."

She nodded weakly.

"I will come to you in a more palatable form then, so we may speak."

Moments later they heard footsteps approaching. The nausea and weakness left and Adora was able to stand. Ninazu and the monks also arose to their feet as the girls began to stir from their unconsciousness. They were soon approached by a tall, strikingly handsome black man in an army general's uniform. He adjusted his tie and smirked at Ninazu, "Is this not a form that commands respect in this realm, Ninazu?"

"Yes, my Lord," answered Ninazu as he bowed his head.

The general then turned towards Adora. Her mind itched as she felt him probe her thoughts. He nodded seemingly with approval. "Adora, Ninazu tells me that you wish to be freed from the service of The Nachash."

"Yes, my family has served Lord Lu– The Nacash, as you call him, for centuries. Faithfully doing all and more that was ever asked of us, even to the point of supplying our children for his enslavement and plans."

He looked at her intently and unblinkingly as she spoke, "I see. And what would cause such a faithful family member to seek, how should we say, service? Elsewhere?"

Sweat began to bead up on Adora's forehead and her heart raced as she felt the question might be a trap, "Well, Lord Azazel, it's very clear to me that I cannot hide even a thought from you, so I will be direct. It's simply about survival. After Lucifer gets my eldest daughter back, I am of no more use and I desire to live."

Azazel tapped his chin, "Hmmm, yes straight to the point. Good. I also understand the base instincts even though I am not mortal like yourself. I'm sure Ninazu informed you that I was imprisoned for over 5000 years in darkness. This is why I must reside for a time in this underground stronghold until I can adjust to sunlight again, I can only bare to go outside at night. I know fear, desperation, and... desire." He looked at her and then over at the girls again with intense, unblinking eyes. Adora was uneasy. This seemed to be going well so far, but what she had felt coming in here was unpredictable. That kind of darkness could easily consume all life in its path without pause.

Still looking at the girls he stated, "Tell me of your eldest daughter and why the Nachash desires her so intensely."

"Amora is the culmination of generations of royal bloodline perfection. If there were to be an Empress of Europe today, she would be it. Not only is she the heir of what was the Byzantine Empire, but she is also the most powerful of us all. He plans to make her his wife, raise her to first in the Order, but then to impregnate her with the male antichrist child."

"How Ironic." Azazel clasped his hand behind his back and began to pace. "Lucifer is engaging in copulation and impregnation of human women. A crime that I was imprisoned for. And yet! Here he is freely planning a coup with his progeny!"

Again, Adora wondered about the power of this other God who judged and punished these powerful ancient entities.

Azazel continued, "Ninazu, my first desire when learning of this is to plead my case in the heavenly court against the Nachash! But surely Yah must know already!" He stopped pacing, but continued to talk, almost to himself more than them.

"It's not possible that He doesn't. No... no. I've forever lost favor in that court. I will instead ruin Lucifer's plans and rule the earth realm in his stead."

Ninazu said nothing.

Azazel then addressed Adora again, "You will bring me the girl. If you succeed, I will take you into my service and reward you handsomely. If you fail, I will kill you and your daughters and put an end to your entire bloodline. You will leave these other two with me as a guarantee."

Adora's heart dropped, but somehow, she kept her composure. Now she had two dangerous, psychopathic egomaniacal gods wanting to kill her and though she may walk away from this alive today, it still seemed her death was imminent. She kept her mind calm and clear, with no ideas of escape plans, knowing that this entity could read her thoughts.

Azazel smiled, his eyes revealing nothing, "I hope you've been thinking of how to draw out the girl, Amora is her name, correct?" Adora nodded. "I understand she has come under the protection of our enemy. Is that the case, Ninazu?"

"Yes, My Lord. Not only is she shielded, but they seem to be one step ahead of us at every turn as of late."

"Well, it sounds as though you'll need my help with that as well. Did you say that the girl is gifted? Tell me more of this."

Adora cleared her throat, "Yes, Amora has many giftings, but her strongest is as a clairvoyant. She can see the future as well as she can see things that are happening presently especially to those she is connected with. She has even communicated with her sisters since she's been gone, and I believe she does it in dreams."

He seemed to be thoughtfully listening, his dark unblinking eyes staring intensely at Adora as she spoke. He paused before responding, "That would also explain why she seems to be a step ahead. Very interesting. So, she is concerned with her sisters' safety? Perfect. I know how to speed up this process now and solidify our . . ." He grinned wickedly. "Agreement." He then turned to the monks, "Take the girls and put them in my entertainment room."

The monks, who had been standing silently nearby, bowed and then approached the little girls. The monks began to shape-shift as they got nearer to Anna and Alanna. Their faces began to lengthen, while long, curled horns sprouted from the sides of their foreheads, then their robes disappeared revealing goat-like legs and hooves. The serene monk faces were replaced by wicked, drooling satyrs that looked at the little girls as if they were the creatures' next meal. Alanna and Anna began to scream as the goat-men roughly picked them up and carried them away.

Adora stood speechless at what she had just witnessed and wondered again how she would get out of this alive.

Chapter Sixteen

Hickory, North Carolina

Alvin's thoughts were foggy, his eyelids heavy, and his muscles sore. They had spent much of the night searching for the creature that killed Jesse, to no avail. The sun was breaking over the hills, and the birds were flitting from tree to tree in song, both which Alvin usually enjoyed. But true joy was hard to come by in this new age of shadow and living nightmares. *Ironic*, he thought, *so much death and horror, and still, He gives us beauty with the dawn.*

He didn't want to rest until he found and destroyed the murderous villain, but weariness was quickly overtaking him. He found Lincoln and some of the team that was still searching and told them he was heading back for some rest. Earlier, Lincoln had a few volunteers set up a new trailer for Alvin and Jaque to move into later that day, since it would be impossible for them to live in the old one after Jesse's murder. Until the clean trailer was ready, both Alvin and Jacque opted to sleep in one of the men's bunkhouses.

Jacque was quiet as the two of them strode back, but Alvin could tell the Creole wanted to speak. "Speak your mind, soldier." He said.

Jacque looked at him, his usual joking smile and bright jovial eyes, were now dimmed with pain and glassy with anger and unshed tears, "I should have gotten there sooner, I might have been able to save him." A few tears escaped as he continued, "This guilt and anger is eating me up inside, sir!" he clenched his fists, "I've got to kill it! I should have killed it." Jacque whispered.

Alvin stopped, he faced Jacque and squeezed his shoulder, "You listen to me, soldier. Jesse was a skilled and dangerous warrior. For him to have been taken out like that . . ."

Suddenly, a deep sob rose in his throat. He clamped his mouth shut as the words, his grief, anger, and weariness converged. He shook his head as all of it rose from his belly, and he pulled Jacque into an embrace, and they both wept. All of the faces of their fallen brothers began to come to his mind, first Jesse, then each of the men and women killed in combat played like a movie in his eyes. Jacque cried silently, but his tears fell on Alvin's head as his much taller friend bent over him, and they held each other. Alvin couldn't ever remember being this vulnerable and broken in front of anyone in his life. He began to make excuses in his head that he was exhausted and maybe should see someone for PTSD symptoms. Then he chuckled to himself. *Who are you going to see in the middle of the Apocalypse, dummy? Maybe Asheville has a VA.* Then, he began to laugh out loud.

Jacque stepped back, wiping his eyes on his sleeve he eyed Alvin warily, "You, okay, Chief?"

Still laughing, Alvin shook his head and looked down, "No. No, I'm not okay." He put his hand on Jacque's back and they began to walk again towards the bunkhouse. He finally caught his breath, "Dude, I need some sleep, and probably a counselor after that."

Then Jacque started to grin, "Yeah me too. Maybe we can both go after the end of the world is over, huh?"

They both started laughing as they entered the bunkhouse.

***

Lincoln had just dismissed the last of the team that had been searching for the creature to go get some much-needed rest and was going to head back for some sleep himself when it occurred to him that he had never checked on the women's dorm to see if everyone was alright. He quickly changed direction and headed that way. Before knocking, he stopped to listen for any noise or talking coming from inside. Nothing. He tapped lightly hoping only to get the attention of those who were already awake. The door opened, surprising him and he jumped back. Emily's pale face peaked through the doorway.

"Hey." She said with no emotion or interest, as if he was the pizza guy dropping off an order.

"Oh! Hey Emily." He took a step towards the doorway. "Everything good here? Did you sleep okay?"

"Yeah, I slept okay. Why?"

"Is anyone else up? Mae? I wanted to let y'all know something happened last night. Something bad."

She looked intrigued, "Oh yeah? What?"

"Well, I'd much rather tell Mae, so she can tell everyone else. Do you mind getting her?"

Emily rolled her eyes, "Sure, hold on." She stepped inside, leaving Lincoln shaking his head. One of his biggest pet peeves was women rolling their eyes at him. It got under his skin more than anything.

Moments later Mae and Emily appeared back in the doorway. "Good morning, young man," Mae greeted

124

him smiling despite the early hour and the possibly dour news.

Lincoln responded, "Mae, I'm sorry it's so early and I have terrible news to deliver." Her face grew serious, "Well, don't sugarcoat anything, dear. Just give it to me straight."

Lincoln nodded and continued, "Jesse James was killed last night in his room."

"Oh, my Lord! Who did it? Did you catch him?"

Shaking his head, he answered, "Unfortunately no. And it wasn't a who, more like a what. And I also wanted to warn you and the girls. I'm going to put a couple extra guards at your bunkhouse tonight because whatever it was may still be in the compound. I have no idea how it got past all our security and I'm worried."

"That poor young man." She shook her head sadly. Emily didn't say anything and looked as interested in the conversation as he imagined she looked in Algebra class.

Mae continued, "Well, some of the girls and I will be praying today for this servant of Satan to be exposed and for y'all to dispose of it promptly."

Lincoln nodded, "Thanks Mae, please do that. We've stopped the search for a bit so everyone can get some sleep. I have a feeling this creature is most active at night anyway." He yawned.

"Well, you get to bed, Mr. Lincoln and the girls and I will get to work as soon as I rouse them."

He guessed Emily took that as her dismissal as well. Without a word she turned and ducked back inside. He noted how much he didn't understand the lack of manners of this younger generation as Mae hugged him and he finally turned and headed back towards the main house and his bed.

***

Alvin settled into the bunk and began his deep breathing ritual awaiting the sweet oblivion of sleep to overtake him. As his eyelids grew heavy and began to close, the scenes before his mind's eye were suddenly filled with blood and death. He began to smell the stench of burning buildings and bodies, and to hear the screams of victims being devoured by the hordes of hell. His heart rate began to accelerate in response, and he opened his eyes and switched positions four times. Each time praying a silent prayer to dismantle the siege on his senses.

Alvin was on the verge of panic. It had been months since he suffered from PTSD symptoms that used to rob him of sleep and peace. He figured the murder of Jesse James set him back into more shock and stress than his mind could take, especially right after the event at Asheville only hours before. The exhaustion was overwhelming. He had to sleep.

After several more turns, Alvin finally recognized he was in panic mode and stopped moving. He took another deep breath and willed his body to relax, pushing all the memories out, and began to refocus his thoughts. He pictured himself in a favorite place from his childhood that he used to run to and play for hours: a wooded creek behind his home. He even imagined himself at his happiest age, around ten years old. In the spring and summer, he would wander into the woods that he knew so well, find the small flowing creek and immediately wade into the ankle-deep water, since it was rare that he wore shoes.

The Waking Part II: Withstand in The Evil Day

The water was ice cold at first sending a cold shiver up his legs, but soon his feet and ankles were numb to it. The squish of mud between his toes and tiny fish touching his feet made him giggle. He would spend hours stepping on rocks, looking for crawfish holes and unsuccessfully catching them, humming to himself as he had no cares or worries. Alvin soon fully relaxed as the blissful memories took him further away from the pain of the day. He began to hear the birds in the trees, to feel the wind blow over his skin, and was about to reach for a smooth skipping stone at his feet when he heard a whisper. "Alvin."

Alvin stood back up and looked around, seeing no one. He shrugged and began to reach again for the rock. The wind blew through the trees, making them dance above him. "Alvin." came the whisper again. He looked up, "Hello? Who's there?"

A gentle breeze carrying the scent of apples and cinnamon, swirled around him and he inhaled deeply and smiled. "Alvin, my son, I am with you." said the soft voice.

Alvin's heart leapt in the vision and in his bed, as he recognized the One who was calling him. "Yes, Lord." He said as the boy in his vision.

"Alvin, my son, I have called you and I have healed you. The enemy desires to control and destroy you, but you must overcome."

"What should I do, Lord?"

"You have done well coming here. You won this battle against your mind and emotions. Now I need you to see, my son."

"What do you want me to see, Lord?"

"Come out of the water and to the trail ahead."

Alvin looked up and nodded as he spied the trail marked by well traversed ground. He made his way out of the cool water, his feet quickly picking up mud and dirt from the trail. As he walked, he waited for more instruction, but Holy Spirit was silent. He picked up an interesting stick along the path and began to wave it around like a sword, then smacking it on some tree trunks as he defeated an imaginary foe. Large crispy leaves crunched under his feet, and he kicked at a pile watching with delight as the leaves caught the breeze and scattered in different directions.

"Help! Please help!"

Startled, Alvin looked up. The call for help sounded like a young girl, and he quickly ran to the sound. As he turned a corner, he caught sight of a pretty brown girl about his age in tears. Her long hair traveled down her back in waves, and she wore a simple dirty white dress.

As he approached, she looked up, her almond shaped green, gray eyes glassy with tears. "Can you help me? I'm lost. I was playing in the woods, and I don't know how to get home."

Alvin smiled at her, "Don't worry, I know every inch of these woods. I can get you out and back to the road. I'm Alvin, what's your name?"

The girl wiped her eyes and smiled back. "Thank you. I'm Penny."

Something in Alvin's stomach didn't feel right, like the sour feeling one gets after drinking bad milk. For a second he rubbed his belly and the feeling seemed to pass, so he shrugged it off and hoped it wouldn't return, he definitely wanted to help this pretty little girl.

The Waking Part II: Withstand in The Evil Day

He urged her to follow as he began to lead them back down the trail towards the main road. She followed closely behind him in silence for a little while until his mind was lost in his own breathing and the feel of cool dirt and crunching leaves under his feet. This path would eventually come out onto a main country road which would eventually lead back towards his neighborhood and the main town. Soon he remembered that Holy Spirit had wanted to show him something. He wondered, *was it her?*

She spoke then as if she heard his thoughts, "I'm tired. I need to rest."

Alvin nodded and stopped turning towards her, he immediately noticed something different about her and rubbed his eyes. She leaned against a tree and looked at him casually and didn't seem out of breath or tired at all. She looked older. Where there had barely been slight lumps of prepubescent breasts under her dress earlier, now appeared well pronounced plump mounds. She was definitely shorter than him when they met and now her lengthy athletic legs were clearly visible beneath the now very short white dress. He quickly averted his eyes from her body and looked her directly in the face. His heart thrummed rapidly with a mix of uneasiness and excitement.

"What happened to you?" He asked with wide eyes.

She seemed confused. "What do you mean? I told you I got lost."

"You look different."

She shook her head, "I don't know what you're talking about. Are you feeling okay?"

He frowned, looking her up and down, "You look older than a few minutes ago. I know what I'm seeing."

Penny was incredulous, "I'm the same as when you met me. This is weird and makes me feel uncomfortable. Maybe I'll try to find my way back without you."

"No. No, I'm fine and I'm going to get you out of here. Let's just keep going." He finally shrugged and moved her to walk in front of him rather than behind him. Maybe he was losing it a bit. He also reminded himself that this was a vision or dream and things here weren't the same as in real life. They walked in silence for a while, Alvin keeping a close eye on Penny to see if he could catch her in the act of changing. Even thinking about that had him feeling like he was losing his mind a little. He wondered if he was going to hear from the Lord again and maybe if he should try to wake himself up from this dream. Feeling that he was actually asleep and wasn't seeing horrific bloody visions, he opted to continue whatever experience this was. He noticed the light fading and began to realize that he'd probably been in the woods for hours for it to be getting closer to sundown. He mentioned the time to Penny and asked her to pick up the pace so they could get to the road before it got dark. She only nodded and walked a bit faster but after a few minutes slowed down again. He decided to take the lead in hopes of motivating her to move faster. He walked ahead briskly, still not winded at all from their easy trail walk. She seemed to linger back a few paces, and he just wanted to continue.

The light faded even more, and he wondered at the speed it was getting dark. "Come on, Penny, we don't want to be caught in the woods at night." He urged.

Her answer came from a distance, and he turned, barely able to make her out on the path behind him by a few yards now. He frowned. It was almost as if she wanted to be out here when it was dark. His frustration and uneasiness were mounting by the minute. He waited a bit for her to catch up but no longer saw movement.

"Penny?"

There was no answer. *Seriously, she was just there!* He thought.

"Penny?" He listened and stared down the path in the rapidly fading light. He reluctantly decided to walk back to where he last saw her. He thought she must be messing with him because she thinks I'm scared of the dark. He called her name a couple more times, and now he was concerned. No answer and no sign of her anywhere. He thought through the best course. He didn't want to leave her scared and lost at night in the woods, but he also wanted to get home himself before he lost the path completely in the dark.

He shouted out, "Penny if you're playing a joke, stop now. I'm going to leave you. We need to get out of here!"

He waited again. He smelled something foul and strange. It was familiar, but he couldn't put a finger on what it was. His heartbeat began to accelerate with anxiety bordering on fear. The hairs on his arms and neck rose to attention, and he felt the need to flee. He quickly turned back the way he'd come and began to run towards the road. He heard what sounded like an animal racing towards him from behind. His heart pounded in his ears, and his lungs burned. He felt the breath of the animal close at his heels, heard low growls, and the foul smell grew stronger. He wanted to know what was chasing him,

131

but he knew he would be devoured if he turned. His legs moved swiftly, powered by pure fear and adrenaline, his bare feet flying over sticks and rocks. He knew were cutting, but he felt nothing. He prayed the road was near but also wondered if he would be saved if he came to the road. He looked up and saw it only steps away; he felt a burst of energy as if coming to a finish line at a race. As he crossed the road, a huge, bright light shone around him, and he heard the animal behind him yelp in pain. Then something flashed by his face, ending with a thump behind him and a woman's shrill scream.

As he struggled to catch his breath, he turned around. His mouth dropped open and his knees grew weak, as he took in the sight of a bright ten-foot angelic warrior standing over the body of a female creature. The angel's spear was still protruding from the chest of the monster. Alvin first looked at the creature then up at the angel who regarded him stoically, "Come closer young one." said the warrior. Alvin nodded and walked slowly towards him and the dead thing.

As he got closer, he could see that the creature looked like a mix between a woman and a huge wolf. One thing he could tell from the shape and coloring of it was that it was Penny. He frowned, feeling a mix of shame and frustration with himself.

"Child, you could have died."

"I-I didn't know."

The warrior's eyes briefly glowed with golden light, and a shiver traveled down Alvin's spine. Alvin perceived he was seeing an emotion from the angel flash from his eyes.

"The Spirit warned you when you approached the creature, and you ignored Him."

"What? No, He didn't.. I..." But his words trailed off as he remembered the sour stomach he got upon meeting Penny and how he had ignored it. He looked down and rubbed the back of his neck.

"You err in expecting Yah to speak to you with human words at all times. If you cannot discern all the ways He speaks to you, then it will not be long before the enemy will take your whole team out, and he will overrun your entire organization."

Alvin nodded as he thought deeply about what the angel was teaching him.

"Pay close attention to this lesson, child."

***

Lincoln showered and crashed into bed right as the alarm clock went off for Charlotte to get up. She kissed him and tucked him in, telling him she would take the kids out for some garden work after breakfast to give him some quiet time to sleep. He nodded gratefully and began to drift into dreamland even before she made it out of the room. Minutes later, Emily stood over his deeply sleeping form. Her eyes glowed red in the darkroom as her body began to elongate and morph into succubus form. She purred like a feline hunter. Her reward for this kill would be great; she desired to take her time with him and enjoy the process.

Chapter Seventeen

Springfield, Missouri

Amora had fallen into another waking dream. She was aware of Diego and his soothing voice as he guided her through prayer to healing, and yet she was also fully immersed in another place. It was familiar. She had been here many times before in her training. It was a long, dimly lit hallway with different colored doors lining each side that went on further than her eyes could see. Usually, she was alone, but this time, she knew Jesus was with her. Even though she couldn't see him, she sensed him. He was closer than the atmosphere around her. She didn't understand how, but she knew he was in her and they were one like the cells in her body were her, yet also something else.

Amora waited, as she had always done, for the white rabbit. All of her senses were amplified, and her heart beat in her ears. Soon enough, she heard the familiar light hopping come from behind her, and as the snowy bunny hopped past her, it quickly picked up speed, and she followed. Her pulse began to race with fear and adrenaline, knowing that whatever door it disappeared through would begin a harrowing test of fighting and survival skills, usually leading to the death of someone in the scenario. So far, she had managed to survive, but she never knew if she would.

The rabbit phased through a red door that she had to open, and her heart fluttered from the chase and the fear of what was on the other side of that door. Amora gritted her teeth and opened it.

"Amora! It's about time. We're up next." said Luka with a grim-faced nod. She nodded back, already swept up in the scene. Luka, her duad, the Brotherhood's name for paired children who were psychically bonded from infanthood to fight as a team, took her hand and pulled her onto the gravel-covered training field. His hand was damp, and she saw great drops of sweat trailing down his flushed cheeks. He must have already been practicing. He was only wearing a light pair of running shorts, a white t-shirt, and a large knife the size of his arm strapped to his side. She noticed that she was now wearing white linen pants and a shirt along with a purple quartz necklace; both of them were barefoot.

There seemed to be hundreds of spectators seated around the field this time. Most of the time there was no one watching except the programmers. Today would be long and arduous with a crowd. Many coven leaders would be here, as well as government leaders, intelligence representatives, the military and more. The best of these trials would be integrated into military and secret spy programs for every country. From the large dark splotches on the ground, Amora could see that a few teams had already gone before them, and some had been carried off of it, never to be seen again. Two other duad teams walked up and stood near Amora and Luka. They were dressed in similar garb, and she only knew their code names: Blaze and Starfire from America and Nighthawk and Phoenix from Germany. She and Luka were Ares and Athena. If all three teams were being sent in, they would have to work together to defeat whatever came at them.

The sun was blazing high and hot above them, and she had to squint to see. She spied her parents in the stands watching her with cold, expectant gazes. She turned away, not wanting their presence to influence her performance. Soon, men or monsters would come out into the arena to attack them. She and Luka had to survive using magic and the physical combat training they had learned for years. Amora closed her eyes as she felt the psychic connection to Luka engage. Now, they barely had to speak to know what the other's next move was. Each could perceive the other's emotions and pain. Amora felt Luka's fear and excitement ramping up by the second. They both eyed the side doors warily.

The signal came for the teams to get in place. Amora and Luka walked towards the center along with the other two teams. The arena was paved with gravel, about half the size of a soccer field, with stands built around it in a circular pattern. It mimicked a Roman colosseum but smaller. What took place there was similar as well, but on a much higher scale. The gladiators of old could fight back, yet the men and beasts that attacked them were of traditionally birthed earth material. What came through these doors was engineered in a lab or off-world and was an unholy mixture of beast, man, and or "alien" material. Worse was the creature was usually completely mind-controlled and evil. Nothing made by "them" ever came out with such human weakness as mercy, kindness, or empathy. The fighter could never hesitate, even for a second, when in battle with the hybrids. Such hesitations meant death.

The Waking Part II: Withstand in The Evil Day

The head programmer stood in the stands directly in front of them. He raised his arm, all three teams bowed, then immediately got in fighting stances with six pairs of eyes laser-focused on the immense metal door that would soon roll back to reveal their opponents. Seconds before the door slid back, Amora saw a picture of what was coming through, and thereby, so did Luka; three massive hybrid super soldiers. One was bigger than the other two by about a foot. As the door slowly slid open, the larger hybrid lept out and came right for her and Luka as if it were targeting them specifically. Amora noted that all three were male and dark-skinned, wearing army fatigues combat boots, and sported no weapons. She knew from experience that these creatures were living weapons and needed no man-made defense. She and Luka had fought and defeated many, but these seemed different.

The larger soldier growled as he sprang towards them, bearing a mouthful of pointed teeth, and his eyes were yellow reptilian slits. Amora could sense the evil exuding from him, and she and Luka both shivered. Luka responded quickly to the attack with a roll and fast strike at the leg, which the hybrid soldier dodged easily. Amora, feeling the power rise within her, attempted to control the dark soldier's mind but was blocked. Feeling the probe, the hybrid growled in response and leapt an inhumanly long distance towards her, and she immediately cloaked herself with an electric force shield. As his fist contacted her shield, a pulse, like a lightning bolt, shot through his entire body. He screamed and fell to the ground, convulsing. Luka darted to the attacker's throat to slit it, but he was dropped by the programmer before he could make the kill.

Luka wasn't hurt but had invisible bonds on his hands and feet. Amora quickly assessed the field. The American team seemed to have the upper hand on their hybrid opponent. The male, Blaze, was on top of the hybrid's shoulders with an arm around its throat, while the female, Starfire had stunned it with a blast similar to Amora's electric shield. The Germans had lost the female, Phoenix, who was lying in a pool of blood on the ground with a torn-out throat. Their hybrid opponent was pursuing Nighthawk across the field, blood dripping from its mouth like a rabid dog. Nighthawk was only inches in front of the soldier.

Amora acted quickly. Using her magic, she broke Luka's invisible bonds. He immediately sprang up. She and Luka sprinted towards Nighthawk in hopes of saving him before he was killed. The hybrid's arms seemed to have lengthened, and before their eyes, he shapeshifted into a wolf. Nighthawk seemed to sense the shift and dove off, somersaulting to the side as the creature's jaws snapped the air, and it crashed into the wall. Stunned for a mere moment, it shook its massive head and continued the chase.

Luka helped Nighthawk up, and they both turned to face the hybrid, their knives ready. Amora put an invisible wall around the beast, and it stopped. Angry and confused, it tried moving forward twice more to no avail. It suddenly turned its attention to Amora and growled low and threatening. She was unmoved and put all her thought and energy into the invisible cage. Using the opportunity, the boys crept forward, both hoping to get a killing blow in before the cage failed. The beast ceased growling and stared menacingly at Amora. The boys were almost on it when suddenly Amora felt a searing hot iron slice through her mind, and she screamed. The invisible cage failed, and the beast was instantly on Nighthawk's throat. Blood spurted everywhere, and the boy didn't even have time to scream before he was dead. Luka lunged while it was killing Nighthawk, and it snapped at his arm.

Luka and Amora screamed as the razorlike teeth tore through flesh and bone. She flung Luka out of the way with her power just before the wolf went for his throat. Luka cradled his bloody, mangled arm to his chest and moved against the back wall. Amora, feeling Luka's fear and pain, became angry. Her body filled with rage, which she cast at the creature, who yelped and began to roll. It was on fire, and as it rolled, it shapeshifted back into a man. The officials attempted to send people to put him out, but by the time they reached him, it was already too late. All that was left was a black, steaming skeletal husk.

The workers removed the bodies of Nighthawk and Phoenix and the American male, Blaze, who had died killing the other hybrid. The only remaining trainees were she and Starfire. After removing the hybrid bodies and the surviving hybrid opponent, they took Luka back with them as well. Starfire and Amora were left on the field. When Luka left the field, the psychic connection between them severed.

Amora trembled from the exertion, her breath coming in heavy gasps as the anger slowly drained. Starfire walked slowly up to her, her short black hair sticking up all over from sweat and blood, and her large brown eyes were wide with fear. Amora had trained with Starfire a few times and had also been sent on missions

139

with her, but they had never spoken to each other, as they could only do what they were programmed to do.

"Remember me," Starfire whispered.

Then all went black.

Chapter Eighteen

Hickory, North Carolina

Charlotte had been humming as she pulled weeds in the vegetable garden next to the house, every once in a while, glancing up to see the boys. Chris, the oldest was, for the most part, on task and working on the weeds in the potato patch. The other three had worked for mere minutes before the twins began to wrestle, and Petey, the second oldest was loudly refereeing. She smiled, thankful again that she was a boy mom. The energy, noise, activity, and dirt constantly confirmed that there would never be a dull moment in their home, not to mention a little boy's pension for adoring his mom above all others in the world. They were always running back for comfort and kisses in the midst of rough-and-tumble play, bumps, and bruises.

Suddenly, a searing pain shot through Charlotte's head. She yelped, placing her hand on her forehead. The pain was gone as suddenly as it came, but she was confused, "What was that?"

A single word came to her mind, *Lincoln.* She had learned from experience not to ignore anything strange coming to her mind. Charlotte immediately stood up, "Chris, watch your brothers, please, I'll be right back." The responsible ten-year-old responded, "Yes, ma'am." And walked over to where his brothers were playing. She hurried inside, praying, for once, that it was just a weird

141

feeling, and he was fine. As she approached the bedroom door, the feeling of dread amplified, and she all but ran through the door.

There was a large shape seemingly sitting on top of her husband, making a disgusting slurping sound that immediately set the hairs on Charlotte's neck to attention. Her eyes adjusted to the dimness as the shape sat up and faced her with glowing yellow eyes and blood dripping from its mouth. "I rebuke you in the name of Jesus Christ!" Charlotte shouted. The creature screeched and backed quickly against the wall, its eyes darting around, looking for an escape.

Charlotte's heart raced with fear and revulsion, but she wasn't going to let this thing get away to possibly hurt or kill anyone else. She pointed at it, "I bind you in Jesus' name!" It screeched again and froze, unable to move. Charlotte attempted to inch closer to the bed so she could see if Lincoln was still alive. So far, she saw no movement. Slowly pulling her phone from her pocket, she dialed the first number that came up, Alvin. As it rang, the creature hissed and glared at Charlotte with murderous intent; she had no doubt she would be dead if not for the power of Jesus' name. Alvin picked up after the second ring, "Charlotte?"

"Alvin! Get over here right now with weapons and back up."

"I'm already heading your way."

She dropped the phone and inched even closer to the bed, while praying for Lincoln and that God would come into the room. It was still too dark to clearly see the monster, and in a way, she was thankful because she may have lost some of the courage she was experiencing if she was actually able to see it clearly. Lincoln still didn't move, but she could make out the shape of him.

The monster was still hissing and squealing, so she didn't want to take her eyes off it for too long in case it could get free of its bonds somehow. What would she do if he was dead? Her stomach dropped as the thought emerged, and she shook her head slightly. No, she wouldn't think that way right now. She couldn't. He's still alive, and they would save him. She turned to him again, searching for the shape of his shoulders and chest, willing it to rise with breath. How long had it been? Minutes or hours? The squealing creature had to be loud enough for the kids to hear. Oh, God. What if they came in looking for her? *Please God*, she pleaded. *Don't let them come in.*

Suddenly, a shadow darkened the doorway, "Charlotte?" She relaxed a bit. It was Alvin.

"I'm here, Alvin."

In moments, he and Jacque were next to her, aiming their guns at the creature. She ducked and covered her ears. It squealed louder right before they put numerous bullets through its head, and it slumped over. When they finished, she turned the light on and went to Lincoln.

"Oh God! Help!"

Blood was pouring from a gash in his neck and deep scratches across his whole body. Charlotte pressed a part of the sheet onto the neck wound to stop the flow. "Lincoln, baby wake up. Can you hear me?"

Jacque quickly left the room to keep the boys out and call for help. Alvin tried to feel for a pulse. Lincoln's body still felt warm, but Alvin was worried. There was no pulse.

"Come on, brother. It's not your time yet, man."
Alvin prayed, "God, Lord Jesus. He's got more to do.
He's got kids! Lord, don't let the enemy win here."
Charlotte was weeping and kissing Lincoln's face. Alvin
shook his head, his face determined as anger burned deep
in his gut. He bent to speak into his friend's ear,
"Lincoln, you listen to me, brother. You will not die! Do
you hear me? You are going to live. Come back!"

Chapter Nineteen

Springfield, Missouri

"Why did the Lord bring you to this memory, Amora?"

Amora could hear and focus on Diego's voice again. Her heartbeat had slowed, and she felt the Lord with her. She looked at Diego, "I think He wants me to remember something that I did with Starfire after that training. Starfire and I were sent as spies to different politicians and world leaders. We carried information, were used, then sent back. Our programmers would then erase our memories."

Diego frowned, trying to push aside his personal feelings about the horrors that this little girl had witnessed in her short life. He felt helpless, knowing that he could do nothing for the many children like Amora who were trapped in Satanic Ritual Abuse and sex trafficking around the world. He hoped that helping her would also be a way for him to also help others like her. He patted her hand gently, "There's a part of you that remembers these missions. I'm going to speak to that part of you. If she doesn't answer me directly, I'm going to need you to tell me what she is saying."

Amora nodded. Diego looked into her eyes and spoke again, "I want to speak to the person who takes over when Amora goes on secret missions. Are you there?"

Amora's eyes widened, "I see her. She's taller than me and older. She says her name is Athena. Oh, that's my code name." Amora paused for a moment, then frowned.

"What's wrong?"

"She says I'm not supposed to know about her, and we'll both get in trouble."

"Athena, you're safe. Amora isn't with the programmers anymore. She is with us, and we are protecting her. Will you come forward and talk with me?" asked Diego.

Amora shook her head, "She says eventually they'll find us."

Diego continued to address Athena, "Athena, we need to talk with you. I know you want to protect Amora and yourself, but you know something that's very important. Jesus has led us to you. Do you know him?"

The young girl shook her head again, "She only meets people the programmers send me to."

Diego had an idea. "Amora, can you introduce Athena to Jesus?"

She was quiet for a bit, then she smiled and nodded. "He's here, and he's speaking to her."

"Tell me everything you're seeing and hearing."

"He's telling her that He knows all the pain and suffering she has been through over the years and that He can heal all her wounds and memories. She's asking how he can do that. He's now sharing with her what He did on the cross many years ago to heal the pain of everyone and reunite them with God forever. He's showing her how great His love is for her. . . and me," at this, tears began to run down Amora's cheeks, and she rubbed her nose across her sleeve.

"She doesn't understand why He would do that for her. She feels like she's not worth anyone to do anything like that for her. He's telling her that she is a treasure to him and worth dying for, that He already did it. He asked if she would let him in? Would she let Him take her pain and heal her? She's shaking her head and telling Him that she's done a lot of bad things. If He knew them, then He wouldn't want her near Him. She's crying, and Jesus is looking into her eyes. He tells her that He knows everything that she's done and what has been done to her and that He still loves and accepts her. He asks again, will she let Him in? Will she let Him heal her? She's crying more, but now she is nodding her head. He hugs her and tells her that he forgives her and is taking all of her sins and pain."

Amora stopped talking for a few moments and continued to wipe her teary eyes with her pajama sleeve. Diego waited patiently while also wiping a few stray tears from his own eyes. After a few minutes, Amora began to speak again, "He's calling me over to them. He said that Athena now belongs to Him and He's healed the pain from the bad memories. He says that Athena and I now need to be whole. Athena will no longer need to hold the bad memories and missions because we are done with that forever. He asks if I will accept Athena back to me and if she will agree to let me take her and finally share all her knowledge and memories. He assures us that we are both safe and He is with us and will never leave us. Yes, Lord. We both want to be united."

Amora stopped speaking. She was still in the vision with Jesus and Athena. She knew without words what they were to do, and she turned to Athena and looked up at her. Athena nodded and embraced Amora.

As she did, the older girl disappeared, and Amora was suddenly flooded with memories from the last three years.

***

Gianna sat in her favorite chair, sipping coffee. She opened the Bible sitting on her lap, and she heard the highlighted words spoken out loud, "I saw Satan fall like lightning from heaven. . ." The power of the words shook the room. She gasped in wonder as the words pulsed through the atmosphere like a heartbeat. She felt them ripple through her skin and bones, then outward. The house continued to shake with their power. She noticed something strange through the window, so she got up and walked out the front door, the ground still rumbling beneath her feet in a rhythmic pattern.

Gianna stood on the porch and watched as hundreds of shooting stars fell towards the earth from the tumultuous gray sky. The giant full moon shone bright seemingly right above her head. Suddenly, the moon split in half and pieces of it broke away and separated from each other. The sky thundered, and the stars continued to fall. Gianna put her hand to her mouth, her eyes wide with shock.

"It's the beginning of the end of all things." A familiar voice next to her said.

She turned, and Lincoln was standing with her on the porch. He looked down at her, his eyes shining with light from the falling stars, "Stop their plan. Save Amora. The lost ones still need more time before He comes to judge it all, Gianna."

Tears began to fall from her eyes like rain; she couldn't stop them, and she didn't know why she was suddenly struck with such sadness. He smiled, one of his friendly Lincoln smiles that always warmed her heart, "Don't cry. I came from Him, and now I'm going back to Him: my Treasure, my King."

He touched her face lightly, "I'll see you again, dear friend."

And he was gone.

Her voice had been trapped somewhere deep in her belly. She finally heard herself screaming his name over and over, "Lincoln!"

"Gigi. . .Gigi."

She continued to cry, even though she began to awaken as she felt hands on her shoulders and heard David's voice from far away, "Gigi. It's okay. You're dreaming. Wake up, baby."

Realization came as she finally awoke in bed with David. He hugged her, "Are you okay? You kept saying Lincoln's name. Did you dream about him?"

She laid her head on David's chest as he held her, and she wept. "He's gone. . . he's gone."

***

"I remember the last mission Starfire and I were sent on," Amora opened her eyes, speaking quickly of the downloads she was getting. "We were sent to Sedona, Arizona, to participate in some blood rituals by some rock formations in the town, and afterward were sent to an underground military base for more programming. And I don't think Starfire came out with me. I think she had to stay and continue in some other program. That place was horrible. I have the memories like a movie. Even though it was me, I don't remember the feelings and experiences as if I lived them myself." She paused, considering her next words.

149

"Athena's programming was military intelligence, so she basically recalls everything she sees, reads, or is told almost like a computer. I now know everything about this bunker, from where it's located to the top-secret map of the whole interior, and it's as big as a city under there!"

Diego considered all that she said with interest and some fear, "Do you think you're supposed to go back there?"

Amora pursed her lips thoughtfully and finally nodded, "I've been experiencing brief visions of my sisters the last few days, and now that I have Athena's memories, I am almost certain they are being held in one of the rooms in this underground base."

Just then, they heard footsteps coming down the stairs. They turned, and Gianna stood with David supporting her as she wiped her eyes and her nose, "Lincoln's dead."

Chapter Twenty

Hickory, North Carolina

A little over 200 people had gathered at the compound if Darrel's estimation was correct. Everyone was standing in clusters around a giant oak tree on one of the back acres. A few of the team had worked diligently that morning digging two six-foot holes near the base of Lincoln's favorite tree. Darrel, Alvin, Jacque, Drake, and two others had carried each of the wooden boxes over and carefully, with more help lowered them into each hole while the others watched solemnly. Charlotte and the boys were up front, the twins too young to even understand yet that they would never see their dad again, stood quietly next to their older brothers. The only family Jesse had left was a sister who he hadn't seen or talked to since before the Breach, and no one knew how to get ahold of her. Alvin, Jacque, and Kat were the closest family Jesse had, but all the others who had gotten to know him the last six months now mourned for him as well. Two of the strongest warriors the slayers had, killed in one day was almost too much for many to bear.

Darrel was numb. Was Lincoln really gone? He couldn't accept it. Lincoln had been such a natural leader and always such a great friend. Who could fill that void for him? For all of them? What about his kids? *God, how could this happen? How could You let this happen?* He felt guilty for feeling that way, but he couldn't deny that he felt that God had let them down. All that they had been through in the other realm and all that they had been doing here the last six months to fight this dark battle, there was no way Lincoln was finished. No way!

Then there was the guilt that maybe he could've saved him somehow. They were all still in shock that a dark creature got through all the base's extensive security. No one had an explanation for it. Alvin was heading up a team that was looking into it in detail, and the body of the creature had been saved to examine as well. Darrel balled his fists over and over, trying to suppress the sorrow and rage that was skating at the very surface of his thoughts and emotions. He took a breath and scanned the area again.

Diego, who was presiding over the service, had arrived earlier that day with Gianna, Lucy, and the rest through a portal that Drake had made. He was also able to bring the five other teams here that had been trained by them from Europe, Asia, South America, and Africa. Those core fighters, along with the refugees living in their compound, had made the count for the funeral over 200. Darrel had counted at least four times already. For some reason, getting the exact numbers mattered to him. It would have mattered to Lincoln. They had just talked about how many soldiers they now had for the Giant Slayers team.

Billie Jean stood beside him, her nose, and eyes red from crying since they found out about Lincoln and Jesse two days ago. Darrel hadn't cried. Instead, he had an uncomfortable ball of pain and anger sitting like lead in the middle of his chest. Billie Jean had asked him last night why he was holding it in. She was afraid it would come out in some unhealthy way. He had no answer for her. He didn't feel like he was deliberately keeping the tears in. He just had no tears, yet he felt the sting of the loss very deeply. He stood looking at the two holes, then across the crowd of faces, stopping at each of the individuals that he hadn't known a little over six months ago but that now were so dear to him. As dear as his grandmother had been. He sighed to himself. He missed her a lot lately, even more during times like this.

Diego began to speak, "Dear brothers, sisters, and friends, as we gather on this somber occasion to remember our brothers Lincoln and Jesse, I ask that you turn over the pain and shock of your loss to our gracious and loving Father in heaven. He is close to the brokenhearted and comforts those who mourn. . ."

As Darrel struggled to stay focused on Diego's words, his mind began to drift to a few of his last conversations with Lincoln, "Man, I'm struggling with being happy about this baby coming." Darrel shook his head, "How am I going to protect them? What if we die, and the baby ends up being an orphan?"

Lincoln and Darrel had gone on a perimeter check together, examining the fences, traps, and monitors. They often did this together to debrief. Lincoln squeezed Darrel's shoulder and stopped walking to face his friend, "Darrel, don't think those thoughts don't cross my mind constantly either, brother. Listen, there are all those real dangers and possibilities, but guess what? That's why we have to continue to fight and win! We run into the fight while others are running away because God is with us, and He's equipped us to beat back the darkness for our kids and everyone else's kids, too."

"I know, Link, I know that, and I would never shrink from a fight. But Billie Jean and this new baby have got me on edge all the time." He sighed. "I want to be happy. And part of me is so happy at even the chance to be a dad and with BJ, who's so amazing. But I'm way more afraid than I should be, man."

"Hey, brother, a little fear never hurt anyone. You just don't want fear to control you. Like Jesus said, 'Don't yield to fear.'" He poked Darrel's chest, "You, my friend, are going to be an incredible dad, and we're here to support you too, right? You know we are all family. Even if something happened to you or BJ or both, you know that your child would never be an orphan, right?"

Darrel nodded, smiling down at this long-bearded, country white man whom he would have never even looked at a year ago. "Thanks man. I love you, bro."

Lincoln smiled and hugged Darrel, "Love you too, man."

It had really eased his mind immensely knowing all the family his baby would have here with everyone that had quickly become closer than any blood family he had ever known. As Darrel mused over the memory of this conversation, he looked over at Charlotte and her four young boys. His heart stirred. *Your boys will have a father, Link. I will love and protect them like they're my own.*

***

Later, Diego, Gianna, Darrel, Lucy, and Billie Jean met privately in Charlotte and Lincoln's home. Charlotte was invited to sit in for Lincoln. They all sat comfortably on couches and chairs in the ample farmhouse-style living room with a stone hearth and bright white wood paneling on the walls. The sun shone through wide windows, casting cheerful light and warmth throughout the room. The contrast between the current mood and the beauty of the day was not lost on those gathered. It was rare that the original team were ever together without a full entourage of new members and those in training as well as family attending as well. Under the circumstances, they felt the need to have some private time to express their thoughts and emotions about Lincoln's passing and what had occurred in their separate groups in the last couple of weeks.

Each of them took turns talking about Lincoln and telling Charlotte about their adventures with him in the other world. He had told her some, but she was amazed and grateful for all they were sharing that she didn't know. In the last few months, all of them had become like family to her, and she was so grateful that they were here during this horrible loss.

Charlotte finally got to share in detail about Lincoln's murder, which resulted in more tears and questions from the team.

"Do you all know yet how the creature breached security?" Gianna asked.

Darrel shook his head, "Alvin has a team doing some deeper investigating, but nothing solid yet. Our systems were above military level, as well as putting in many spiritual blocks. It doesn't make sense."

"Did you pray for the Lord to expose the breach?" Asked Lucy.

Charlotte, Darrel, and Billie Jean exchanged looks that went from shock to sheepish. Finally, Darrel answered, "I know that seems like an obvious first step, but honestly, I think we've all just been in shock and survival mode the last few days, and we seriously have not gotten together to do that."

Diego stroked his beard and added, "It sounds like you fell into the enemy's trap, and it's still working. Don't worry, we will pray right now."

They all got quiet, and Diego began, "Father, we come before your throne in the name of our savior Yeshua, and humbly ask for forgiveness for not seeking your help and counsel on this grave matter. We ask that you bring to light the way that the enemy was able to infiltrate this compound. Thank you, Amen."

"Amen. They all agreed." And then they all sat quietly waiting.

After a few minutes, Diego looked at Darrel and Billie Jean. "Tell me, was there a significant event that took place before the death of Jesse?"

Billie Jean nodded, "There was a huge attack on Asheville, and we took a team and put a stop to it."

"Yeah, we took out a mega-giant and a few small ones, along with tons of monsters," said Darrel.

"Sounds like something might have come back with you." Added Gianna.

Diego nodded, "It could have been something one of you picked up from somewhere in the city that was cursed. A cursed object will allow the enemy to get a foothold into someone's life."

"But this is bigger than a cursed object," added Lucy as she scanned all their faces. She looked as if she was in deep thought, "This was a physical breach. You actually killed a monster, not like casting a demon out of a person."

They all nodded, then Billie Jean's eyes got big, and she tapped Darrel's arm, "Oh, oh, oh, Baby, remember that girl that Lincoln brought back to the compound?"

"Oh yeah." He snapped his fingers, "What was her name. . .Emily? Yeah, the little college girl he saved."

Charlotte looked horrified, "Is she still here?"

"Come to think of it, I haven't seen her since the night we got back. . . the same night that Jesse was killed." Darrel shot up from his chair, "I'm going to get Alvin and check on the women's bunkhouse."

Everyone else quickly got up and followed him out.

***

Jacque and Alvin joined the group at the women's bunkhouse. They had all gathered around Mae, who was the resident coordinator for the compound and lived in the women's bunkhouse. Mae had met everyone before the funeral, so Darrel went right into questioning her. "Mae, is the young girl still here that Lincoln dropped off a few nights ago?"

She took a deep breath and shook her head, "No, honey, I'm sorry I haven't seen her since the morning after her first night here. I figured she didn't like us much and ran off. I was going to tell Mr. Lincoln. . ." she trailed off sadly after that.

"Can you please show us which bunk she slept in?" Alvin asked her.

She nodded, "Of course, follow me."

Alvin, Jacque, and Darrel followed her, and the rest stayed in the foyer area.

When they got to the bunk, Alvin pulled his flashlight out of his back pocket, "Did you change the sheets since she slept here?"

Mae shook her head, "Unfortunately, no. The girls are each responsible for their own spaces, and I wasn't

157

going to strip it until I knew she wasn't coming back. With all the chaos, I just didn't know who to ask about the girl since it was Lincoln who brought her here."

Alvin pulled back the sheets and began slowly scanning the white fabric with his flashlight. As he came down to the middle edge, he stopped, "Got something."

"What is it?" Jacque asked.

After he scanned down the rest of the bed, Alvin stood back and pointed at a couple of spots, "There are a few small smears of blood at the very middle edge of the mattress, where she could have grabbed it with her hands. I don't see anything else, but I think it's something besides the fact she's gone."

"Wait, do you think she has something to do with this creature that killed our guys? You looked at the body? Does it look like her?" asked Darrel.

Alvin nodded, "Well, after Jacque and I shot it, it began to decompose very quickly, like within hours, it was unrecognizable as to what it was. It basically became a stinking black hunk of meat, and we ended up torching it. The only thing we could verify was that it was the same monster that killed Jesse and that it was female."

Darrel looked at Jacque. "You got a close-up look at it, right?"

Jacque nodded.

"Can you remember if that thing looked like Emily?"

Jacque flinched at the memories of the creature and then shook his head, "I can't tell you. I looked closely at its face, but no, I wouldn't say it looked like her, although I never got a good look at Emily's face. I do remember she was super pale, but blonde girls usually are. The monster was white skinned, but that was the only similarity I could see. It had extra-long limbs, really voluptuous like it was made for seduction and death." He stopped for a moment, looking like he wanted to say more, but shook his head.

Alvin spoke. "Jacque, tell him the rest."

Jacque looked uneasy and nervous, and Darrel wondered what would unnerve a seasoned soldier like him, who had literally seen it all. Jacque blew out a long puff of air and continued, "Well, you remember I told you about my family history, right? The whole voodoo royalty thing?"

"Yeah, of course," Darrel answered.

"So, I grew up hearing about different spirits and gods and one of them was called a succubus. These things are female spirits that could take on flesh and visit men at night. They would seduce the man and have sex with them, and sometimes, they would kill them after. Even if they didn't kill them, then, eventually, the men would die from the life energy being sucked out of them from the demon." Jacque swallowed, looking grim and fearful.

Darrel rubbed his bald head, his thoughts racing, "Okay, so that's horrible. Do…you know if Jesse and Lincoln had sex with it?" He closed his eyes, not wanting to picture his friend dying in the sinister embrace of a demon.

"When I walked in on Jesse, she was on top of him . . . eating him, and they were both naked. I really will never get that awful picture out of my head." Jacque replied.

"We don't know about Lincoln. We came after Charlotte found him, and she had the monster subdued in a corner of the room." Alvin added.

Darrel crossed his arms and looked up at the ceiling, trying to calm his tumultuous emotions, revulsion, and fear. He finally looked at Mae, who had been standing silently by, her face as troubled as his own heart felt. "Thank you, Mae. Can you please have one of the girls change these sheets out, and will you get your prayer team together and seek the Lord for us while we figure out what we're doing?"

Mae smiled and put her arms around all three men, "Absolutely. I have faith that the Lord knew what He was doing when he put your team together, boys. He will give you the wisdom and understanding that you need at this time." She said a quick prayer for them, and they all exited to rejoin the others.

Outside, Darrel told the rest of the team what they had seen and discussed.

"If the conclusions you're drawing are true, which they seem to be, the reason the creature was able to breach your security was simply that the threshold covenant was circumvented," Diego observed. They looked puzzled, except for Gianna, who nodded.

"Y'all know what that is. You've seen it in vampire movies. They can't enter your home unless you are tricked into inviting them in. That is actually a spiritual law that has stayed in our cultural vernacular even if we don't really know the law."

Jacque looked surprised but soon agreed, "Yes, of course, this was a common understanding in my family. Of course, it's also why we always had extra protection of amulets and wards against evil placed at doorways and windows, but yes, if you invite a demon in, it can and will wreck your house."

"So, you're saying that Lincoln basically invited the devil to have his way with us by offering refuge to this young girl that he thought needed help? That seems unfair, doesn't it?" Darrel countered, clearly getting upset.

Suddenly, Alvin's eyes widened with understanding, "Listen to this dream I had the morning after Jesse was killed." He explained the dream about him as a child helping a little girl who turned out to be an evil monster and the angel warning him about listening more closely to the Spirit.

Darrel looked at Billie Jean, Alvin, and Jacque, "For Jesse and Lincoln's sake, I'm so sad that we are learning this the hard way, team." He shook his head as the grief and anger stirred under the surface of his heart.

Diego touched him lightly, "Sometimes important lessons must come at a great cost so that they prevent even worse losses later on." He then turned to the rest of them, "We must mourn and heal in the midst of the war, unfortunately, family. We have much more to discuss and plan. Let's meet with all the leaders and our team later today after we've collected our thoughts, eaten, and rested."

Darrel nodded, "We'll get the word out, and we can meet after dinner tonight in the big cafe."

Chapter Twenty-One

Sedona, Arizona

Adora stood on the precipice of a cliff overlooking a calm sea. It seemed that the sun had just gone down, and the stars had begun to twinkle into sight. The horizon still boasted a gleaming golden strip of light that painted its hues across the calm, dark waters. A breeze danced lightly across her skin, and a faint voice tickled the very edges of her thoughts as it passed over her, *I AM whom you have been seeking.*

Goosebumps stood up on her arms, though she was not cold. In fact, the temperature was pleasant and perfect. *What was that?* She blinked and rubbed her arms. *Where am I?*

You are beyond where your gods can hear or see. I AM the Most High God . . . the Creator and Judge of the Universe.

Adora began to tremble uncontrollably until she fell to her knees, her heart racing in fear. *Are. . . you going to kill me?*

Peace, child.

Again, the gentle breeze lighted her skin, her heart slowed, and she took a deep breath.

God spoke again. *You have wondered what kind of God can imprison the ancient ones who seem to be powerful. Truly, these gods live in constant fear of my final judgment when they all, yes, even Ha Satan, will be cast forever into the lake of fire and suffer eternal torment. You have a choice, child. Will you follow the fallen ones to their final fate? or will you repent of your ways and follow Me?*

Adora paused, considering all that He had said, then answered. *Can You truly save me from them? From Satan? From Azazel? and all those that follow them?*

You desire to be saved from the first death only, child. What does it profit you if you gain the whole world, and yet your soul is still lost?

Adora pondered His words again. She had never thought about life beyond this one. The elders, spirit guides, and others never spoke, at least to her, of an afterlife. Only prolonging the pleasures of this one, killing, stealing, and lying to gain possessions and positions. Self-preservation mingled with fear was all she knew.

Is there truly life after death? She asked.

Yes, child. You were created to live forever. Those who choose Me will spend eternity with Me. Those who choose their own path will follow Satan and his angels to his judgment.

If this truly was the God who could imprison and destroy other gods, then He would be her best chance of surviving. She wondered what choosing Him would mean. She was in awe that *He* had found *her* and that He didn't seem like the other gods at all. Adora inquired, *What must I do to be your servant and to choose You?*

Repent of your sins, forsake your evil ways, and believe in Jesus the Messiah, the One who died for you, rose again and is coming back to judge all at the end of days.

She hissed under her breath. That name! The one who was not to be spoken of. The enemy. The one whom Amora saw before she escaped! Yes, it all began to make sense now. From childhood, she had been taught to hate this name and all who bore it. She never questioned why. They always had enemies. What was it to her which name was a god or a man? But this now made sense. The God who would destroy Satan is the one he would hate the most. Her thoughts now ran rampant of the things Satan required his followers to do that were to fully dishonor this God:

The Black Masses, the desecration of churches and holy sites, the torture and blood sacrifices of animals, babies, and children, the cursing and ruination of Christian people's lives and businesses, and this was just a small percentage of all of it. This God should hate her and want to destroy her, and yet He was offering her a *choice.*

She began to wrestle with thoughts of her past deeds and the seeming conflict of the Creator's offer. Suddenly, she heard the deep rumble of thunder throughout the sky, which echoed all around her. Adora looked up, for she was still on her knees at the edge of the cliff. The amber sky had turned gray and was now filled with storm clouds that covered the stars. A dark and wicked storm had rolled in fast, and the gentle breeze had become a strong wind. Adora trembled and wondered if the Creator God was still there. What if He took the offer back? What if she was still going to die?

Lightning streaked across the sky, followed by the deafening crash of thunder. To her horror, the cliff underneath her broke away, and she began to fall. Adora screamed.

The Waking Part II: Withstand in The Evil Day

She shot straight up in bed, her heart beating wildly as sweat drenched her nightgown. She reached for the lamp and flipped it on. The cheap side table clock read 3:33AM. She scanned the unfamiliar, eerily quiet room containing a basic military dresser, side table, desk, bed, and small bathroom. Not the luxury she had always been accustomed to, but she wasn't dead. . . yet. Getting out of bed, she slowly shuffled over to the bathroom, turned the light on and splashed her face with cool water. Her thoughts were a fog of voices mixed with fear and thunder.

Eventually, she decided to make her way back to the bed, where she sat and focused on clearing her thoughts and remembering what she had dreamed. She began to breathe deeply to calm her body and shut out the chattering of her inner voices and demons. Finally, after a few minutes of quiet, flashes of her dream came back to her, and she spent some time replaying the conversation with the Creator God and carefully weighing the offer against her other options. She wondered if it was even possible to choose the offer since it ran contrary to her programming. There had to be a fail-safe that would result in either instant death or an alert for someone to kill her. Either way, death seemed to be waiting at all doors.

Frustration at her limited options began to consume her. In the past, she had survived by being shrewd and adaptable to all situations. Pain and bloodshed were part of life, and she had taken it in stride. Of course, it helped once she was able to wield it against others, knowing she, at least for a time, was essential to Lord Lucifer's plans, had given her a bit of misplaced confidence. Adora's thoughts began to drift towards her daughters.

Her concern for their safety had never been a blip on her radar before. After all, in the Brotherhood all must pay their dues for power and position, and maternal affection, or any human affections, for that matter, was not something any could afford to get entangled with. Her own mother had gladly exchanged her, at the age of 18 months, into the hands and beds of the programmers and handlers. Adora had never known a touch, human or otherwise, that wasn't brutal or sexual. She had just learned to shut off all weaker emotions. . . again to survive. Did she really want Amora to be found? Or should she desire her to stay where she was? In relative safety with the people of this more powerful God?

"Mother." A little girl's voice whispered, seemingly close to Adora's ear.

Startled, Adora looked all around and saw no one. "I must be hearing things." She said out loud to the empty room.

"Mother," said the voice again. Adora's heart thumped. There it was again, and it sounded like Amora's voice.

An almost imperceptible orb of light shone near the foot of the bed. Adora noticed it and would have turned away had it not fluttered slightly. She continued to stare at it, and as she did, a faint line formed from it. After a few moments, the outline of a small person appeared. Adora's mouth dropped open as the full body, although ethereal and ghostlike, of her daughter Amora materialized in front of her.

Adora was about to speak when Amora put her finger to her lips, "Don't speak, Mother. I can't be seen or heard by the dark ones, but if you speak, then they'll know I'm communicating with you. Just listen, I don't have long."

Adora nodded slightly.

"We are coming to get my sisters. I know my Father contacted you in a dream. You should turn to Him, Mother. If not, you will be doomed to the same fate as Satan and all who follow him. I cannot promise that you will survive or be safe, but you will not go to judgment with the rest. We are coming soon. Goodbye, Mother." Amora's eyes were sad and imploring. Then she faded and was gone.

Adora stared at the empty space where Amora had been for a long time. She didn't know how long until finally, the alarm clock sounded on the bedside table: 7:00AM. She was due for a meeting with Ninazu and Lord Azazel in 30 minutes. She quickly got out of bed and began to mechanically change into a black suit and fix her hair and make-up.

Soon, there was a sharp knock at her door. Adora had pulled her hair up in a tight, no-nonsense bun, causing the corners of her eyes to turn slightly hooded while also emphasizing her sharp chin and jawline. She furrowed her brows, threw her shoulders back and set her mind to stun. She had always been able to command a room and intimidate most men, except her husband Viktor, of course, who never cowed to anyone, no matter what their status. Even kings had trembled in his presence. This attitude, of course, eventually led to him overstepping with Lord Lucifer himself and to his recent demise. One must tread lightly in the presence of ancient powers, showing enough strength that they are confident

167

in a person's abilities yet still willing to yield to their whims as law.

She opened the door to a soldier waiting with a car to escort her to the meeting. She climbed in, still puzzled about what to do, but her face betrayed nothing but cool passivity. Once they arrived, she was escorted into a large boardroom with a meeting table that seated several scientists and military commanders, as well as Azazel in the military general form she had seen him in yesterday and Ninazu still in the form of a secret service agent. To the left of the table were a leather couch and a few cushioned chairs on which sat Alanna, Anna, as well as a young black-haired girl around Amora's age who looked familiar and Luka, who had been Amora's duad. The children all looked like they'd been drugged very recently and sat with blank stares, saying nothing.

The group at the table all stood up when Adora entered. She nodded at them and sat on a chair next to Ninazu. Azazel nodded back at her. He was wearing dark glasses, and she was thankful his eyes were not showing. He addressed the table, "I am pleased with the progress that we have made so far for our plan for further infiltration into the American government and military. I understand that you've made great strides in enhancing human DNA for the super soldier and super spy programs. What I'm about to give you will advance those programs 100 years beyond where you are today. It will be impossible for the people to resist what is coming, and once it is rolled out here, all other governments will follow or be consumed."

Although the room was large and at a pleasant temperature, Adora began to feel as if the walls were closing in on her and sweat dripped down her back. She wondered if her face was red and flushed, so she took a cloth handkerchief out of her purse and began to dab at her neck and forehead. Azazel was still talking to the table, but his voice seemed far away, and she was struggling with hearing all of his words. Her demons began to chatter nervously, arguing with each other and others, telling her to get up and run. She willed her hands not to tremble and dabbed her upper lip. She scanned the table. The military brass and the scientists were hanging on every word of Azazel. No one seemed to notice her discomfort, and she was thankful. She then glanced across the room at her daughters, their vacant eyes giving no indication of the horrors they must have seen and participated in the night before. It was probably best that they were so drugged they couldn't think. Not for the first time, she wondered why she suddenly noticed or thought about her daughters' suffering. Ninazu bumped her arm sharply, and she quickly averted her gaze from the girls and turned back to him. The full lips of his avatar were pursed into a line. Azazel and the others were looking at her.

"I apologize. Could you repeat the question?"

She could feel Azazel's penetrating gaze through the dark glasses, "Do *you* have an update on your eldest daughter's status?" The tone of the god's voice was restrained, but his voice amplified in her head was tinged with anger, and she jumped slightly, her hands trembling again, and she tightened her fist around her handkerchief.

"Yes," she half grinned and took a breath, "I heard from her, and she has said that she and those whom she is with are coming to save her sisters." Adora felt that telling it was the only choice, as this god seemed all too

169

capable of reading thoughts or at least could easily tell if a person was lying.

Azazel grinned, "Excellent. After we have secured her and killed those she is with, I have decided I will keep your other daughters as well. It seems there is use for them in the cloning program." One of the scientists, a blonde, middle-aged man with glasses and dead eyes, nodded enthusiastically. Adora's heart dropped in her stomach, and she frowned and drew her breath in sharply.

Azazel looked at her intently through the sunglasses, "Do you have any objections, Mrs. von Braun?"

Ninazu shook his head at her. She looked away from him and back at the god, "We had an agreement. . ." she swallowed, "And you said you'd keep my other daughters as a guarantee until you got Amora. There was no mention of keeping them. . . or giving them to this program."

"The agreement was that if you gave me your eldest daughter, Amora, you could then live under my service and protection. Serving me means that all you have belongs to me, just like you and yours belonged to Lucifer." He folded his hands and smiled, sending a cold shiver down Adora's still sweaty back. "Now, do we still have an agreement, or have you changed your mind?"

She tried to keep her shoulders erect, but she cowed, bowing her head slightly, "Yes, of course, I understand and agree to your terms."

"Perfect. Now, since we will be expecting these visitors who are with Amora, it will be perfect for testing the Nephilim super soldiers against a formidable opponent." He called on the female, raven haired scientist at the end of the table, "Doctor, the plan for the child soldiers is in place?" He looked at Luka and the other girl.

"Yes sir, the duad will be in place when his counterpart arrives, as well as Starfire, whom Amora knows as well. Both children have been modified with the most advanced neural implants. These implants will actually grow and improve along with the subjects' brains and bodies. The AI interfaces with their brain implants in real-time. In theory, they can outthink and outmaneuver even the DNA-modified super soldier. We're very excited to put them on the field and compare their performance alongside each other."

"Is there a danger of their . . . feelings getting in the way of their orders?" He asked her.

The scientist smiled coldly, and Adora wondered if the woman also had a chip implant in her own brain, "Not at all. That part of the brain has been shut off. We've done it often in the past. They may recognize the girl, but it will not inhibit them from acting on whatever they've been programmed to do."

"Excellent. I look forward to observing them as well as the DNA-enhanced soldiers in action." He addressed the whole table, "Let us prepare for war." With that, he dismissed the meeting.

Chapter Twenty-Two

Hickory, North Carolina

The compound's cafeteria was in a 3000 square foot, modified metal building that contained rows of long wooden picnic tables and sat the over 200 residents and guests with more room to spare. The plan was for 300-350 residents to eventually occupy the safety of the compound. Lincoln, Darrel, and a few others had made extensive plans over four months ago, and this cafe was one of the first things finished after the bunkhouses. The celebration on the opening of it was still a recent happy memory for Darrel, and every time he ate in here, he was reminded of the amazing connections that had come out of their little, odd team of giant slayers. He had mixed emotions as he finished his wonderful home cooked meal of chili and cornbread that Janine and her kitchen crew had put together. Janine had joined them just a couple months ago from Virginia after most of her hometown was overrun by vampires. She managed to escape with her sister and two kids, who all now helped in the kitchen to make two full meals a day for all the residents.

Alvin, Jacque, Darrel, Billie Jean, and Diego were at a single table, along with Charlotte and her boys. Charlotte was in an intense discussion with Diego. Gianna, her husband David, their son Dylan, Amora and Lucy were at a table directly behind him. Darrel had yet to have a chance to meet Gianna's husband and wondered if there would be any time. The teams from the other countries were also sitting close by. Billie Jean intertwined her fingers into his, "You've been so quiet today, babe. Please tell me what's going on with you. I want to help."

He looked into her striking blue-gray eyes and squeezed her hand, "You're so beautiful." He kissed her lightly on the lips, and she blushed, "Thank you, but you're deflecting."

Darrel grinned, "I can't tell my wife how beautiful she is?"

Billie Jean rolled her eyes and shook her head. He kissed her on the cheek, "Baby, I'm kidding, okay? Well, not about how beautiful you are."

She punched him playfully on the shoulder, "Darrel!"

"Okay, okay." He held his hands up in surrender, "Serious. I'm serious now. Yes, I'm a mess right now, and I'm sorry I haven't shared with you much. That's wrong of me." He scratched his thick beard. "I just don't want to upset you more than you already are."

"Darrel, I'm not some delicate flower that will crumble at any moment. Give me some credit, will you? After everything we've been through?"

He kissed her hand, "Baby girl, yes. I definitely know that you are *not* a delicate flower. Look, you're just as upset as me about Lincoln. . . and BJ, to be honest, you feel things very deeply. Honestly, I'm just trying to keep it together myself and to not break down every five minutes. . ."

"You mean like me?" She chuckled as she sniffled and wiped a stray tear away.

Darrel stroked her cheek tenderly, and then they both looked over, startled as Diego stood up and Mae joined him, blowing a whistle that Darrel wasn't surprised she had around her neck. Everyone went silent, and turned her way, "Listen up, Y'all. Mr. Diego needs to address the soldiers. Please clean up your plates and head out if you are not part of the Giant Slayers team or their families. Thank you!"

Diego nodded and thanked her, "Family, please gather closer so we can speak about what the Lord is leading us to do next." He waited as some people filed out, and others got up and sat closer to him. The teams from other countries had people with them to translate the meeting, so Diego spoke slowly and paused after every few sentences to allow for clarity.

He continued, "I believe that all of us have been given pieces of a humongous puzzle, and it was imperative that we come together and share all that we did today. I have spoken to most of you," He looked at specific leaders as well as Charlotte and Gianna. "And from Gianna's and Amora's dreams to the Satanic group that is pursuing Amora and the strategic attack on this compound, I believe our next and most important task has presented itself. As many of you know, before the Breach, my team was tasked with saving a little girl from the clutches of a worldwide Satanic Network of which she was raised, trained, and programmed to eventually become the bride of Satan. Had they had their way, she would have eventually become the most powerful witch in the world and bearer of the anti-Christ child, fathered by Lucifer himself. So far, we have kept her safe and out of Satan's hands. Unfortunately, if they don't get Amora back, they still have her two sisters to fulfill this plan with. Their ages will only buy the world a couple more years at most. It's my understanding that only very few in the world have the bloodline that can bear a hybrid baby, and even less with royal lineage who will give the offspring ruling rights. We know where they are keeping Amora's sisters, and we believe we are to rescue them."

Darrel looked over at the little blonde girl sitting next to Gianna. She had gained a little weight since he had last seen her a few months ago when she was painfully thin and about the size of a nine-year-old. Now that she was almost twelve and having been with Gianna for the last six months, he could see she looked much healthier and could almost pass for her age. He didn't want to even think about all that little girl had experienced in her short life. Darrel began to burn with anger at the thought of so many innocent children just like her who were subjected to sex trafficking, abuse and worse.

Diego continued, "We want to give you all the choice whether to go with us or not. This is more dangerous than you can imagine, and many will not return. This fight will take place in a deep underground military base. We'll be dealing with military soldiers as well as monstrous experimental creations of the government, Nephilim creatures and even worse."

"What could possibly be even worse than what you just described?" A woman with a Russian accent asked. Diego's face grew even more serious than previously, "An ancient evil has recently been awakened. One, I believe, that is more evil than Lucifer, if that's even possible. A fallen angel referred to heavily in the book of Enoch named Azazel. He has been chained in darkness since before Noah's flood, and Enoch describes him as the one who corrupted the whole earth, and the Most High said to ascribe all sin to his doing."

Gianna responded, "That's what I saw coming out of the pit in my dream?"

Diego nodded, "I believe so."

She shivered and rubbed her arms, "There's no way we can survive that, Diego." She answered.

Darrel felt a stab of fear in his belly at the thought of going against such a powerful enemy with his wife and unborn child at his side. As if she heard his thoughts, Billie Jean squeezed his hand.

There was a murmur of concern among the group.

"For the last six months, all of us have faced some of the darkest dangers that hell could conjure and have prevailed. The Lord our Father has equipped us, been with us, and prepared us for all. We must not yield to fear. All of the gods of this world will fall! They all will bow the knee to the Name above all Names! We must entreat God to help us and provide the aid we need from the Heavenly Host when the time comes." said Diego.

Amora stood up, "Please, everyone . . ." Her face flushed and you could tell she was nervous. "I... I'm Amora, who they have been talking about. My sisters are only 9 and 6, and they have already been through so much pain and suffering. They will have no choice but to do what the bad people tell them and become what Satan makes them. It will be dangerous, but please, anyone who is willing, please help." After speaking her mind, she quickly sat down next to Gianna, who kissed her cheek and hugged her close.

The group began to pepper Diego with questions about bunkers and government and then monsters and fallen angels. A man from England raised his hand and addressed the whole group, "Who here has special abilities, and what are they? I think it would be helpful to know and strategically place them where they can be the most utilized for offense and defense." Of the about seventy present, Darrel estimated around 25 raised their hands.

"That's a great idea." Diego looked at Mae, "Mae, is there a white board that we can use for recording names and powers?" She nodded, but Jacque popped up, "I'll get it, Ms. Mae." He sprinted to the back of the cafe, where there was a huge storage closet with extra chairs, cleaning supplies, and a large white board on wheels that he had out in front of the team in minutes.

Diego nodded, "Thank you, Jacque. Okay, please raise your hands again, state your name and special power." He looked over at Charlotte, who was close by, "Ms. Charlotte, would you please record for us?" She nodded, picked up a dry-erase marker, and began to organize the board with categories.

NAME	ABILITY	TEAM
Diego	Seer/Various	USA
Darrell	Fire/Flight	USA
Billy Jean	Shape Shifting	USA
Gianna	Power/Speed/MA	USA
Lucy	Force Field/Flight	USA
Alvin	Matter Absorption	USA

Jacque	Influence	USA
Li	Night Vision/Super Jump Climb	USA
Drake	Portal Creation	USA
Amora	Seer/Knowledge	USA

After some time, the list contained 20 more names, with a handful of those with special abilities from each of the continental groups represented. The abilities ranged from a man from Africa named Bakari, who could breathe underwater. A girl from South America named Luna who could create EMPs. Sophia from Europe, who could read minds, and Bao from Asia, who could manipulate the weather. As they were finishing off the list, an unexpected hand went up. David, Gianna's husband with a look of embarrassment. Gianna's eyes were wide with shock, "David, why didn't you tell me?" He stood up and looked at her apologetically.

Diego addressed him, "David, it seems there's something you've been keeping from us?"

David ran his hand through his hair, again looking a bit embarrassed, "Well, it's been a really recent development, you see. I, uh…had this amazing experience with God at your house…and I haven't even tested it to see if it's a for real thing. And well, when was a good time to bring it up, ya' know?"

"David, quit beating around the bush and spit it out," Gianna said with a hard edge of frustration.

"Okay, Gi...well, it seems that the Lord told me that I can grow as big as any giant that attacks us. He also told me that we'll be needing that for whatever is coming."

Murmurs of surprise and concern peppered the room. Darrel spoke up, "So, how does that work exactly? Can you only use it when attacked?" Billie Jean elbowed him, "What, babe?"

Billie Jean said something inaudible. "Oh, okay. Hey, I'm Darrel, by the way."

David scratched his beard, "Hey, nice to meet you. In answer to your question, I have no idea if there's an on/off switch. I assume when the time comes, and I'm needed, I'll know what to do. . . at least I hope that I will."

Charlotte wrote David's name and information down on the very full board. Diego addressed the group. "Let's thank the Lord for adding to our arsenal, I'm sure it will be necessary for what's coming. Now, I want to give anyone an opportunity to opt out of this mission before we begin to plan. If this is not something you want to join us for, please feel free to leave now. We will understand and not judge." He stopped talking and waited. No one moved.

"Okay. Let's begin our planning session."

***

It was three hours later, and more food and much coffee had been passed around as the group came up with a possibly good plan that everyone agreed to. The powers list on the white board had been erased to be replaced with the plan and the divisions of two separate teams. Drake, of course, was an important player, as his portals

179

will be how the teams get to and away from Sedona. One team was going inside the base to extract Amora's sisters, while the other team would be sent outside the base in order to provide a distraction. They would be tasked with engaging most of the enemy forces, while the inside team would work on the rescue and getting everyone out alive.

The inside team consisted of Amora, Alvin, Jacque, Li (Cat), Gianna, and six others from the other teams from Africa; Yuusuf (Illusion construction) and Omari (Night vision/stealth) from South America; Jose (Phasing through matter) and Luna (EMP), from Europe; Oscar (strength/speed) and from Asia; Viti (Strength/speed).

Once inside the base, the team hoped to be able to knock out its electrical systems with Luna's EMPs and then make their way by stealth to where the girls were being held. Since Amora knew the layout of the base, they hoped it would not take too long to find and free them. They knew there were many possibilities that they couldn't account for, including the fallen angel that was darkness incarnate. They talked about the fact that this entity was powerful enough to kill them all before they got past the first access door. Another possibility was that the beast was using the sisters as bait to trap or kill them all and that this was the most likely scenario. If that were the case, they would have to hope and pray for divine intervention to help them survive and complete the rescue.

Chapter Twenty-Three

Sedona, Arizona

The palms of Adora's hands were slick with sweat and her heart thrashed wildly. Way too fast. She knew that the stink of fear was wafting off her like a rabbit cornered by hungry wolves. All her techniques for masking it had failed. She had been called to appear before Azazel again and she knew that if he could read her mind, he would know she had had contact with his enemy and that she had been contemplating swearing allegiance to the Creator God in order to live.

Instead of the military soldiers who had been her escort wherever she went in the base, she was now following one of the Buddhist monks, who she now knew were cloaked vicious satyrs. She shivered a bit as she remembered seeing their true forms a few days prior. While pushing the thoughts quickly away as to what her daughters may have endured at the hands of the creatures.

She had already followed the monk, who hadn't said anything since he was first sent to fetch her, through three guarded doors and was now in a wing that was mainly military offices. The names on the outside door frames read Colonel Hanson, Major McDonald, Captain Thomas, and many more. She wondered if Azazel had given himself a human name in order to hide his true nature from some of the underlings in the base or if they all knew exactly what the entity that was running this place was.

Eventually, they stopped outside of an office with the name plate General Hurai. The monk knocked lightly and then entered. Adora wiped her palms on her dress, threw back her shoulders, raised her chin and followed him. The office was immense, with high ceilings, sleek black leather couches with marble side tables, plush white carpet and what appeared to be a jet-black onyx desk with leather chairs in front of it that matched the couches. The general, who was Azazel, looked up from stacks of books and parchments as they walked in.

"Welcome, Adora. Have a seat please." He continued to read a parchment in his hand as she obediently sat in a leather chair in front of him. The monk stood to the side of the desk; hands clasped behind his back. He commenced to stare at the wall behind her or at nothing. His eyes seemed glazed over and dead, making her wonder if the body was just some sort of drone piloted by a dark spirit waiting for commands. Adora assumed she would never find out the answer and switched her focus on the godman in front of her. He had definitely created himself a large and intimidating physique. Even seated, he towered more than a foot above her, and his thickness engulfed the desk. Conversely, there was an attractiveness about him as well, the kind that comes with great power and authority.

He finally looked up and stared at her for a moment before speaking, and in that instant, she felt him probe her thoughts. His human, dark brown eyes changed briefly to reveal the inhuman entity within, and her stomach immediately clenched with terror. He smiled and sat back, seemingly satisfied with her response to him.

The wordless exchange lasted mere moments, but in it, she understood volumes.

Azazel touched his fingertips together, forming an A with his hands and began to tap them as he spoke, "I believe our plan has worked, and your daughter and her . . . *companions* are coming to rescue her sisters." Adora said nothing and didn't think he was looking for a response since he continued with a confident smirk, "Soon, we'll have your eldest daughter and destroy the Enemy's chosen ones all in one day. It's a wonder Lucifer let such an easy win go because he's too lazy to work a little himself." He grinned widely now, "I'm very pleased that Ninazu brought you to me. He will be richly rewarded."

He leaned back and placed his hands on the leather arm rests, looking intently at her again, "Now, about our agreement. I could just kill you and still have everything I need and want, which is your daughters and your demons." Suddenly, the voices in her head began to scream in protest. She closed her eyes briefly, closing off the areas of herself that kept the demons restrained when needed. The rising terror in her belly flushed her chest and face with blotches of pink. She still stayed silent.

He showed no sign that he sensed her inner turmoil, "But I am a man of my word. That you may know that serving me will be more to your benefit than to Lucifer or anyone else . . ." He paused after that phrase for emphasis. He did know then and yet hadn't killed her for it. . . yet. "Once your daughter is in my possession, I will grant you safety in my employ and provision for a good life, wherever you choose to settle, until I need your services again, of course."

She bowed her head, "Thank you, Lord. You are very gracious."

"I'm glad we were able to come to an understanding. Now, I wish you to prepare for your daughter's impending arrival. She will have to be. . . re-educated. Especially since she has been with the Enemy's people for such a long time. To prove your loyalty, Adora, I want you to be the first to inflict punishment for her treachery. You and the duad will inflict the first rounds of her initiation back into the brotherhood."

Her stomach turned, but she nodded stoically.

"Does this trouble you, Adora?"

"No, not at all. Of course, I'll do what needs to be done."

"Good. You will be escorted to the programmers to prepare."

"Will I be able to see my other daughters, Anna and Alana?"

He smiled, and his eyes flashed red for a moment, "Of course, they and the duad are with the programmers. You'll see that they've been well taken care of."

Her stomach felt like ice inside her. She simply nodded and stood up. The monk came to life and escorted her out of the room. She didn't look back.

***

Hickory, North Carolina

The teams gathered in the fields beyond the residences. It was early morning. They all thought it best to go with as much daylight as possible, as a lot of the creatures and Satanic entities thrived and were empowered by darkness. They felt this may be true for the fallen angel as well. Diego suggested since he was locked in the bowels of the earth for thousands of years, that sunlight may have a negative effect on him. There were around thirty giant slayer warriors with various abilities divvied up amongst the two teams, as well as another forty trained soldiers and militia.

Darrel was suddenly nervous and worried. He was looking at the majority of the world's giant slayer forces all gathered together for this rescue. If they became overwhelmed and overpowered by the enemy's forces, it would wipe out most of the world's defenses. It would be a perfect way for Satan to gain the upper hand and take over all the earth with little resistance.

Diego gathered them close and prayed, "Father in heaven, we gather in your Son's holy name to ask for your divine protection, guidance, and victory. We ask, Oh God, that you would release your heavenly host to go before us to make war against the enemy forces who would seek to inflict terror, violence, murder, and darkness against us, the innocent ones, and the entire earth. Make us shrewd and stealthy like serpents and vicious and strong like lions. Grant us victory in the rescue of the innocent children and the destruction of the plans and programs of the wicked. We thank you for hearing us and answering, Yahuah Tseva'ot, Almighty Lord of Hosts! Amen."

With that, Amora and Drake stepped forward. Drake, who was six foot tall, knelt down and bent his head for the little girl to put her hands on. She pictured one of the outside entrances to the deep underground base which was a large doorway wedged in a cavern just outside of the city of Sedona. Then she pictured a storage room on the inside of the base that she felt was safest to open a portal for their team. It was on the topmost level of non-military government offices, directly into a large warehouse that contained thousands of shelves of food and drug supplies for the base that would probably last hundreds of years. As she pictured these areas, Drake received those pictures as if he himself were seeing them. After a few moments, he nodded and stood up. Diego asked the teams to split into two, the smaller inside team waiting while the outside team prepared to go first.

Gianna pulled David to the side before she joined Amora and the others, "David, I know things are still strained between us," She looked into his eyes, hers filled with fear and feeling. "I just want you to know that I do still love you. I... never stopped, but the hurt..."

David interrupted and didn't care if she protested as he pulled her close. She didn't resist. "Gigi, you don't have to explain anything. I messed up, and I may never get a do-over for that, but I want you to know that I never ever stopped loving you and I love you more now than I ever could before... and if we live through this, I hope to be able to show you." A tear fell slowly down her cheek, and he wiped it gently away with his thumb as he cupped her face in his hand, "Can I kiss you?"

She nodded lightly and he pulled her closer and leaned in brushing her lips lightly with his. She moved up on her toes planting her lips fully on his and cupped her hands to his bearded face. Their lips and breath expressed months of feelings in a few urgent moments. She finally pulled back and said, "Come back to me, David Shepherd."

"I wouldn't dream of disobeying such an order." He smiled.

Squeezing his hand one more time, she walked away to join her group. David watched her, and a seed of hope burst like a new bloom in his heart, and he prayed a quick prayer that he wouldn't die.

The teams split up according to the plan; the ones going inside the base joined Amora to one side, and the larger team stood ready to move forward. Drake closed his eyes and began to move his hands in a circular pattern. A large portal opened and gradually, they could see a vast landscape of red-orange rock formations and spatterings of red earth and green vegetation. Darrel, Billie Jean, Diego, and Lucy led the forty-plus member group of soldiers slowly through the portal into the beautiful, rugged Arizona landscape. The outside team was to go in first and make a bit of an obvious show of force. They were to draw out the worst of the bases' defensive forces and hopefully let them think the whole attack was coming from the outside. When it seemed they were fully engaged, the inside team would go in and immediately, Luna from the South America team would disable the base with an EMP.

As Darrel stepped through, the beauty of the morning landscape struck him. *It would be a shame to die on such a beautiful day,* he found himself thinking. He immediately felt guilty for the thought, as if it showed his lack of faith in God and the team, but it was hard not to contemplate the reality that they were about to come up against the worst that hell and the government could produce. This time there was no visible evidence of angelic warrior assistance. Billie Jean squeezed his hand and kissed his cheek, "I love you." she whispered. Before he could respond, she transformed into her white gryphon and blasted into the sky. The resulting wind sprayed a smattering of dirt and rock toward him and the others.

He furrowed his brows, left his doubtful thoughts behind and set his mind on the task at hand. His eyes became orange flame that spread from his head to the rest of his body, until he looked like a human torch that was not consumed. He looked at the rest of the warriors, "Alright, Slayers! Listen up, we have one objective, draw them out and fight! Spread out and let them know we're here!" At that, he took off after Billie Jean into the sky.

The ground troops spread out. Some went to the large, armored door of the base and began to hook up C4 explosives on multiple parts of the door. Others picked large rock formations for cover when the enemy monsters and soldiers emerged. David had decided to stick close to Lucy and Diego since his combat experience left him a little wary of engagement. Diego and Lucy had moved by a rock formation in plain view of the door. His staff in hand, he and Lucy had decided to join powers and try to magnify her force field around the group. They had never tried it before but had discussed it as a possibility. She had been able to hold a force field around their team before, for short time frames, but found that she tired very quickly and it weakened the strength of the shield and after about 20-30 minutes, it was gone altogether. This also left her too weak to fight and protect herself afterward for another 15-20 minutes. She felt that it wasn't worth the exertion in the long run.

David watched as they talked through the plan, the young girl who had done so many brave acts in the last few days that he'd known her and the kind and wise grandpa who also stood against an evil entity with such impressive power and strength. These people amazed David. He was in awe that his wife was among their rank. He hoped when the time came for him to act, that he would, in kind, show as much courage as they did. He prepared himself for a battle that he couldn't wrap his mind around with powers that he'd never used. When he thought about it too much, it definitely sounded insane. What if he imagined everything that happened at Diego's? What if it wasn't real, and he didn't have powers? Was he a lunatic about to commit suicide?

The ground began to rumble. The sky started to glitch like an old VHS tape, and a strange frequency made David's ears ring to the point that he felt it in his toes. He looked at Diego and Lucy, "Do y'all hear and feel that?"

Lucy and Diego nodded; their faces solemn.

"They're coming," Diego said.

Chapter Twenty-Four

Sedona, Arizona

Adora passed through five guarded doors in which the guard had to scan his wrist on an electronic panel in order for the door to open. Apparently, the monk had above top-secret clearance. After the fifth door, she was escorted to large double doors that opened up to a lab. It had white walls and metal tables, a few men and women standing around in lab coats, and smelled of bleach. They were approached by the female, raven haired doctor who was at the meeting a couple of days ago. "Ah, Mrs. von Braun, I was told you wanted to see your daughters."

Adora nodded, her face a mask of cold indifference.

"Please, follow me." She said.

Adora followed behind the woman and the monk stayed by the entrance doors. She was glad of that; the creature had her always on edge. She felt her shoulders relax a bit as she left its presence. The woman took her through two more doors, passing through one lab with caged animals. Her brief glance was enough to understand that many of the animals in those cages were genetically engineered, unnatural hybrids, and smelled evil, almost as strongly as Azazel had the first time she encountered him. In her seemingly brief 38 years, Adora had seen demonic entities, alien beings, genetically modified super-soldiers, and more, but what they were doing here seemed way beyond even what she had seen in the past. She shivered and breathed a silent sigh of relief after leaving that room. Finally, they entered what seemed to be a recovery room with hospital beds lining the back wall and curtains around most of them.

The woman led her to one of the first beds and pulled the curtain back. Alanna caught her breath as little Alanna laid on her back hooked up to monitors, and IV drip, with bandages around her head. Adora walked over to the bed, Alanna looked small and frail, and for the first time, Adora really saw her daughter. Anger welled up and she snapped at the doctor, "What the hell did you do to her?"

The woman didn't react to Adora's tone but stated matter-of-factly, "She's had a brain implant. It won't hurt her. In fact, she'll be able to process at 50 times organic genius levels. If she passes all the training and testing, she will eventually be a part of the elite world leadership."

"Completely controlled by your employers, no doubt. What is your name, anyway, *doctor*. I don't believe we were properly introduced." Adora stated.

"Doctor Shelley," she smiled, "I assure you, Mrs. von Braun, your daughters are very valuable to many important people..."

Adora stared at the doctor icily, "Yes, I know. What about my other daughter, Anna? May I see her?"

Dr. Shelley nodded, "Of course. Follow me."

After passing through a couple more rooms, they ended up in a small room that was locked from the outside. Inside was a small bed and chair. Anna was sitting on the bed, staring at the blank wall. The room had

191

barely adequate lighting and of course, no windows since it was so far underground.

"Has she been drugged?" Adora asked Doctor Shelley without looking at her.

"Just a mild sedative to calm her."

Adora grimaced and spoke to her daughter, "Anna, it's mother." The girl made no response.

Adora approached her, sat in the chair, and looked her daughter in the eyes, which were glazed and unfocused, "Anna, can you hear me?"

Anna's eyes began to focus, and she looked into her mother's face. When she finally registered who she was seeing, she suddenly looked alarmed, "I'm sorry, mother! I didn't know!" She shrank from Adora.

"It's okay, you're not in trouble." Adora took Anna's hand gently, but the girl pulled it away as if burned. "I'm sorry, mother!" she said again.

Adora began to panic. She had so much she wanted to say to her daughter but couldn't because the girl had no connection to her besides fear. She stood up and took a step away from the young girl, "Anna, please, listen. I'm not going to hurt you. Look, I'm backing away."

Her daughter seemed to calm slightly as she backed away.

"Very interesting relationship you seem to have with your daughter, Mrs. von Braun." Doctor Shelley commented from the doorway.

Adora ignored her, "Anna, are you okay?" the girl nodded slightly in answer.

Adora turned to the doctor, "Can I please have a few moments alone with my daughter?"

"Of course, I'll be right outside. Just let me know when you are ready to leave by knocking on the door." She left and Adora heard the door latch behind her.

"Anna, have you heard from Amora?"

Anna pursed her lips and shook her head.

"It's okay if you have. You can tell me."

Anna was silent for a moment, then whispered, "I only hear from her when I sleep, and I haven't been sleeping much."

Adora searched the girl's face. It was pale and dark shadows sat under her eyes. Of course, this was not unusual for Anna, but Adora had never before wasted a second thought for the child's well-being. Something was different today and the last few days. Adora was seeing her daughters, not as she had once done, as objects and afterthoughts, but truly seeing them as people. Adora blinked and took a breath. *Something's happening to me*, she thought; *something's wrong.* She took a couple steps back from Anna and crossed her arms, *I must get out of here, and I have to get my daughters out. What do I do?*

***

Back on the surface, Darrel and Billie Jean hovered above the highest rock formations. Dark creatures and army soldiers were pouring out of holes in the ground and caves in the nearby hills. The ground began to shake right below them as a large pit opened up and Nephilim giants of all shapes and sizes began to climb out of it. He and Billie Jean dove in different directions. Darrel towards some of the soldiers and creatures, blasting them with flames, some screaming and burning and others just changing direction with no visible damage; Billie Jean towards the Nephilim coming from the pit. She screamed her strange eagle-lion sound that sent the enemy fleeing seven ways with their hands covering their ears.

Lucy and Diego stood with hands clasped behind the stone formation, concentrating on a power shield to cover the team from pulse and fire attacks that were beginning to come from the surrounding creatures; it would also protect them from bullets as well. David looked at Diego, "When should I transform? Now?"

As Diego felt the glorious power from heaven enter him through the staff and pass into Lucy, his eyes briefly glowed, and all time seemed to stand still. He heard David's question in real-time, but the brain process from the thought to his mouth seemed all at once trapped in time and above time. He couldn't process if the simple answer, yes, would come out of his mouth now or at the end of time and space, so he simply nodded, hoping David would eventually either see it or decide that now was the perfect time to begin to fight.

To David, the nod was instant, and he shivered a bit as he saw Diego's eyes glowing. "Okay." He said quietly to himself, trying to calm his doubts because he wasn't sure what would actually happen when he transformed. He shrugged. Either way, now was the time to act. He closed his eyes, said a quick prayer, and stepped forward. David instantly began to enlarge, and within seconds he had grown to over twelve feet tall. He looked down and to his chagrin, he had outgrown his clothes and was in nothing but his skin. He flexed his stronger, larger arms and decided that now wasn't the time to worry about modesty, "Let's see how this giant body fights!" He said and ran forward to face the first of many giant foes of different sizes and shapes coming his direction.

***

Minutes after the outside team stepped through the portal, the inside team prepared to walk through the doorway that Drake had created into the underground military bases' storeroom. Gianna, dressed in her battle gear, stood with the other soldiers and Amora. Gianna's thoughts raced to Dylan, and she prayed that he wouldn't lose his parents today. She had left him with Charlotte and her boys, whom he'd grown very close to in the last couple of days. She was glad he was too caught up with his new play buddies to be very concerned that both his parents were going away to a battle. Charlotte was thankful for him as well, as her boys seemed wonderfully distracted by their new friend.

Amora seemed calm, her pale blue eyes strong and determined. Again, Gianna was struck by her courage and maturity. She planned to stick as close to the girl as possible, not letting Amora out of her sight no matter what. Alvin, Jacque, and Cat, who were dressed in black from head to toe as well as body armor, checked their sidearms, their MK18 rifles, as well as various knives, flash grenades and other items that Gianna had never seen before. The other team members, military and otherwise, were doing the same. Finally, Drake nodded to them as he got the portal stabilized. Alvin took the lead position with his rifle ready. They all waited as he and Jacque stepped through and assessed the area. Gianna and the others could observe the other room as if it were just a window to the outside rather than a wormhole to a destination over a thousand miles away.

Alvin looked back, nodded, and waved them forward. Gianna, Amora, and the others quietly stepped through the portal. As the last one of them came through, Drake pointed at his ear, indicating for them to call him on comms when they were ready for him to bring them back. Alvin nodded and the portal disappeared. Even though there were 12 of them, there was ample space in the gigantic room. Bigger than any warehouse that Gianna had ever seen, the ceilings could have been twenty feet up with full shelves lining the walls that went as high. They had arrived in an area where several unused forklifts were parked alongside pallets of water bottles that had not been shelved yet.

Thankfully, there didn't seem to be any workers in the room. They had already agreed beforehand to only talk when necessary. Alvin gestured for Luna to engage her EMP, electromagnetic pulse ability. Once engaged, the whole power grid to the base should go down, at least for a time. There was a slight chance the base had EMP protection for their systems. Amora had no knowledge of any protocols for an EMP event, but they had deduced that since the base was so deep underground, they may have believed the depth alone was enough protection from a surface EMP attack. Luna had agreed to set it off and stay in the warehouse until they returned, since she had no fighting abilities. She would stay hidden and if no one returned and she felt in danger, she was to contact Drake and be pulled out.

Luna, a beautiful college-aged woman from Chile with sleek jet-black hair, had said little since Gianna had first met her. Jose said that her English wasn't great and though she could understand very well, she was embarrassed to practice speaking. She mainly nodded or shook her head when addressed. She knelt on the floor and looked at everyone. Alvin signaled and Jacque took a lined duffel bag out of his pack. Everyone deposited phones, night vision goggles, and comms into the bag and he sealed it, to protect their electronics from the pulse. Luna then put her hand on the ground and closed her eyes. After a moment, she opened her eyes, nodded, and stood up. An electromagnetic pulse is almost imperceptible to human senses and only affects unprotected electronics and systems.

Alvin signaled for the rest of them to move towards an exit. He looked at Amora and signaled her to walk next to him and the others to follow as they made their way towards a door. A few minutes of walking led them to a set of double exit doors that may be immovable because of electronics. First, they tried the doors, and it turned out that they opened from the inside pretty easily. Before they walked through, though, Jose moved forward and phased through the doors to check on outside activity. He was back quickly, "No activity on this level, but no lights either." He whispered.

They all retrieved their equipment from the duffel bag and those who couldn't see in the dark quickly donned night vision goggles. Those without, like Amora and Gianna, followed closely behind the others. The hallway was eerily quiet. Amora had directed them from this level because it had the least amount of security and activity, but it was also a higher level, and her sisters were being held in one of the lowest levels. Unfortunately, without elevators, they would have to take the stairs, many many floors of them. The stairwell was straight ahead, and they found it quickly.

***

Adora had just made it back to her room when she heard the alerts sounding in the hallways. Her heart began to pound, and then the phone rang. She jumped for a second and then caught her breath before she answered.

"Yes?"

"They are here, witch." Ninazu's voice, as usual, was oily and dark, making her stomach turn, "Lord Azazel wants you to report to the training center on the same floor as the labs. No one is available to escort you right now, I trust you remember the way?"

She cleared her throat, "Why, yes, of course. I'll come right away." The phone went dead. Adora's thoughts raced. What was about to happen and the side that she would choose were still unknown to her. Only one thing she knew with certainty: she would do whatever it took to survive.

She exited and made her way to the closest elevators, quickly pressing the down button until it lit in response. Adora was thankful for many reasons that she had no escort. The first was to know if she had remembered where the labs were on her own. She had been paying particular attention to every path she was taken on to get anywhere since day one and felt certain that she could get to where the girls were being held and back to the upper levels on her own. She also felt she could make her way back to the surface if necessary.

After many minutes of silence as she descended to the lowest levels, the lift stopped, and the doors opened. The training area for the children, soldiers, and other experiments was past the main labs at the end of the hallway. There were no alarms going off on this level. Adora assumed they were disabled because they would probably interfere with the programming. She entered the doors and surprisingly, the woman Lilith that they had met when they first arrived greeted her with crossed arms and a look of disdain. "Follow me," she stated coldly as she strode forward towards an ample meeting room equipped with a wall full of screens and a large black table that contained internal controls for what seemed like every screen on the wall as well as anything in the whole complex.

Half a dozen men in lab coats along with Doctor Shelley, Ninazu still in the form of a secret service agent and of course, Azazel as the general, were all seated around the black table. Lilith sat at the table and Adora followed and sat as well. No one from the table had looked up when they entered. Their eyes were locked on the wall screens that showed the outside surface. There wasn't anything that Adora could see happening except a couple of dark figures hiding behind some stones.

"Release the first wave of super soldiers, then wait a few minutes and release the Nephilim warriors," said Azazel.

The black table's controls were above the table, like a hologram of screens, switches, and dials. The scientists spoke the commands, some things changed on the light screens and as she looked on the wall of televisions, suddenly there were swarms of soldiers pouring out of crevices and doorways that she couldn't see. Minutes later, the men spoke other commands and one of the screens showed the ground opening up and giant humanoid creatures climbing out of it. She was mesmerized by the sight. She had heard the great ones were back but hadn't seen them with her own eyes. The scientists enlarged the screens of four different angles of the outside fighting, so they had a better view.

Adora could finally see a few of the invading soldiers' guns firing and explosive weapons deploying at different points on the TVs. Suddenly there was a great flying lion and a man of fire fighting the giants and Adora's mouth dropped, "They have super soldiers and mythical beasts fighting for them?" She questioned in astonishment.

"Ah, yes, this is what I was waiting for. He has equipped his followers with special abilities to fight us. I must see all their warriors' power." Azazel looked at her and smiled confidently, "They'll be overwhelmed with our power before we've even spent a small percentage of our soldiers."

They were all focused on the screens, where Azazel and some of the scientists would point to one of the enemy fighters and call out an ability they had seen. Azazel pointed to two figures who were holding hands, "These are sharing power." He watched a little longer, "They have some sort of shielding. Send some warriors in their direction. If they disconnect, they may lose that power."

It's true Adora had not seen one of the enemy soldiers fall, though there were already quite a few casualties on this side, which didn't faze anyone. Suddenly, a figure ran out from a nearby rock formation and grew to giant proportions before their eyes. Everyone remarked on that with interest. They immediately ordered Nephilim warriors to attack the giant individual. As they came at him, he seemed to easily block their blows and throw one then the other with ease, and when a bigger nephil warrior came at him, astonishingly, he grew again to outsize it. One of the scientists looked up suddenly as three separate wall screens turned red and began to pulse.

He looked at Azazel, "Sir, there's been a breach in one of the upper floors."

Azazel leaned back and smiled, "Ah, she's here."

Adora frowned. The demons screamed in her head in fear. She rubbed her temples and swallowed. She felt their fear in every nerve in her body and just realized that she hadn't heard or felt them for days until now. Why were they fearful?

"Mrs. von Braun?"

She looked up, startled that she hadn't heard someone address her, "Yes?"

Azazel eyed her through his dark glasses, and she shivered.

"Are you unwell?"

She shook her head slightly, "Just a bit of a headache, I'm fine."

He nodded, "We'll have her soon."

She didn't answer.

The head scientist asked him, "Do you want us to send soldiers to retrieve them?"

As he was about to give his answer, a static buzz went through the room. Every screen paused, glitched and then the room went black.

Chapter Twenty-Five

Sedona, Arizona

David had never felt this powerful in his life. He knew the element of surprise was about to wear out as he lifted the sixth giant off the ground with ease and slammed its back down hard upon his knee in what must have been the best backbreaker move anyone would have ever seen. His years of childhood wrestling fandom were finally paying off as a pile of monstrous bodies were left writhing on the ground behind him. He continued to plow forward into the line of Nephilim warriors ahead, laying one then the other down with no feelings of weariness or overexertion slowing him down.

Soon, he had laid out two more, and as he was about to take down another, two more jumped on him from behind. They slammed him hard into the ground, his face and teeth ground into the dirt as he struggled to breath. His mouth filled with dirt and blood and tried in vain to spit it out. For the first time since he transformed into a giant, he began to fear. One giant bent his arm back while the other bit painfully into his left leg. David screamed, but it was exactly what he needed to push through the fear and explode upward, punching and kicking with new adrenalin-induced energy.

As David punched the one who had his arm in the ugly face, he became overwhelmed with the stench of sulfur, so strong that he became light-headed and nauseous. The one who bit him in the leg got a kick in the face right before another green two-headed ghoulish horror jumped onto his back. David again thought he was done for and began to panic and pray at the same time. Suddenly, a stream of fire engulfed the heads of the giant on his back. Their dual roar almost burst David's eardrums but did temporarily dislodge the monster so he could roll out of the way of a few more of them coming at him. Darrel had come in and overwhelmed a few Nephilim with fire while six warriors from their team began to slice the heads of the fallen monsters with what looked like samurai swords.

Darrel hovered briefly near David's head as he leaned against a hill to catch his breath. "I've assigned these guys to you, man. Sorry, should have done it in the beginning. I just wasn't sure what you were capable of."

David raised his eyebrows, "Neither was I."

"Just FYI, the only way to really take out a giant is to decapitate it. What you were doing was just making them mad."

David shook his head, "That would have been great info to have before I got started."

Darrel shrugged sheepishly and continued, "These guys from Japan are amazing with the samurai skills, and they volunteered to be your guard. So, keep knocking these evil bastards to the ground, and they'll take care of the rest."

David looked down at the black-clad, masked team at his feet and bowed to them. They bowed back and then crouched in anticipation of what was coming. "Got it." David nodded and ran forward as another dozen or more various-sized giants headed his way.

***

Inside the base, Alvin's team carefully climbed down their thirtieth flight of stairs in the dark. They had yet to run into anyone else coming up or down the stairs from inside the base, which was a little concerning for Alvin. The consensus among them was that they were running right into a trap like mice. Since there were no other options to get to the girls at this point, they kept going, praying that God would make a way for them. There was little chatter as the team wound down flight after flight, except every few floors, Alvin would call out the number for those who did not have night vision goggles.

"46" was the most recent number he called out as he estimated they had been walking down stairs for at least thirty-five minutes straight. Amora said floors 62 through 68 were the labs, training, and programming facilities of the base, so they were going to begin on 62 and work their way through until they found her sisters. They continued.

"55," he said as his mind continued to wander to the fact that he had been a career military soldier just months ago, and here he was now, breaking into an above-top-secret government facility. He was ashamed of giving half of his life, sweat and blood to a false organization acting as a freedom-defending government for and by the people. Knowing now how closely this government colluded with tyrants, mafias, and criminal organizations for power and money, trading innocent lives like commodities and becoming an arm of Satan himself was more than he could stomach. He hoped that what he had been doing with the Slayers and ultimately for God himself these last few months had and was making a difference in the world for the help and redemption of many people.

The Waking Part II: Withstand in The Evil Day

The team finally arrived at level 62 with sweat-soaked armpits and backs and achy legs. They stopped on the platform for a breather and allowed Jose to phase through the door to check for safety before any of them walked out. He came back a couple minutes later with a thumbs-up. Again, Alvin wondered what they were walking into. One by one, they eased out of the stairwell, Alvin then Jose, Gianna then, Amora, Jacque then the others behind. All of them stayed close to the walls of a wide hallway leading to some double doors. They had only walked a few steps when Amora pulled Gianna's hand. Gianna turned and Amora whispered in her ear, "No one is on this level. We need to go to the next one." Gianna nodded and tapped Jacque. He stopped and Gianna shook her head and pointed back to the stairway. He nodded and grabbed Alvin. They quickly signaled to the others to go back.

When they got back to the stairwell, Alvin questioned Gianna in a low whisper, "How does she know there was nothing back there?"

Amora responded, "I can feel what's there or not."

Alvin nodded and they all continued down to floor 63. Again, Jose phased into the next room, and they waited. When he came back through, he again gave them the thumbs up. Alvin moved Amora up behind him. He then went through the door in a crouch, his gun out as he slowly scanned the room, which was very similar to the one above. It was dark and quiet, and the only thing he could hear was his own heart beating in his ears. He had a feeling Amora would "feel" plenty on this floor. He signaled for her to come out. She inched out, and then her small hand touched his arm. She paused for a moment, then nodded her head to him. He nodded back, then signaled for the rest of them to come through one by one.

Jacque, Gianna, and Jose came through the door. Alvin had a sudden thought, and when Cat came through, he whispered to her, "I need you to engage comms from this point on. You take the other half of the team and go to the next level, clear that one and the next unless you hear from me to back us up." Cat nodded and went back.

Alvin turned to the others with him and pointed at his ear. They all turned on comms. A small two-way communication device that fits inside the ear and could be used on a localized hidden channel. From now on, any whisper would be heard by the whole team. Alvin moved forward, and the others followed. Gianna whispered, "Why did you send the others back?"

As an A-team commander, Alvin wasn't used to being questioned, but he understood that this was not a military op, and he wasn't leading a full military team anymore. He answered, "If it's a trap, there's no use in all of us being captured together. If we're split up, it may give us a chance, at least, of not being completely wiped out."

Gianna was silent. They walked forward towards a set of doors. Alvin's breathing got shallower and more strained the closer they got to the doors, and he struggled to move his legs as they seemed to weigh a hundred pounds each. He gasped, "Are you feeling this?"

Jacque responded, "Like a thousand-pound weight is on my back and crushing my lungs? Yeah."

Gianna croaked a weak "Yes."

As they finally made it to the doors, Alvin called Jose. He came forward and stood at the doorway for what seemed like an hour, but checking his watch, Alvin was taken aback that only two minutes had passed. Jose finally looked back and shook his head, "I can't get through…it's like I have no power here."

"Okay, get behind us," Alvin said. Jose turned and shuffled back weakly.

"The dark ones are inside," whispered Amora. "That's why you feel weak and heavy. Your weapons won't work with them."

Even though it went against all his training, Alvin holstered his weapon. Jacque followed, and Gianna sheathed her swords. "Will our powers work?" Gianna asked.

"I think so, but really, it will be Jesus' light that will scare them the most," Amora answered.

Alvin tried the doors, which were unlocked and unmanned on the other side. It wasn't surprising, given the ease with which they were able to make it this far. He had no idea what they were coming up against in the next moments, and he suddenly had a premonition that coming out of this alive, let alone with the girls, was going to take a supernatural act of God to accomplish. His heart hammered in his chest, and he decided to enact his powers, which he rarely did. The walls were made of cement blocks and stone in some places. He decided that was better than fighting with flesh and bone at this point. He touched the wall and absorbed the cement, which then became part of him, making his exterior composed of the hard material.

Suddenly, a red pulsating light began to flicker on and off, and they felt and smelled a smoky mist filling the hallway. "Cover your nose!" Alvin barked. He pulled his neck gaiter over his nose and mouth but doubted it would be enough to block whatever poison may be pouring over them. It didn't seem to burn or itch his skin, so there was that, but he knew they were either about to pass out or worse. They continued forward, and each time the red light pulsed, he caught a shadowed glimpse of the room they were in, which was an outer area that led into what seemed to be glassed-off laboratories filled with cages. The red light reflected on the surrounding mist, creating ghostly movement that unnerved him. He wiped his eyes to get the moisture out and checked that the others were still behind him.

The sound of knives being dragged across the rock walls reverberated through the room, and they stopped. Fear sliced through his stomach like a blade. He looked at Jacque, "Spread out. I think something is coming." Jacque nodded. He and Jose split to the right, while Gianna and Amora stayed next to Alvin.

Cat's voice came over comms, "Sir, do you need backup? We haven't found anything on floor 64. We can backtrack and get back to you in ten minutes."

"No, not yet," He answered. "Standby. I'll let you know if we need backup shortly."

"Yes, sir." She replied.

Gianna blinked, then squeezed her eyes shut for a second before opening them again, "The walls are moving," she said. She knew the substance they had inhaled was having an effect on her, and she willed her eyes to see clearly, but to no avail. Every time the red light pulsed, the walls undulated back and forth as if made of liquid and in some instances, they swirled with black vortexes. The scraping sound was getting closer, and she set her mind to attack whatever came down that hallway. She pushed fear away and grasped onto anger, knowing that those innocent girls were here somewhere being held captive, and only God knew what else had been done to them. She was determined to not leave without them. She squeezed Amora's hand reassuringly, wishing somehow that she could protect the girl from what was about to happen.

Amora sensed the great blanket of evil as soon as they set foot on the level. She had never felt so much darkness all at once, and it unnerved her. She had come in so sure of Jesus' presence that no fear had entered her mind. When she felt the stomach-turning atmosphere here, that instantly began to change. Her heart still clung to the memory of His presence and the hope that her sisters could soon be saved, but fear was quickly consuming her. She prayed.

Dark figures with yellow eyes crawled on the walls and ceilings. Demonic whispers echoed throughout the room, speaking words of fear in English, French, Latin, and Arabic. Alvin and Jacque understood some and so did Amora, who all spoke or were exposed to multiple languages. Gianna understood fear very well. The group continued to walk forward until the source of the scraping finally revealed itself. A seven-foot-tall black figure stood before them, with unnatural long legs and arms and an enormous crown with snake-like appendages protruding from it in all directions. As the light pulsed, they caught a full picture of the ghostly pale female demonic being. The scraping sounds were the razor-sharp nails protruding from the tips of her six lengthy fingers. She remained still for four full red-light pulses, and in that time, two more figures appeared behind her, literally out of nowhere. First, she was alone, and one pulse later, they were there. Only slightly shorter than her, but menacing and thick satyrs that smelled as dangerous as they looked.

"Give us the girl, and we'll let you live." The female said.

***

Lucy's body ached and sweat-drenched her clothes and dripped from her face in huge droplets, watering the ground around her feet. She and Diego had been linked and holding a protective shield over the team for close to an hour now. She knew she would give out soon and worried that it just wasn't long enough to carry them long enough in this battle. Lucy looked at Diego, who held his staff in one hand and had his other rested gently on her back. He was calm and unstrained, keeping his eyes fastened on the skirmishes going on around them. All enemy attacks aimed specifically at herself and Diego, and there had been quite a few, had been thwarted by David in the first few minutes. After that, a handful of others stood stationed around them at different intervals.

Some of these soldiers Lucy knew and had helped train, like Henry and Matt from the European team, who had powers of strength and invulnerability. They were guarding her and Diego along with a few of their trained militia, and some soldiers from Africa had joined them. They were taking some sniper fire from the upper left side, but the bullets could not penetrate the shield. The gunfire would stop in intervals, where more monsters would be sent in to take them down. When their warriors sliced through the monsters, the gunfire would start up again.

Lucy worried that once her shielding was down, many of them would be dropped by the hidden snipers in minutes. "Animo, Lucita! Don't fret. I'm praying for supernatural strength for you. I know He will provide what we need to overcome the enemy."

She simply nodded. Talking and thinking took too much energy. She closed her eyes and just inhaled and exhaled. With each exhale, she thought of Jesus' face. His kindness and love were palpable to her at times, and she hoped it would extend her energy.

"Look up, Lucy," Diego said.

She opened her eyes as the great gryphon Billie Jean landed in front of her, and an Indian teenager jumped off of her back. Then Billie Jean shot back up to the sky and right back into the fight. The bronze-skinned young girl headed towards Diego and Lucy, stopping just in front of them, "I am Miral from the Asian team," She smiled. Her long hair was tied back, but wisps of black had flown everywhere from her flight on the gryphon, "I can also create a shield. The gryphon brought me here to help you."

Lucy's mouth dropped open, "No way!"

Miral nodded.

"Get over here," said Lucy with relief.

Miral stepped over to the other side of Diego and put her hand on top of his staff hand.

He nodded as he felt Miral's shield engage over them. Lucy released her shield and sat down with her back against the rock formation. She asked Diego, "Are you sure it's working?"

As if in answer, bullets ricocheted around them, with a few hitting the top of the rock formation, sending dirt rock shards flying, but nothing hit any of their team.

"Sweet," she said as she took out her water bottle and drank it dry. Then she leaned back and watched four different areas of fighting going on around them that she hadn't seen earlier. About a football field away to her right, David, who was at least 12-14 feet tall, had piles of Nephilim to the left and right of him, all decapitated and was working on wrestling an eight-footer to the ground while a handful of samurais worked around him cutting heads off of the ones that had fallen earlier. Lucy gagged as she looked at the monstrous bloody heads, whose mouths and eyes still moved after being severed from the bodies.

She looked up to see Billie Jean and Darrel dipping down into different frays of skirmishes. A group of their own militia was fighting a few humanoid reptilian creatures that weren't affected by bullets. Darrel's fire caused them to scream, and Billie Jean swooped down, grabbing one or two at a time and pulling them apart with her beak and claws. Lucy shivered and gagged again as she saw Billie Jean eat some of the pieces before scattering them on the ground. She had no idea that BJ ate *things* when she transformed. Maybe it was the pregnancy. Lucy quickly turned and saw another team of about 7 or 8 of their team surrounded by hundreds of demon rodents, triple the size of city rats with glowing red eyes and horrible sharp teeth. The team stood back-to-back, facing outward and shooting automatic rifles, killing many of them, but more were scrambling forward. A few of the warriors had hand explosives and began to throw these into the piles of rats, exploding tons of them. The strategy would work as long as they didn't run out of ammo and explosives. This scene worried her a bit, and she began to think.

Lucy stood up, "Diego, how do we know if we're drawing out enough of their defenses? This is a lot, but it doesn't seem like the kind of forces that an army base would send out. Do you think they might just be testing our strength before they release the real defenses?"

Lucy raised her eyebrows and looked at Diego. He became thoughtful for a moment. "I've been watching everything since the beginning, hija, and have been wondering the same since the first few minutes of the battle. You are right. We need to make sure we are drawing all of it out to give the inside team the best chance. Please call Darrel over so we can discuss it."

She nodded, shielded herself and flew towards Darrel.

***

Jose phased through the side wall. The demonic satyrs advanced toward Alvin, Gianna and Amora. Gianna withdrew her swords, ready to strike the abominations down. Jacque ran over and stood in front of the team. The satyrs stopped inches from him, and Jacque whispered something that Gianna could not hear. The goat-men stared at him with their yellow-slitted eyes, shaking their heads in confusion.

"What are you doing? Kill him!" shouted the female creature.

They turned back to her, claws extended and ran towards her as if to attack, "Stop, you fools!"

They came at her, and there was a chaotic scramble. She knocked both of them easily to the ground, and when she did, they quickly arose in confusion.

"Enough, I'll do it!" She walked forward, and for the first time, they got a good look at her. Skin as pale as a corpse, blood-red lips and fiery eyes, with a serpentine neck and appendages. As she spread her black-horned

213

wings, she glared at Jacque and Alvin, "You killed my daughter; I will have my vengeance and feast on your flesh!"

Alvin sucked in his breath. She's the one that sent the creature to murder Jesse and Lincoln and probably more of them if they hadn't stopped it. Oh, he would see her die before he left this God-forsaken hole today. He advanced towards her with a cement-filled punch. Jacque stopped him, "Wait."

Alvin hung back but was eager to destroy this demonic woman. Jacque tried to influence her like he did the goat-men, but she lunged with speed that Alvin had never seen before. Her claws had pierced Jacque's sides before he even had a chance to scream, and she tore through him like he was made of paper. His blood splattered the whole hallway as he fell.

"NOOOOOOO!" Alvin screamed as he ran at her. She moved before he reached her, sending him smashing through the wall behind her. Gianna sprang forward with super speed, her swords slicing downward, Lilith caught the first slash with her wings, and they began to fight. Gianna's speed and sword skill were able to match Lilith's powerful blows, and they traded hits and parries for some time.

"Gianna!" Amora screamed behind her, and she turned to see that one of the satyrs was running down the darkened corridor with Amora in its arms and the other following close behind. Her heart froze in her chest, and she thought, *oh my God, I lost her.* An excruciating pain slammed into the back of her head, pitching her into blackness.

Chapter Twenty-Six

Sedona, Arizona

"Amora! Get up!"

Amora heard her name from somewhere far away. She was tired and didn't want to wake up.

"Amora!"

There it was again. A familiar voice that she couldn't quite place. She squeezed her eyelids, not ready to open them, but attempted to move. Dirt and gravel pressed into her face and skin like nails. She finally sat up and slowly opened her eyes while wiping dirt from her face. Luka stood in front of her, fighting blade in hand and next to him stood Starfire, a look of concern on her face. Luka reached down, and she grasped his hand as he pulled her to her feet.

Amora looked around as she got to her feet. She was on the combat training field. "Luka? . . . what's happening? Why are we all here?" she asked.

"What do you mean, Amora? You know we're training. Get ready. They're about to send out the next creature for us to fight."

Still confused, she nodded and stood ready, awaiting her psychic connection to Luka to engage. Moments later, she felt him, and to her surprise, she also connected to Starfire. Their minds and emotions were all one. She looked at Starfire questioningly.

"We are now a triad. *They* want us to work in bigger teams from now on." Starfire said flatly, her eyes focused on the doorway.

The training arena was empty except for the three of them. Amora looked at the outskirts, where there were normally spectators, usually government officials and handlers, as well as members of the brotherhood and, of course, the programmers. Today, there were only two programmers in view, and because of the lighting, she could not see their faces.

The electronic doors began to open, and she crouched, all her senses focused on feelings that could be coming through. She felt hindered and clouded, where normally, she could feel the anger, agitation, hate, or other emotions projecting from the person or creature that was sent to fight them. Now, she only felt her own confusion, Luka's determined strength, and Starfire's willful purpose. She was unnerved by feeling a third link and thought that may be why she was struggling to see or feel what was coming through.

The doors began to open, and she received a split-second picture of a horrible nightmare of a creature. The ground rumbled as the giant, two-headed, feathered serpent barreled into the arena. Sprays of gravel and dirt splayed in every direction as it moved like a slithering freight train around the perimeter of the fighting area, its bulk leaving deep creviced tracks wherever it crawled. The two heads constantly moved side to side. Its slitted yellow eyes missed no movement, and its perpetually darting tongue absorbed every scent in the room.

Amora looked intently at the creature; the chaos of its bloodlust projected louder than any other thought or feeling in her perimeter. She narrowed her eyes as she projected a psychic shield over her mind and body. She could now only feel her own, Luka's and Starfire's emotions. The serpent shot toward them, Luka sprinted to the opposite side of the arena from Amora, and Starfire stood her ground at Amora's side. The creature stopped in front of the girls, its front end rising four feet above them. One head had its yellow slits focused on them, while the other tracked Luka.

Amora attempted a psychic hold on the serpent in order to control it. It spread its colorful plumes and shook its body at her in response. Apparently, it was intelligent and not a base animal like common snakes and other animals that could be controlled psychically on some levels. At least to turn them away and keep oneself out of danger. This was not that kind of creature. She felt Starfire join her, and they both willed the creature to back down and run. It continued to shake its plumes, and then it began to move both heads from side to side in unison.

Submit.

Her mind felt as though a thousand pounds of pressure had just fallen on it. The serpent had somehow penetrated her mind shield and was now bending her will to yield to it. She looked over at Starfire and Luka. They both stood in place, with limp limbs hanging at their sides, blank eyes staring forward at nothing. She was alone.

Yessssss. Utterly alone. She heard its oily voice again in her head.

Amora knew she could not allow this dark one to take her mind. If she did, she may never escape again.

Closing her eyes, Amora pulled deeply from her will to project a secondary shield around herself. She felt the serpent's mind move back slightly.

The black voice spoke again, *you are weak. You will submit. No one is able to resist for long.*

She knew it was right. She had never felt something so strong in her life. The thoughts of what would happen to her if she failed began to seep in, and she felt a wave of fear overtake her, and she began to break.

Yessss, the creature said. *You are alone and weak. You will yield.*

Tears began to run down Amora's face as she felt the fear and loneliness form deep in her chest. She was still holding onto the shield for dear life but felt it weakening by the second. She began to question why she thought she could come here and win. She had been so sure that Jesus would make way for them and that He had wanted her to come. Now, it seemed so foolish.

She heard a snickering and the voice again. *Did God really say He would be with you?* It paused and then snickered again. *Where is he, then? Hmm? He knew you would come here and fail, and yet you trusted his word, and here you are, utterly helplesssss.*

The tears were flowing freely now, and the creature's words were like a knife in her heart. She trusted Jesus. She still trusted Him, didn't she? He had helped her before, and he would again. Wouldn't He?

She was about to call out to Him when a picture of her sisters was projected into her mind. They were naked, bloody, and chained to a table where horrible goat men were abusing and torturing them. "Noooo!" she cried out in anguish. Her psychic wall came crashing down, and complete darkness consumed her.

One of the programmers stepped forward, a wide grin crossed his beautifully dark features, "Excellent. Prepare her for the wedding ritual." Said Lucifer.

The other programmer stepped forward, "As you wish, my Lord." Answered Azazel.

***

Cat, Jose, and the others were finally able to revive Alvin and sit him up. The crash through the rock wall had knocked him out cold. Cat and the others had made it to them soon after Amora and Gianna were taken. Jose had guided them to him after he had phased through the wall and ran back to the stairwell.

"Where are they?" Alvin stammered.

"They were taken further down this hallway," Cat said.

Alvin attempted to get up, and she pushed him back down, "Sir, you may have a concussion. You need to sit for a few minutes."

Alvin shook his head, "There's no time. . . Jacque?"

Cat shook her head, "He's gone, sir. It was horrible...his body–"

"Stop," Alvin shook his head, and tears began to fall from his eyes. "I saw it. I was hoping it was a nightmare."

No one spoke for a few moments. Finally, he wiped his eyes and looked up, "Get me up. We can't stay here. We've got to save Amora, Gianna and the girls."

Suddenly, lights in the hallway blinked on, and a deep voice bellowed from speakers that they couldn't see: "If you come any further, you will die. Leave now, and we may let you live."

Alvin stood up, leaning on the hard rock wall. As he touched it, his body transformed into the same substance. He felt solid and immovable. He was determined to do everything in his power to save those girls and was unafraid of what may come. He looked at Cat, Jose, Yuusuf, Omari, Oscar, and Viti, his dewy eyes still soft and human, staring out from a stone-hard face, "I'm not backing down, team. If any of you want to leave now, I don't blame you. There's a good chance none of us are coming out of here alive. So, who is coming with me?"

One by one, each of them raised their hands. He nodded, "Okay. Let's move."

*****

Gianna's head hurt. In fact, it was throbbing, and she was almost certain she was bleeding from the back of it. She was going to touch the back of her head to see if there was blood, but her arm wouldn't move. She tried to move her other hand, but no. She finally decided to open her eyes, and the pain was so much worse when she did that. She was looking up at a plain white ceiling, and she was definitely strapped down to a hospital bed. She looked around, and there were other beds in the room. It seemed like a military hospital of some sort. The beds had human shapes in them, but when she tried to make them out, it hurt her eyes and her head too much. She closed her eyes again and tried to think.

She remembered she had been fighting that tall demon witch who shredded Jacque like paper and shivered at the memory. Somehow, she was still alive. Alive was good. Alive meant there was still hope. She may be able to escape and get to Amora. Someone had to come along sooner or later to check on her. She tried to move her legs, but they were strapped tightly, too. She began to breathe deeply and pray silently. For Amora and for herself, she could get past the pain of her head to figure out a way to escape. Then she recited her favorite psalms in her head: *even though I walk through the valley of the shadow of death, I will not fear, for You are with me. Your rod and your staff comfort me. For You, Oh Lord, are a shield about me, my glory and the lifter of my head. Blessed be the Lord my Rock who trains my hands for war and my fingers for battle...*

After some time, the head pain began to wane, and with it, her thoughts began to clear. She suddenly remembered that she had powers. She would have smacked herself if her arms weren't strapped down. Gianna began to engage her power, and a tingling sensation started in her hands and traveled up her arms and she snapped the restraints like breadsticks.

"Where do you think you can go, my dear?"

Gianna sucked in her breath and looked up. A beautiful blonde woman, her hair pulled back in a perfect French twist, stood at the foot of the bed. Her arms were crossed, and her cold blue eyes assessed Gianna scathingly. If she was human, Gianna was sure she could take her down in seconds, and she had just managed to snap the flimsy belt that had tied her feet down.

She spoke again, and this time Gianna picked up a slight accent, "You would never find your way out, even if you managed to make it past the guards, scientists, and . . . mythical creatures." She smirked slightly as she said the last phrase. *French? She was thin and tall. It would be hard for her to put up much of a fight in a dress and heels*, Gianna thought.

She was about to spring out of the bed and go for the woman's throat when she said, "You are the one who has had Amora these last few months, no?"

Gianna raised an eyebrow, "Who's asking?"

"I am Adora von Braun, Amora's mother."

Gianna scowled, "What have you done with her?"

"You care for her, that's good."

"Yes, I care for her! I protect her, and I fight for her. That's more than I can say about you!" Gianna stood up, anger burning in her gut as she stepped closer to the woman, "You will tell me where she is, or I'll kill you!"

Adora stood like stone, arms still crossed, but her eyes suddenly softened, "I want to help my daughters escape."

Gianna scoffed, "You can't seriously think I'm going to fall for that. I know you don't care a thing for your children. I know what you've done to them and what you've allowed to be done to them!"

Adora nodded, "I know what I've done. I don't understand what I am feeling now, but I regret it, all of it." She wiped a stray tear from her cheek and, for a moment, looked at it, almost as if she didn't know what it was. Then she shook her head and looked back at Gianna, her full crimson lips becoming a line of concern, "I don't have much time in here. I told them I was going to interrogate you for information. I can get you out of this room and tell you where they're keeping the girls, but they are not together. I also don't know how you will get to Amora without me. So, let me think of a way while you get Anna and Alanna."

Gianna was torn on whether to trust Adora or not. She certainly seemed sincere, but these servants of Satan were adept at deception. If she didn't agree to work with the woman, what were her other options? Wait for the mad scientists who worked in this facility to use her for their demonic experiments? Or worse, use her against Amora to force her to comply? That was a more likely scenario. She decided to at least act like she was going along with whatever the woman said, and she could always overpower her and try to run if it started to look bad.

Gianna crossed her arms and nodded, "Okay. I'll go along with this," she pointed in Adora's face, "But if it looks like you have set me up, I will make you regret it."

"Understood," Adora answered flatly as she pulled a set of electronic shackles out.

Gianna glared at her, "What are those for?"

"I've got to make it look convincing. Surely, you didn't expect me to just open the door and let you walk out."

"This is the only way?"

"If they know I let you out, I'm dead. There are no questions."

Gianna sighed, "Fine." and stuck her hands out to be cuffed.

"Turn around, please. It's got to look like I know you could escape."

Gianna grumbled and turned around. Adora put the cuffs on her wrists and edged her forward. At the door, she knocked, and a guard opened it and let them out into a hallway. As they walked, Gianna noted the lack of personnel and guards for such a super-secret base. She whispered, "Where are all the people?"

"Many have been sent to the surface to fight your army. Others, the most important personnel, have gone to other bases throughout the world to move the assets and experiments in case this base gets shut down or destroyed."

They took about ten different turns, and Gianna lost track after five. She had no clue how she would get out of here if and when she even got the girls. Her communication device had been taken, along with her weapons, so getting a hold of Alvin and the others was not an option either. She hoped and prayed the Lord would make a way for them. She reminded herself that they still had the upper hand with Him on their side. It would be nice to have some assurance that He was coming through for them here, though.

Adora looked straight ahead the whole time, even when she spoke to Gianna. "Listen carefully," she said in a whisper, so low Gianna had to move a bit closer to hear, "I want you to engage the power you used to break those hospital bonds to also break your wrist restraints. We're coming up on a guard at my daughters' room. When he unlocks the door to let us in, you'll need to overpower him, take his weapon and act like you are forcing me to comply with you. Clear?"

Gianna nodded just slightly. After another turn or two, they finally arrived at a guarded door. She had already snapped the cuffs but kept her hands behind her. Adora told the man to open the door. He nodded and did so. He was knocked out and disarmed in seconds. Gianna made a big show of pointing the gun at Adora and yelling, "Take me to the girls! Now!"

To which Adora put her hands up and led Gianna into the room. They left the door cracked so it wouldn't self-lock. Inside, the girls were strapped to beds and looked asleep. The little one, Alanna, had half her head shaved, showing a line of stitches over her left ear. She looked too small and very frail. "Oh my God, what did they do to her?" Whispered Gianna, her stomach clenched and a mix of sadness and rage welling up.

"A cybernetic brain implant. I did not consent to this surgery. I was told after it was done."

Gianna exploded in rage and pinned Adora against the wall by her throat, "Don't play innocent with me, you witch! You've already allowed irreversible damage to be done to these innocent girls for years, and I'll see you pay for it!"

The cold indifference returned to Adora's eyes, "Is this the way of your God?"

Gianna blanched, then slowly loosened her grip on Adora's throat, "No..." She sighed and walked to the other girl's bed. Her thoughts and feelings were a mess of anger, sadness, and guilt. Adora massaged her sore neck, "What *is* the way of your God if not taking vengeance against your enemies?"

Gianna thought for a moment. Was there hope for someone like Adora, who had spent her life worshiping Satan by committing horrendous crimes against children and living completely for power and riches? Would Jesus offer her grace?

"My God is holy, good, and kind. He's all powerful and all knowing, and He allowed His only Son's blood to be shed so that His vengeance against sin could fall on Him and not on sinful humanity. We all would have been destined for an eternity of punishment and separation from Him along with Satan, the so-called other gods and demons, had He not paid the price Himself for it."

Adora stared at Anna thoughtfully, "Well, perhaps if I help my daughters to safety, I may escape the fullness of His wrath."

Gianna shook her head, "No... Adora, that's not how it works. You could never do enough good to make up for even one sin, let alone all you have done. And neither could I or anyone. It's why He had to take the wrath of God Himself. You can be forgiven of all of it if you repent of your past and serve Him."

Adora chewed the side of her cheek, still avoiding Gianna's direct gaze. Finally, she shook her head slightly, "We've already taken too long here. Help me wake them."

Gianna nodded and began to rouse little Alanna, "Wake up, sweetie, we need to leave."

The girl turned over and opened her eyes slowly, "Please. . .I don't want to go to the goat monsters again."

"Oh, sweetie, no, we're going to get you out of here," Gianna answered. Alanna closed her eyes again.

Adora had Anna out of bed and was supporting her. It looked like both girls had been drugged and were having a hard time coming out of it. Gianna scooped Alanna up, "Let's go, I'll carry her."

"No, let me," said Adora, "So your hands are free."

Gianna nodded and handed the girl to her mother, who cradled her close, and another unbidden tear slipped down the woman's cheek. Gianna cocked the pistol and led the way out.

***

There were slimy creatures crawling on the walls. Alvin couldn't see details in the quick moments when the red lights flashed, but there were hundreds of them. Every so often, they would drop from the ceiling and land on one of them or on the floor. Someone screamed every few minutes when one landed on them. They bit and latched on like vampire slugs. Alvin was the only one who did not suffer from the bites because he had absorbed the rock from the walls again, and his skin could not be penetrated by the little beasts.

That didn't stop the feelings of revulsion when he stepped on one, or it fell on him. He had no idea if they were ever going to escape from the creatures, but they kept moving forward. They had walked down various hallways. Jose had tried to save them some time by phasing through doors. Most of the time, he came back saying the rooms were abandoned. The place was built like a labyrinth. Alvin couldn't figure out why a government facility would be designed this way, almost with no logic. After turning that thought around for a bit, he stopped walking.

"Everyone, stop," he said.

They stopped and looked at him. "They're messing with our heads."

"Wait, what?" asked Omari.

"Government and military facilities have certain schematics for how they design floor plans, for offices, labs, all of it. There's logic to it because people need to be able to get in and out fairly easily. The way we've been going just doesn't make sense."

"Wait, I've been going through walls and doors, and it all looks like this, but empty rooms and hallways," added Jose.

Alvin nodded, "See, that also doesn't make sense. Even though they've sent a lot of force up to the surface, there should still be some manpower down here. This is a medical floor. Where are all the scientists? Or the experiments?" As he finished, the creatures on the wall began to pulse and gel together into one huge black oozing blob.

The team moved back behind Alvin as the blob poured from the ceiling onto the floor in front of them. It pulsed and writhed until it formed into a bodily shape. The thing's head was just under the top of the ceiling, which Alvin estimated to be ten feet high. It had sprouted four arms and stood on long insect-like legs. It gurgled and hissed fiercely, and Alvin wondered if fighting this thing was the only way of getting out of whatever simulation they were trapped in. Well, it didn't seem like they had a choice at this moment, so he lunged at the monster with both fists raised to pound it into the ground. Oscar and Viti, who had super speed and strength, came on either side of it and ended up hitting it before Alvin did.

Oscar and Viti made contact almost simultaneously. Viti's fist and Oscar's kick seemed to sink into the flesh of the creature. As they attempted to pull back for another hit, their eyes widened. Viti's arm was covered in the ooze up to her elbow, and Oscar's leg past the knee. The flashing red light beat in time with Alvin's heart in his ears as he stopped just short of making contact with the entity and watched as the ooze made its way up their limbs. The creature itself stood still as a statue but continued with the hissing sounds. Cat began to shoot at it with no apparent effect. Viti and Oscar began to try to take it off with their hands, resulting only in spreading the ooze to the other limbs. Then they looked at Alvin and the others, "Help us! Please! It burns!" The inky goo had now taken over half of their bodies.

Jose, Omari and Yuusuf stepped towards them, and Alvin raised his hand, "Stop! Don't go near them."

"What? You're just going to let them die?" yelled Omari.

Alvin didn't answer but took a step back. Viti was crying and Oscar was screaming, and intermittently they would ask for help again.

"This isn't right, man! We need to do something!" protested Jose.

Alvin turned to him, "Look at them. Do you want to end up the same way?"

He was losing hope quickly, no way to go forward with that thing there, can't turn back because they were stuck in some mind maze. He was at a loss and rubbed his eyes trying to think, "Please, God help us. I don't know what to do. Please Jesus, come to our aid."

As he said the name, Jesus, the creature screamed and took a step back. Alvin shook his head, "I can't believe I forgot." He took a step forward, "In the name of Jesus Christ of Nazareth, I rebuke you!" It screamed and backed up again. Alvin took another step forward, "I command you to go in Jesus' name!" It immediately returned to a blob of black goo, separated into multiple portions, and dispersed into several different directions until it was completely gone.

Jose and Omari ran over to Viti and Oscar who were laying on the floor, no sign of the black goo on their bodies now. They didn't move. Omari checked for a pulse on Viti's neck, then Oscar's. "It's very faint, but there is a pulse." Cat bent over them and shined her light in their eyes and felt their hands. "They're in shock." She loosened their shirts and pulled out her canteen then she looked at Jose and Omari, "Elevate their legs please." They nodded and each lifted the legs of Viti and Oscar.

Cat poured some water over each of their foreheads and said, "Viti. Oscar. Are you okay? Can you hear me?" Alvin chimed in as well.

Viti's eyelids began to move, and she turned her head and moaned. Oscar soon responded with coughing. They finally gently sat the two up and leaned their backs against the stone wall. The two looked like they were slowly coming around. Alvin was beginning to worry that if they didn't get out of here soon, they would never find the girls. He looked at Jose, "Hey, man, can you stay with them while we move on to try to finish this?"

"Of course." Jose nodded then added, "If they feel up to it soon, you can guide us to you on comms."

"Absolutely." He patted Jose on the back, "You're a good man."

Alvin stood up and nodded to Cat and Omari, "Let's go."

They moved forward down the stone hallway, that although it was still pulsing red lights like a heartbeat, presently seemed clear of any enemy occupation. Alvin whispered, "Lord, help me to see. Help me to find them."

Within minutes they came upon a door to the right or they could keep going straight. The metal door was locked, which immediately made them want to go that direction and he regretted not waiting for Jose and the others. *Time to try out the stone skin suit*, he thought.

He backed up and ran into the door and succeeded in making a human sized dent. He backed up to do it again when a noise came from the other side. Some shuffling ensued and then the door began to slide back. Alvin, Cat, and Omari crouched to the side of the door, ready to spring on whoever came through.

The door opened, "Alvin?" came a woman's faint call.

He instantly relaxed as he recognized Gianna's voice. She came out the door and holstered a handgun in the front waistband of her leather pants. He gave her a quick hug. "I'm so glad you're okay."

A blonde woman came out behind her with a child in her arms and an older girl at her side. He looked behind her expecting to see Amora walking through. Instead, he saw a long surprisingly normally lit hallway with a few bodies of military guards laying here and there along the way.

He looked at Gianna, "Where is Amora? What happened to you?"

"No time to explain," She took the older girl's hand, pulling her gently forward. She attempted to place her hand in Alvin's, but the girl pulled it to herself and backed away after she touched the stone hand. He quickly changed back to his natural form.

Gianna took her hand again, "It's okay, Anna. See he turned back. He has the power to make his skin like rock or metal, but he's a normal person."

Anna took a tentative step forward and touched his outstretched hand. After feeling the warm human skin, she let him hold her hand and stood with him. He smiled down at her and squeezed her hand gently.

Then Gianna looked at the blonde woman, "Give Alanna to the lady here." Indicating Cat.

The woman placed Alanna gently into Cat's arms. "Take them out of here, now. She and I are going back to get Amora." Gianna said.

"You can't go back there alone and with no comms. We're coming too." Alvin replied.

"No, too many of us would never get in and out of there, and we have these two and can literally get them out now. I'm not taking a chance that these monsters could get them back."

"Okay but take Omari at least. Cat and I can get the girls out and we have to check in on Viti and Oscar anyway." She gave him a questioning look. He shook his head, "Tell you later."

Omari nodded, "I'm ready, Ms. Gianna, plus I have comms, our team will know if we need back up."

She nodded, "Thanks, Omar. Okay let's go, we don't have much time."

"Wait," said Alvin. "How do we get back? There were like twenty different turns."

The blonde furrowed her brows at him, "How could you miss it? It's straight down the way you came, there's no turns at all to get back to the entryway where the stairs and elevators are."

Alvin, Cat, and Omari looked at each other and shook their heads. "Okay, we'll take the girls back now. Keep us updated on your status. I will come back after I bring them through the portal to the compound." They were about to go, when the other woman spoke, "Wait, please."

She walked over to Alanna who was still in Cat's arms. She smoothed the hair back from the girl's face, "Alanna darling, can you hear me? It's mother." The girl's eyes slowly opened. "I . . .I love you, Alanna." She kissed the girl's forehead lightly then turned to the older girl and got on her knees in front of her, "Anna, I have so much I want to say to you, but no time." The girl looked shyly into her mother's eyes. "This may not mean much to you now or ever, but I'm sorry for what we've done and what you've suffered. Please tell Alanna when she can understand it, okay?" Anna nodded but said nothing. Then Adora hugged her quickly and stood up.

Alvin didn't know the story behind all of that, but from the look of that hug, it may have been the first time the woman had hugged anyone or anything in her life. He definitely wanted to get the story from Gianna later. He prayed that they would all make it out of here and be able to share stories later. He nodded and led Anna forward. He and Cat made their way back down the hallway, hoping it truly was as the mother had said, straight ahead. He looked back as Gianna, Omari and the woman re-entered the doorway.

"Please, Lord, help them get Amora back. Protect them all with your strongest angels. Amen."

Chapter Twenty-Seven

Sedona, Arizona

David wiped sweat, dirt and blood from his forehead. Every muscle in his body ached and several scratches, bites, and stab wounds began to burn and sting as the adrenaline dissipated from him. The ground around him was littered with torsos and severed heads of dead, smelly giants and festering pools of black goo that he supposed was their blood. The samurai team around him began to clean their swords of the stuff and were finding it difficult to completely remove the dark slime from the blades. Rather than resheath the contaminated weapons, they chose instead to carry them unsheathed.

David hadn't changed back to his natural form yet, wondering if more soldiers or nightmare creatures would soon come out of the caves and holes in the ground in the cliffs around them. Diego, Lucy and another young girl approached him. By the time they reached him, he had shrunk back to his normal size and surprisingly, noticed that his cuts and bites healed almost immediately after changing back. The muscular soreness still remained, though, and he began to stretch his aching arms. The bullet fire had stopped within an hour after Miral had taken over shielding for Lucy.

Darrel and his White Gryphon wife landed nearby. "We feel it's time to draw out the rest of the enemy. Perhaps it will be just what Gianna and the others need to rescue the girls and get out."

David raised his eyebrows, "You think there's more than what we just handled?"

"We're not dead." Darrel answered flatly, "That's definitely not all they got."

"I feel dead." David said, "I could use a break before getting into it again."

"Even though we've suffered surprisingly few losses; even those few are too many. We're going to take the brunt of the next hit." Diego indicated he, Darrel, Lucy, and Billie Jean. "We feel exposing ourselves fully will draw the enemy to us, based on our reputations."

David furrowed his brow, "I'm still new to all this, but what makes you think that you'll be the only ones getting it?" He gestured to everything and everyone around him, "We're all here."

"Sure, there's no guarantee, but we're a formidable force on our own and can take most of what comes." Said Darrel.

By this time, about 20-30 of the other soldiers had gathered to listen. A South American leader chimed in, "We didn't come here to play. We know the risks. We're ready to die to bring these dark ones down." They all nodded agreement around them.

David sighed and ran his fingers through his sweaty, bloody hair, "Okay, let's finish this and bring my wife and daughter out."

***

Diego rode on Billie Jean's back, while Darrel and Lucy flew by their side. The team had taken out most of the ground and air troops. Surprisingly, they had only suffered a few losses, mostly due to Lucy and Miral's shielding. They hoped to keep it that way and they prayed that Gianna, Alvin, and the inside team were able to find the girls and escape. Diego and Darrel thought by exposing themselves completely in the air, they may draw out the rest of the worst the enemy could throw at them. Their reputation as chosen leaders with special abilities had preceded them in most fights. This was the first time they were at a government facility with fallen angel influence.

Darrel shook his head sadly. "Lincoln should have been here for this."

They all nodded in agreement. Diego looked at Darrel with a slight smile. "I believe Lincoln, if he were here, would say, "Knock on the door, and let 'em know we're here, brother.""

"Let's do this!" Darrel responded with a shout. Burning brightly, he flew into an iron door on the hillside, causing a huge dent. He drew back for another try.

***

"Sir, the leaders of the attacking forces are attempting to infiltrate the western bay doors."

Azazel smirked, his dark glasses covering the flash of fire in his eyes, "Let's finish this. Send out the Nachashim. Make sure they take the young girl and the gryphon alive; we would like to add them to the collection."

"Yes, sir." The uniformed young man closed his eyes. He was wired directly into the system through an implanted neuralink. He and the computer could interface with no need for input devices.

***

236

The Waking Part II: Withstand in The Evil Day

I'm with you, daughter, no one will snatch you from my hand.

"Jesus," Amora whispered as she woke up with a start. She was in a large candle lit room with black robed and hooded figures standing in corners and seated in a giant candle lit circle around her. They were chanting quietly to themselves. Their shadowed faces did not turn towards her as she sat up. They were all in a trance. Her heart grew cold, and fear pierced her belly like a knife, she was being prepared for a blood ritual. She looked at what she was wearing; an identical robe as the others, except it was white.

She couldn't recall how she had gotten here, just a vague memory of a giant snake and Luka. She strained her eyes in the dim light to find a door to run to. None that she could see from where she was. She stood up and no one reacted. Amora stepped gingerly around the people and candles, her feet were bare, and the floor was like ice. The further she went from the circle, the darker the room became. It was larger than she first expected. Soon she could barely see where she was going, but kept her arms outstretched in front of her as she kept moving forward hoping to eventually feel a wall or door.

"Ah, the bride is awake." A woman's cold voice startled Amora and she stood still, her heart beating wildly in fear.

A tall woman, the tallest Amora had ever seen, stepped out of the shadows. Amora recognized her pale face. The one who attacked them in the hallway earlier. The horrible woman's face was lit by a candle in the hand of a goat faced man standing next to her. The scent of evil and blood overwhelmed Amora and she swooned. The goat-man caught her arm roughly in his iron grip.

Her senses both supernatural and natural filled her mind with dark voices, monstrous desires, and evil glee mixed with her own amplified fear and dread.

"She's ready. Bring her to the wedding feast." said the woman.

**

Alvin, Cat still holding Alanna, and Anna had been walking the straight hallway for about fifteen minutes in silence. The lighting was normal, cheap, fluorescent tube lights, the stone walls were thick and drab, and the gray cement flooring was unimpressive. It was so quiet, that their rubber soled boots' scuffling and squeaking noises were painfully noticeable. Alvin expected soldiers to come down the hall after them at any moment, and he ached to pick Anna up and run the rest of the way. He was aware, though, that she was in a fearful and fragile state and didn't want to frighten her. He looked ahead and thought he could see an end to this ridiculously long hallway.

As they progressed closer to the doors, Alvin noticed that Anna began to slow down and pull back slightly. He tried gently squeezing her hand in assurance, but as they got closer, she almost came to a complete stop and actually dug her fingernails into his hand, which were surprisingly sharp considering he hadn't noticed long or sharp nails on her hand earlier. He finally turned to her, "Anna, are you okay sweetie? We're getting close to getting you out of here."

She didn't answer but squared her shoulders and looked up at him defiantly. He was in shock that this nine-year-old frail thing was squaring up to him as if she wanted to spar.

"What is she doing?" Asked Cat, also in disbelief.

"I don't know, maybe they did something to her, so she couldn't leave." He answered.

"Just pick her up and let's go."

"Okay, okay. I just don't want to hurt her."

He attempted to grab her, but she jumped back and growled. He tried again and she swatted his hands away with surprising strength.

"Sir quit messing around and just grab her," Cat said, her irritation visibly growing.

He nodded, and without holding back, grabbed her. She somehow wiggled out of his arms and pushed him roughly against the wall, "What the–" and he stopped getting a check in his gut and a brief vision of his dream a few days ago of the little girl that was actually a monster. He looked into Anna's eyes, "What are you?"

Her eyes flashed momentarily and changed from blue to yellow reptilian slits. Startled, Alvin jumped back. She immediately sprang onto him with catlike agility and began clawing and biting his face and neck and he yelled as he tried to pull her off.

Cat gently put Alanna down and pulled the Anna thing off of him with a choke hold around its neck. As she held it tightly, it fought with surprising strength and suddenly shifted into a small green reptilian creature. Cat struggled to keep it in a choke hold as it squirmed and hissed. Alvin withdrew his knife and quickly stuck it through the top of its head until it finally expired and stopped twitching. Cat threw it to the side and quickly got up. "Oh my God. What was that thing?" She asked.

"Some sort of shapeshifter," he answered and spat on the creature.

"Did they turn her into that?"

He shook his head, "No, no. That's not the girl. I can only assume they still have her and replaced her to fool us or to just kill us in our sleep.

Cat looked at Alanna, still asleep on the ground, "What about that one?"

Alvin bent down and gently turned her over, "Hey Alanna, can you hear me?" The little girl opened her eyes groggily, rubbing a little fist into one, "Thirsty." was all she said weakly.

He got his canteen out and lifted her head gently as he held the bottle to her lips, she took two gulps and closed her eyes again. He looked at Cat, "I think she's okay."

Cat nodded, "Okay, let's get out of here."

He nodded, picked the girl up and they jogged to the door and left.

***

The skies filled with unholy screeching. Shivers ran down Darrel's spine. He'd heard something like that sound before in the other realm. When black flying snake-like creatures had come to attack them. They were horrible, fiery evil things. If that was what was coming, his fire would have no effect on them. He shouted, "Get ready! Something horrible is on the way."

The skies became black, though it was barely noon. The screeching intensified a thousand-fold as flying serpentine creatures filled the skies. Fire spouted from the mouths of the deadly screechers. "No way," Lucy whispered, her heart thumping in her ears as terror took over.

***

Lucifer sat on a lofty golden throne atop a stone platform overseeing the giant rock cavern filled with black robed worshippers. Standing thickly at his side was Azazel, still in the form of the tall muscular black man, but instead of the military general's uniform, he was now wearing the opulent robes and armor of the Sumerian gods, complete with a golden circlet sitting upon his head, a long black beard woven with gold flowed from his face, and a gigantic golden scimitar strapped to his side. Next to him, but standing slightly behind in deference, stood Ninazu in his true form, his thick silver black armor and spear glimmered even in the low light of the thousand candles lit cavern. The altar below was bloody with recent sacrifices.

One of the robed priestesses approached the throne with a golden goblet filled with blood, she carefully climbed the stone steps and at the top she bowed, waiting for Lucifer to bid her approach. He nodded at her and she crawled to him on her knees with her eyes to the ground. Once there she lifted the goblet to him. He took it, barely glancing at her and took a large swallow. He then passed the goblet to Azazel, who swirled and smelled it as if it were fine wine, then took a long gulp.

"These *image bearers* of the Most High are just as easily swayed to forsake Him and follow us as they were 5000 years ago," Azazel commented with a smirk.

"Do not speak His name!" Lucifer growled.

Azazel bowed his head slightly, "Forgive me."

Lucifer waved the statement away like a pesky fly, "These fools have been serving me for generations. It's the millions who believe they serve no one but themselves, who are consumed with vanity, greed, lust, perversion, and hate that are the ones I relish the most." He turned towards his cohorts with a grin, "Their negative energy fuels and empowers my kingdom day and night. They have no clue who they are or how truly powerful they could be if they only surrendered to Him. It's delightful."

"What of the ones that serve the Word? The Redeemed?" Azazel asked.

Lucifer scowled, "They can be a problem, but I found that assigning a garrison of troops to them with constant attacks usually keeps them so occupied, they have no will to truly fight back. Many get entangled in sin again very easily and are then enslaved and unable to walk in true freedom."

"But the ones that do walk in freedom, and know who they are? Like those that are fighting our forces above even as we speak?" Azazel asked.

"Only some of them are truly a danger to our plan." Satan answered dismissively, "The most important part, we are taking care of now. The blood rituals will strengthen our forces."

"Doesn't the girl belong to Him? How will you truly possess her if He protects her."

"Sin gives us the door. She will sin, and we will have access. I've already weakened her mind. She will be too confused and afraid to call to Him."

Azazel nodded, handing the goblet back to Satan, "What would you have me do with the mother, Adora von Braun? Is she of any more use?"

Lucifer took another sip of the goblet, "I did enjoy how you toyed with her," He smirked.

"You must force her to participate in the torture of her child, then kill her slowly in front of the other royal households, so they know what happens to any who cross me."

The Waking Part II: Withstand in The Evil Day

Chapter Twenty-Eight

Sedona, Arizona

Gianna, Adora, and Omari had just arrived at a lower level of the base that led to a great cavern. Adora told them that it was where she first met the freed fallen angel, Azazel. Suddenly, Adora turned, raised her arms above her head while chanting under her breath, Omari and Gianna were knocked off their feet hitting the stone wall behind them and landed with a hard thud on the stone ground. Gianna's head and back flooded with pain, causing her vision to darken and bursts of light to appear wherever she looked. Omari groaned next to her. She tried to reach out to him, but her hands were bound behind her back by some force that was stronger than iron shackles. "Omari, call for help." she coughed as she recovered the breath that had been knocked out of her.

Adora reached down and pulled his communication bud out of his ear, "I'm sorry," she whispered, "This is the only way I might be able to get to Amora."

"I'll kill you." Gianna hissed through gritted teeth. She then attempted to break the restraints with her super strength, but the invisible bonds didn't budge. She grunted in frustration, as she realized her legs were bound as well.

"You made the right decision, Witch." The horrible dark voice caused the hair to rise on the back of Gianna's neck, and bile to come to the back of her throat.

"Ninazu, please tell Lord Azazel that I have two of the enemy soldiers. The woman is one of the leaders. I would like to see my daughter."

"You will see your daughter, Witch." The dark voice answered dismissively, and to the soldiers he said, "Bring them to the gathering, and make sure they are bound to a pole with a view of the altar. Bring Mrs. von Braun as well, and make sure she is prepared."

Gianna and Omari were pulled roughly to their feet, and they attempted to fight. Omari was kicked and punched mercilessly, and Gianna was punched in the gut causing her to double over and gasp for breath. They were roughly carried into a dark cavern lit by hundreds of candles, causing shadows to undulate wildly on the cave walls. Multitudes of voices chanting lowly in a dark language Gianna did not understand; her stomach became ice. A rotten smell assaulted her senses. She coughed and breathed shallowly out of her mouth. Finally, Gianna's hands were chained above her head to a thick pillar. Omari was secured to another one nearby, he hung limply from his chains, unconscious from the beating on the way in.

Gianna scanned the shadowy room. A crowd of black robed individuals swayed slowly on their feet as they chanted darkly. In front of them stood an immense stone altar dripping with a dark liquid, she could only assume was blood. She shivered as the evil settled like fog, thick and constricting, causing her to feel that the enormous cavern was but a small iron box from which

245

there was no escape. Her heart pounded and she began to sweat, still only drawing small gasping breaths.

Three individuals in white robes were brought out in front of the stone altar. They were at least a foot or more shorter than all the others around them, so she assumed they were children. Three black-robed women stood behind them. The one in the center pulled back her cowl. Adora's white-blonde hair sat neatly in a tight bun at the crown of her head, her pale features seemed to glow against the dark cavern. All three women pulled the hoods back from the children's faces revealing Amora, a dark-haired girl, and a blonde boy. Gianna groaned as fear and anger gripped her tightly. She prayed short, desperate prayers.

***

Amora's eyes darted across the room, searching for a possible rescuer hidden among the throng. The other two children's faces were slack and staring straight ahead into nothingness. One of the women led the boy to the bloody altar and laid him upon it; he made no sound as she bound his hands and feet to the bloody stone. Adora led Amora to him, "Connect to your duad, Amora." She whispered.

Amora shook her head and began to whimper, "No, please. . . I can't."

"You must."

Tears poured down Amora's cheeks, her bottom lip quivered as she looked down on Luka. His face was relaxed as if asleep. His messy blonde hair stuck to the sides of his face with sweat. She hadn't noticed until that moment how beautiful his face was. They'd been connected psychicly in training since they were toddlers, and it was often used to torture them if they didn't perform well. Amora understood that tonight would be worse. She trembled as fear and dread consumed her. Her mother gripped her arm painfully, "Now." she hissed.

Closing her eyes, Amora reached for Luka with her mind. Instantly she found him, as familiar as the voice of a loved one who was speaking in another room. As soon as she had him, he opened his eyes and looked directly into hers, "Amora." He whispered. As soon as he felt her fear, his eyes darkened, and he looked around. He struggled uselessly against the restraints and Amora felt his anxiety mounting. The other two robed women stood at either end of the altar at his head and feet. One began to slap him in the face, with each slap Amora felt the sting in her own face and cried out though Luka only grimaced and grit his teeth. The other woman began to puncture the bottom of one foot with a long thick needle, he and Amora screamed in tandem. The woman pulled the needle out and inserted it again and again in different parts of the same foot until the whole sole was bloody. Amora swooned and leaned against the altar, her right foot pulsating with pain.

The women then proceeded to strip Luka bare by cutting the white robe off of his body with a dagger. His blue eyes already glazed with pain, now widened with fear as he lay naked and chained on the bloody altar. Amora's heart pounded, knowing that she would probably be completely destroyed from his torture and death. She whispered a desperate prayer to the only One who could save her. As the woman began to cut into Luka's flesh, he and Amora cried out in unison.

Suddenly the woman gasped, her eyes widened, and she dropped the knife. Adora pulled a knife out of her back with a sneer and then threw her to the ground. Before the second woman could even register what had happened, her neck had been sliced and blood streamed from the gaping wound.

Amora looked up as Adora quickly cut Luka free and pulled him off the table, "Sever the connection, Amora!" She whispered fiercely as she pulled the girl to her feet. Amora nodded and cut Luka from her. Adora pulled both children behind her towards the stone stairs behind the altar. Amora tried her best to support Luka as he hobbled as fast as he could on his good foot.

***

"Oh my God!" Gianna whispered as she watched the daring escape of Adora with the children. She looked over at Omari, "Omari! Are you awake! Omari!"

Omari's head flopped in her direction, and he moaned.

"I'm coming! We're getting out of here, Omari. Lord God, strengthen me so I can get us out of here." She breathed out, concentrating on knowing that His strength was made perfect in her weakness. She yielded to Him and the familiar tingling sensation flowed through her arms and she easily broke her bonds. She quickly broke Omari's chains as well and caught him as he fell forward. In catching him she had squeezed a broken rib and he revived with a scream. Gianna clamped her hand over his mouth, "I'm sorry, buddy." She whispered. "Can you stand up?" He nodded and she released her hand. His face was a bloody mess, one eye was swollen shut, but he was still able to crack a smile. "Thanks, Gi." He said as he stood up holding his aching side tenderly.

She patted his shoulder lightly, afraid to hurt him again. "We may have to help Adora get the kids out or die trying. Are you up for this?"

"Sure. I still have some fight left in me. Let's go." He said.

***

Lucifer threw the bloody goblet onto the floor in anger. "Ninazu, kill that witch and get the girl and the woman for me." He looked at Azazel. It is time for you to drink your fill of enemy blood tonight."

Ninazu answered, "Yes, my mast–"

Lucifer turned. Ninazu was on the ground with an angelic spear through his chest. Azazel was pinned against the wall by Raphael. Uriel's sword was at Lucifer's throat. He quickly raised his hands, "You have no grounds to interfere in my domain, Uriel." He said calmly.

"You are attempting to harm His children. You don't have permission to touch them, Ha Satan."

"I have first claim to Amora von Braun. She was mine from the womb." Lucifer snapped.

"She has been redeemed. You no longer have claim to her."

Raphael spoke, "We should bring this one before the heavenly court. He has been released before the time."

Azazel grumbled, "It is almost judgment day. I was to be released for a time before it. Let the Most High stand by His word. I must be allowed to test mankind." Raphael eased off him slightly. "You are on a short leash for a time. Understand that I will not hesitate to come for

you if you touch any of His Beloved without permission."
Azazel nodded.

Uriel withdrew his sword from Lucifer's neck,
"Do not interfere with their escape, and we won't
interfere with yours." The Dark Lord nodded a slight
ascent. "Come, Azazel, we have work to do." Raphael
stepped back.

Lucifer transformed into a dragon, his crimson
wings filling the cavern. Azazel simultaneously
transformed into a fiery goat creature. Large black wings
burst from his back, and his fiery darkness absorbed all
nearby light. They both rose up and blasted like missiles
through the top of the mountain, disappearing into the
sky.

***

Adora's demons screamed profanities at her as she
harnessed all their power to fight her way through an
onslaught of robed witches. Left and right, they fell
before her powerful punches, slices, and fire spells. The
desire to get her daughter and her duad to safety
consumed her wholly and burned like a fire in her belly.
She knew she would take everyone down in her path if
necessary and felt more powerful than she ever had in her
life. They had made it out of the cavern and she
continued fighting her way down a hall leading to
elevators that she was not sure would even work when
they got there. A group of soldiers approached with guns
aimed at her. She easily flung them against the stone
walls with her powers, causing them to crash, screaming
in pain to the hard floor.

Amora and the duad were slowing her down
considerably, and she worried they wouldn't get to the
elevators before more formidable enemies would arrive.

250

She shuddered at the thought of Ninazu catching up with her. She thanked the Maker for the recent arrangement of the demon god working outside of her, conveniently occupying a super-soldier's body, and acting as her guard these last few weeks. If he were still inside her, there would have been no escape for her and no ability to even think outside of her programming.

A foul stench filled the hallway, and the hairs on the back of her neck stood at attention. Adora stopped, and her demons suddenly quieted as well. Amora and the duad clung to each other behind her. Two large dark figures stood directly in front of the opening to the elevators ahead. The lights above them flickered then went out. Giving them the appearance of trolls sculking silently in a cave. She knew the ease of their escape just ended.

"Amora."

"Yes, Mother." The girl whispered fearfully.

"Pray to your God for help. Perhaps He will have mercy on us for your sake."

Amora nodded and grew noticeably less fearful as she whispered inaudibly to herself. Adora surmised that the Creator God favored the young and innocent, and she hoped he would come through for her daughter, at least. She took a breath, clenched her fists and told the children to stay back while she fought the creatures in the hallway ahead.

"You will probably need help with those.... *things*." Said a voice behind them.

Adora turned, and Gianna and her companion stood ready to fight. Though they were badly disheveled from their earlier beating, they seemed determined to continue fighting.

"Are you still going to kill me?" Adora asked.

"I'll let Jesus deal with you instead."

Adora nodded, then turned back around, bracing for the fight. Gianna engaged her power, and Omari, who also had abilities of strength and speed, engaged as well.

"Stay here, kids. And pray." Said Gianna.

Amora nodded and held onto the boy.

The three of them walked swiftly forward, and the dark figures stood immobile and menacing.

"Not these jerks again," Gianna grumbled.

Their foul smell nearly overwhelmed Adora, but she pressed forward, first trying a binding spell, which had no effect. She pulled her blade and began to slash at the first creature as Gianna and Omari took the second. Unfortunately, the goat men were strong and agile, and Adora suffered a deep scratch across her chest before she was able to cast a shielding spell over herself. Gianna and Omari landed a few punches and kicks to the second satyr, only because they outnumbered it, but none of the strikes had any effect either. Adora knew they were being toyed with and that the beasts should have overpowered them quickly. She assumed they were holding back on orders to possibly take them alive. She hoped the Creator God would come through for Amora and save them out of this den of darkness.

Adora continued to slash and dispel lethal blows of energy at the infernal goat-man, slowly but surely beating it to the ground. Behind her, Amora yelped, causing her to pause for a moment. The creature took the opportunity to slash her again with its deadly claws, and blood flowed freely from her arm. Adora growled in rage and blasted every bit of energy she could draw from herself, sending the creature flying into the dark hall beyond. Her demons cursed at her in protest. Ignoring them, she quickly turned to see Lilith standing between the children, her razorlike black claws encircling the throats of Amora and Luka. The demoness looked down her nose at Adora with a fanged sneer.

Omari had the other satyr on the ground in a chokehold while Gianna stood by, ready to face the Mother of Demons to save her charge. Lilith seemed to fill the entire hallway with her malicious presence. Ornate black horns protruded from the sides of her temples, adding another foot of height to her already statuesque 7-foot form; the porcelain white skin punctuated her ruby-red eyes. "What can you hope to accomplish by running away with the master's bride? There is nowhere for you to escape to, my dear." She said.

Adora growled at the patronizing tone of the demoness, she decided she would die before letting this secondhand wench bring her daughter as a prize to Lucifer or Azazel, and now she had no doubt that the two dark gods were working together to use her and her daughter for their shared nefarious purposes.

"She will replace you as head of the Order and bear the Chosen One. A pity you won't be around to enjoy the benefits of the status you were to achieve at your daughter's ascension." the trollop prattled on in her arrogance.

Gianna pointed at the demon, "You will not take that little girl. She belongs to the Most High."

The prattling stopped momentarily as Lilith considered Gianna's statement. She continued, her eyes never wavering from Adora, "You don't dare to think that their God would possibly accept *you*. After all the blood you've spilled for Lucifer? Is that why you've gone on this fool's mission?"

"You know nothing about my God," Gianna said, her fists balled up in rage.

Lilith continued again as if nothing had been said, "Have you figured out yet why Lucifer demands so much sacrifice of the mortals' children?" Adora clenched her blade, her hands beginning to shake, but she did not answer.

Lilith continued, "Because their 'so-called' Most High God hates it. It's the most abhorrent act in the realm and guarantees to incur His wrath." She pointed up and grinned again, exposing her fangs like a maniacal smiling serpent.

Adora's shoulders drooped, and with a sigh and shake of her head, she sheathed her blade at her side.

Gianna raised her eyebrows, "What are you doing? Don't listen to her. There is forgiveness with repentance. There is a place for you." Omari had finally subdued the satyr by crushing its larynx. He threw the foul body aside and stood up next to Gianna, ready to spring forward at a word.

Adora nodded her head, ignoring Gianna. "You're correct. With all the rituals, torture and sacrifice of hundreds of children and my enemies, there is no way that their God would accept me." She lifted her hands as if in surrender, "And yet, after a whole life of service, Lucifer wants me dead, and Azazel would have probably done away with me as well. What choice did I have but to try to go to the enemy?"

"Our Lord is very forgiving, given the right motivation." Lilith chided, her claws still clasped under the children's chins. Tears had begun to fall down

Amora's cheeks as her doom became more and more apparent. The boy had become stoic, almost resigned to his fate, and watched the exchange with emotionless eyes.

Adora began to slowly approach Lilith, her hands still raised. In response, Lilith's grip tightened on the children's throats. The boy was struggling to breathe.

"You can take me to the Master now," Adora said calmly. "I will appeal to him, and I have more information on the attacking forces." Adora was within a few steps of the children. Lilith's hooded scarlet stare bored into her. "I'll consider it. Come no closer." She commanded.

With astounding speed, Adora unsheathed the blade and lopped the horned head from Lilith's long, pale neck. The look of shock became frozen on the fiend's face as her head hit the ground. Wasting no time, Adora pulled the children away as the body fell. "Run!" She yelled at them. Looking at Gianna, she said, "Take them out, now! She'll be back in another form in minutes! I'm going to surrender to the Dark Lord and buy you some time."

Gianna nodded, and she and Omari took the children's hands. "No! Mother, you can't!" Amora pulled back her hand and looked her mother in the face, "He will kill you, and you'll be lost forever." Her big blue eyes were wet with tears. Adora's heart shattered at her daughter's words, and a tear escaped her eye. She wiped it in wonder. *Too late. You foolish woman. You traded what amounted to dung for your precious daughters' lives. Too late to make up for it. Too late to make better choices.*

255

"It's too late for me, Amora. How can you cry for me? I've been nothing but cruel to you." She swallowed a lump in her throat of emotions she'd never felt before. "I'm so sorry for everything."

The girl shook her head, "No, Mother. It's not too late. Jesus forgives evil things if you repent. He does. He'll accept you. Call to Him."

Adora gently cupped Amora's small face in her hand, "You must go now, dear girl." She turned to Gianna. "Please, take her now." Gianna nodded and picked Amora up, "Come on, baby, we have to go." They ran down the hall, and Amora looked at her mother until they were too far to see her any longer.

Chapter Twenty-Nine

Sonoma, Arizona

Alvin's voice came to Diego over the comms, "Everyone still alive from the inside has made it back to base through the inside portal. Diego, you and the outside team stand by for extraction."

They all looked at each other with relief just as the serpentine creatures began to dive for them by the hundreds. The teams gathered together, fighting off the ones they could while they waited for the portal to open. Lucy and Miral did their best to cover the team from fire assault while Billie Jean snapped the creatures up in her beak and tore them apart. The warriors with swords hacked and sliced through as many creatures as they could, with no end of them in sight.

David gathered some in handfuls while getting scratched, bit and burned. He crushed them and threw the dead carcasses at the live ones, dive-bombing them from all around. Diego blasted the creatures with light and disintegrated them with loud screams. Finally, a portal opened just outside the area of attack. Their ground warriors went through first, Diego, Billie Jean and the girls hanging back to make sure nothing followed them through. Darrel hung back, waiting for BJ, though he could do nothing with his fire to ward off the infernal creatures. The ground began to rumble and collapse beneath them.

257

"What's happening?" Lucy asked.

"I think the base is collapsing," said Diego.

Cracks and sinkholes began to appear on the ground around them. "We've got to finish this and get through before we sink!" said Lucy.

The ground shifted and moved. Still, they fought the black serpent creatures. "Come on, let's just run through!" Darrel shouted. Billie Jean roared her Gryphon call, and many of the creatures flew back out of her range. Lucy and Miral ran through the portal, Diego and Darrel followed, with Billie Jean finally coming through. Drake closed it just as a couple of serpents tried to fly through after them; the portal sliced them in two. The severed upper bodies flopped on the ground like a fish out of water.

***

Adora stood amid a crowd of fleeing worshippers. The walls and ceilings were cracking, and pieces of rock fell around her. She had come to surrender herself to Azazel and neither he, Lilith, or even Ninazu were in sight. She didn't feel them either and wondered what her next move should be. A boulder the size of a desk crashed next to her, crushing an unfortunate man who was in the wrong place at the wrong time. She shrugged and made her way back towards the hallway. Based on the rumbling around her, she doubted the elevators would even be working anymore. There may be a chance in the stairwells, but this was at least twenty stories underground, and it would take at least thirty minutes to get to the surface, and that was at a run with no obstructions and other people to block her path. She'd have to chance it if she wanted to live.

The Waking Part II: Withstand in The Evil Day

She began to have hope for the first time since all this began that if she could make it to the surface, she may have a chance to escape with her life. And dare she think it? Another chance to reunite with her daughters and start over? She shook her head. All of that hoping was useless. Even if she managed to escape, Lucifer would come for her eventually. He did not let anyone in the Brotherhood live who even thought of betraying him. She ran towards the hallway behind forty or fifty others as pieces of the rock ceiling crashed to the left and right of them. Some striking a few people around her, she barely dodged one that would've landed directly on her. Her heart pumped wildly and she sent up a quick plea to the Creator to help her out of here, and she would serve Him and make amends for her life.

A few soldiers came through, also running towards the doors but scrutinizing the crowd at the same time. She wondered if they had been sent to find her and was thankful that she was still dressed in the black robes that all the rest of them were. She hoped to blend in and lifted her cowl over her head while she walked quickly next to two other women. They all tried to weave their way through the throng to get to the stairwells and out of danger. There were two stairwells that she remembered, one on this end through the first hallway and one at least a thousand or more meters away on the other side of the labs. She thought to chance heading for the one further away if she could do it without the soldiers seeing her.

The hallway lights flashed on and off every few seconds. The auxiliary power from the generators that the base had been running on for the last few hours would soon turn off. Another block of stone fell, and people scattered. Adora used the distracting chaos to run away

259

and down the hallway towards the other stairwell without being seen. No one followed her as she walked briskly to the end of the hallway. When she turned, she began to jog. The flashing lights and adrenaline had her on edge.

Adora only noticed that her demons and mind had been quiet for the last hour when she began to hear them again. As she got closer to the other stairwell, she heard an evil snickering from her mind, and she slowed back to a walking pace. The hairs on the back of her neck stood up, and she smelled a familiar evil.

"Did you think you could escape me, witch?"

She shivered, and her stomach turned sour at the sound of Ninazu's oily voice. Her demons cackled in her mind as he stepped out from the shadows. Completely decked in his black Sumerian armor, the demon's whole form filled the hallway, blocking her only exit from this death trap.

"Even if you take me back to Azazel and Lucifer, they will never get my children back. The Creator God's people took them and will protect them from now on." She smiled, "I'm not afraid to die now that I've foiled Satan's plans."

He walked a few steps towards her, and she noticed his gait was a bit unsteady. Intrigued, she backed up a couple of steps, hoping to draw him into the light. He laughed, "Oh, you will die, witch. I will bring them your cold corpse. But you will die knowing that you failed. We still have one of your girls, and you will never get her back." His manic smile was terrifying, and her heart sank in her chest like a stone. *Was it possible?*

"You're lying." She said,

As he stepped forward, black ooze dripped from his legs onto the floor. Adora didn't understand what she was seeing at first, but he put a hand against the wall as he walked towards her. *Was he injured? Is that possible?*

He stopped, now leaning heavily on his sickle. He drilled her with his pitch-black orbs, causing her to shiver and look down, "The girl you gave to them was a shapeshifter who has probably killed a few before even being noticed. We took Anna to another facility two days ago. If they ever find her, which they won't, she will already be completely programmed to take Amora's place...willingly."

Anger burned like a furnace in Amora's gut. All she wanted to do was destroy him and all of these evil so-called gods who used, abused and threw away every human that was no longer of use to them. She had to defeat them but was powerless against such beings. But alas, there was a Being that could punish and imprison the gods. She knew one way out and one way to save her daughter and destroy Lucifer's plans for good, "I renounce my allegiance and vows to you, Lucifer, and his whole kingdom–"

"NO! WHAT ARE YOU–?!"

The walls shook and began to split and crack. Her demons screamed in terror in her head to the point she almost couldn't speak out the words, "I repent of all of my sins, how I have murdered, lied, cursed, and any other offenses that I have ever done against the Creator God and His Son."

"I will kill you, witch!" Ninazu lifted his sickle and stalked towards her. Dust and stone began to come down around them.

Undaunted, Adora continued, "I yield all to the Most High God and His Son!"

Ninazu roared. As he got to within steps of swinging his razor-sharp sickle at Adora, a blinding light appeared, causing her to shield her eyes and fall prostrate to the ground. She coughed and wheezed, strained to breathe. Adora's head throbbed, and she gagged as her demons screamed until she thought her skull would crack. Finally, she vomited up a puddle of black phlegm, and the screaming stopped abruptly. Then there was silence. Adora slowly sat up on her knees as the blinding light waned, and the silence continued incredibly amid the rumbling, straining walls. "What happened?" She whispered.

Ninazu was gone, and in his place stood a tall, beautiful, golden-armored angelic warrior. His ebony skin shone with golden light. His hair hung in long, colorful braids, and his silver eyes glowed with heavenly glory.

"You were reborn." He answered.

She bowed at his feet, "Forgive me, Lord."

"Get up, Adora. I am not the Lord Almighty. I serve Him and his children of whom you are now one. He sent me to take you out of here."

She stood up, tears in her eyes, "He sent you? For me? The Lord Jesus?"

He nodded and reached his hand out. "Let's go see Him."

She took the angel's hand, and they disappeared.

Chapter Thirty

Hickory, North Carolina

Gianna

It's only been a few days since Sedona, but it might as well have been years since so much has changed. We've been staying in the big house with Charlotte and her boys. Dylan seems to think he's one of them, and I'm so fine with that. David and I share one of the guest bedrooms, and I have no words to explain what has happened to us. When we both came back from Sedona, we crashed into each other with a gut-burning fire and made love all night. I don't know if it was all that we had been through since we fled our home and then the battle at Sedona and we needed something more to cling to or that my walls are coming down and we're starting over. I'm not trying too hard to figure it all out right now. There's really no time because we're fortifying this compound at the same time as pitching in to build more shelters, cultivate the numerous gardens, help take care of the community farm animals, and more.

It's so much work from sunup to sundown, and we all love it. We're so exhausted by the end of the day that everyone sleeps hard. Little Alanna is starting to play a little with Amora and the boys, and it's heartwarming to see her come out of her shell. I don't think the girl has played a day in her life and probably needs to learn how to be a kid again. Amora is helping with that. Alanna

263

clings to her like a baby to a mother, and sweet Amora does mother her and probably has been for years. I hope to get the little angel to open up to me and let me love her, too. She's been through too much in her seven years. More than I want to even think about. We have yet to address the fact that she has computer hardware in her head and if *they* can control and track her with it. Alvin is looking into it with his military contacts.

David loves the fact that we now have two beautiful girls to protect and raise. Oh, my heart! There should be three. Even as I write this, the tears are dropping on the page for little Anna. When Alvin told us the one we thought we were saving was some sort of reptilian shape-shifter, I thought Amora would crumble into the floor or leave on her own to find her. Satan has her hidden in another of those underground bases, and she could be anywhere in the world by now. We found out that they have portals that they can travel instantly from base to base and there are hundreds all over the world. We've been non-stop praying for revelation on where to go and how to save her. Holy Spirit has given many of us the directive to stay put and fortify.

The boy Luka is another issue. He and Amora have a peculiar connection. It's almost as if they can communicate without words, they are so quiet around each other, and yet they seem to know what each other needs. He's very protective of her and just wants to be where she is and steps in front of her whenever anyone approaches, like a little bodyguard. She doesn't seem to mind. After he physically recovered from that awful torture in Sedona, we have monitored him closely, as we believe his brain has some hardware implanted as well. There's always a possibility that he has physical and spiritual trackers in him. Hopefully, all that Lincoln did to protect this place and what Darrel and the team are doing now, will be enough to cover us until we know more.

Charlotte has been amazing and generous. She wants David and I and the children to stay with her permanently. She doesn't want to be alone in the house with the boys. It keeps her mind out of despair of losing Lincoln. We'll stay as long as she needs us but still work on building ourselves a little home on the property for when she's ready for us to move on. Billie Jean and Darrel are expecting, and I'm so happy we are going to be here when their little one arrives. I hate that such happiness comes in such dire times.

Sometimes, it just doesn't seem like it could get any worse here and in the rest of the world, but it's just the beginning. I'm so thankful for God putting us all together and for being part of his end-times army. Together, with our teams across the world, we will push back the darkness.

Epilogue

"Mama."
Billie Jean startled awake and sat up, "Katie?" She whispered as her heart beat wildly.
She looked around, her hand rubbing her small protruding bump protectively as the moonlight filtered in through the window, just lighting the room enough. "I must have been dreaming," she whispered to herself. Darrel was still snoring lightly next to her in bed. She swung her legs over the side of the bed and sat thinking about Katie for a moment. She would've been such a great big sister to this little bundle. She was so loving. For a moment, Billie Jean was overwhelmed with sadness and longing for the little girl lost years ago. She knew whose hands she was in, though and couldn't stay sad for long.
As she was about to get up to visit the bathroom, she heard a small voice again, "Mama." She sucked in her breath, startled. She didn't hear the little voice with her ears, but in her mind, like the Holy Spirit spoke to her.
"I'm losing it," she whispered.
A brief picture flashed in her mind of a little baby floating gently in a womb. "Mama." Again, the voice came to her mind.
"Is it possible? Am I hearing her?"
Yes. She heard the Holy Spirit say.
"How?"

She is gifted from the womb. She will do much harm to the kingdom of darkness. He said.

Billie Jean's thoughts swirled. She was amazed and afraid. She wanted to protect her baby from the war around them, but it seemed she would be born right into it.

Do not yield to fear, my daughter, am I not with you? Will I not be with her as well?

She nodded, "I'm sorry, Father, I don't want to lose her too."

Trust Me, child.

"Yes, Father."

She felt His love like a blanket, and the babe must have, too, because she felt the butterflies, the first movements of the small baby inside.

"Mama." She heard the little whisper again.

"I love you, sweet girl. I can't wait to meet you." Billie Jean whispered back.

In answer, Billie Jean saw a flash picture in her head of herself and Darrel holding a beautiful little girl's hands. She looked like she was three or four, with lovely light coffee skin, dark curly hair, and light eyes. Billie Jean's heart swelled, and she stroked her belly. Then, another picture replaced it. She saw her Griffin and Darrel flying around a dark sky filled with evil gargoyles and demonic alien beings. She and Darrel were burning and tearing them apart, then the same little girl, but a few years older, flew past Darrel and blasted a gargoyle with light. It screamed and disintegrated, and she went after another. Billie Jean's mouth dropped, and she covered it with her hand. "Oh, my goodness."

She heard a little giggle in her head, and Billie Jean grinned. "She's already dreaming about destroying the enemy."

As she walked into the bathroom, Billie Jean felt the Father's joy in this little warrior forming in her womb. The fear she had earlier was completely gone as His love overcame her.

"What an incredible new generation of warriors is coming, Father." She said,

Yes. He smiled.

About The Author

Cheryl is the author of The Waking, her first novel. She is also a business owner, an ordained minister, speaker, and student of the Word. Cheryl currently resides in Texas with her husband and three boys. She is passionate about seeing people know God deeply while finding true freedom and wholeness in life through Yeshua.

Resources

If you or someone you know needs help, call the National Human Trafficking Hotline toll-free hotline, 24 hours a day, 7 days a week at **1-888-373-7888** to speak with a specially trained Anti-Trafficking Hotline Advocate. Support is provided in more than 200 languages. We are here to listen and connect you with the help you need to stay safe.

Callers can dial 711 to access the Hotline using TTY.

You can also email us at **help@humantraffickinghotline.org**.

To report a potential human trafficking situation, call the hotline at **1-888-373-7888**.

Inner Healing/Deliverance:
https://christianinnerhealing.com/directory/

www.ingramcontent.com/pod-product-compliance
Lightning Source LLC
Chambersburg PA
CBHW051247260626
47162CB00002B/651

* 9 7 9 8 2 1 8 3 9 9 5 0 4 *